D0097674

MAN'S WORK

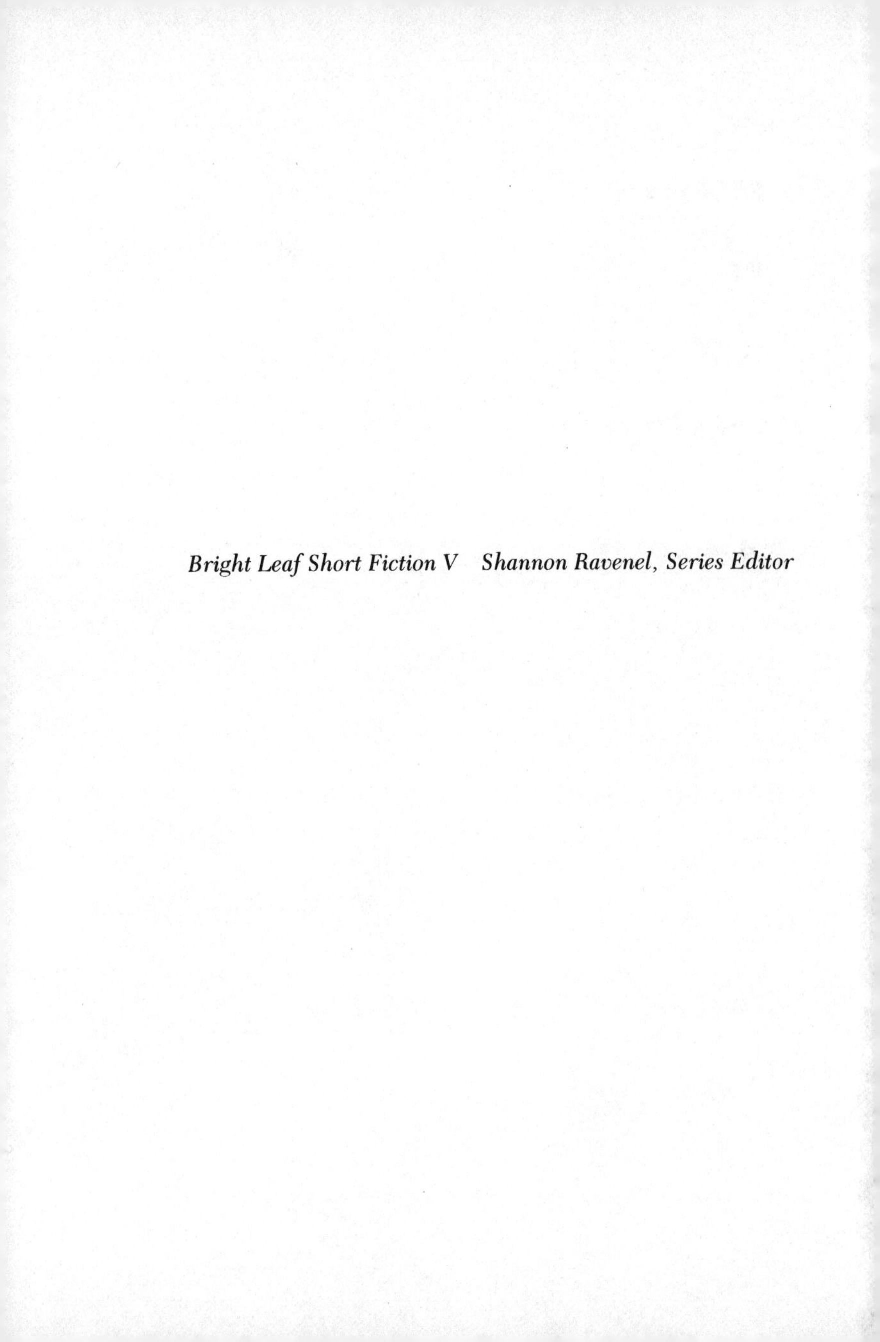

Bright Leaf Short Fiction V   *Shannon Ravenel, Series Editor*

STORIES

BY

JOHN

CONNELLY

MAN'S WORK

ALGONQUIN

BOOKS

OF

CHAPEL

HILL

1987

published by
Algonquin Books of Chapel Hill
Post Office Box 2225
Chapel Hill, North Carolina 27515-2225

in association with
Taylor Publishing Company
1550 West Mockingbird Lane
Dallas, Texas 75235

Several stories in this book have appeared previously: "Basques" in The Greensboro Review; *"Ours" in* Kansas Quarterly; *"The Holidays" in* Indiana Review; *"Partner" in* The Crescent Review; *and "Foreign Objects" in* West Branch.

Design by Molly Renda.

Printed in the United States of America

Library of Congress Cataloging-in-Publication Data

Connelly, John, 1959–
Man's work.
(Bright leaf short fiction; 5)
I. Title. II. Series.
PS3553.O5116M3 1987 813'.54 86-28671
ISBN 0-912697-55-5

for Liz

CONTENTS

MAN'S WORK

BASQUES

We were a little lost, scouting for Peggy's address. They didn't use streetlights out there, three town lines removed from the city bank where we all worked. The houses held tight together along curving streets named for women. I sat carelessly in the back, a leg bent across the seat, an elbow wedged under the slanting rear window. In front, Barry combed his wet hair and called out street names when he could read the night-stubborn, blue signs. Jack drove with reserve; hands symmetrical, he governed the car square as a battleship or a floating village. The windows were rolled tight and the smell familiar, not unpleasant but closed, close.

"Leave gas money in the ashtray," Jack said. "That's a new rule. Nobody bets gas money anymore."

"Lois Street," Barry said. "Colleen or Eileen. Here's Ethel again. Try Ethel."

But Jack was past. His return arc swung so slow and wide that we didn't need to fight our own weight. So Barry faked it violently, all the way across and into Jack's lap. "Easy does it," Barry said. "Don't lose that ranch house we're towing."

It was hard to believe Barry was from the Northeast, with the easy way he put his hands on his friends. By the time of that night out with Peggy, four weeks after we met at the new bank, Jack and I had relaxed about it. I think we knew how it distinguished us, and made our impending clique seem especially fierce.

Jack came to a gentle halt. "So which way on Ethel?"

I spoke up. "I'd keep going in," I said. "Peggy says hers is dead end."

Barry's window stuck; the plastic handle spun for nothing. He said, "How come they don't make those little angle windows anymore?"

"Must be cost-cutting," I said. "One big piece is cheaper."

"Get directions from this guy," Barry said.

"Who?" Jack said.

"On your side." Barry pointed. "Ask Dad up there."

Jack drove as though expecting speed bumps. Slowly, the sweatered strolling couple was overtaken, but Jack never reached for his window. Barry pitied his shyness with a sigh.

Silence excluded me, so I allied with Jack. "Three guys roll up and ask where Pauline's at, how to get on Pauline. I'd call the cops."

"They live here," Barry said earnestly to me. "They know. I bet they're the oldest couple on Martha, or someplace."

"I was kidding," I said.

"You guys," Barry said. "You think if you haven't been somewhere at least a dozen times then it's enemy territory."

Wet hair slapped a little on the vinyl headrest when Barry turned to Jack. "We're respectable everywhere. We're three white guys, we wear ties to work every day. Turn here."

"I'm going to try Lois," Jack said, and he eased the wheel to the left.

Barry thumped his arm. "You especially. You're the guy to do the asking, John-boy. Who gave you that haircut?"

"The mall," Jack said. The mall wasn't much older than the bank. It stood a half-mile away, in a slightly better neighborhood. Most of us went over daily for a safer, enclosed lunch.

"It doesn't look big," Jack said. "But it's got all you want. I don't think I've spent a dollar outside of it since we opened."

"Not counting jai alai," Barry said.

"Not counting jai alai."

"Well they went to town on your head." I reached forward to pat it, but then held back. Instead I skimmed my own shaggy hair. "How's something like that feel?"

"Feels *good*," Jack said.

"Mark would just love it," Barry said jauntily. "Has Mark seen it?"

"Mark called sick today," I said. "And Mark's engaged now anyway. He's ass over kettle for some big guy. He's saying he found Burt Lancaster in a time warp."

"He'll still be checking whatever walks in," Barry said. "He'll keep his glass Windexed."

Fag jokes, I was thinking then, even as I laughed at them. Fag jokes, gas money, weekly gambling. The pinched and tapered world of peers. Around that time, soon after I met Gail, I told her about waiting for everything around me to begin remodeling itself, to start growing up, and how it was taking so long. Gail believed that not much changed; she said that this was more or less it. Gail has older brothers and sisters, and she used to work for her father, downtown, in the summers. She claimed years went by at this level. Peers were all there ever were.

We passed the old couple again, on a different street. On Ethel, facing a third ride past useless landmarks, Jack accelerated some. "This is unbelievable," he said. "Streets just stop and then start again somewhere else. Julia. Did we have a Julia already, or was it Judith?"

"Judith," I said, guessing.

"You know though," Barry said, with the suck of breath that means return from daydreaming. "There's something there, with queers. You kind of pick up when they look at you. Not that you lead them on, or anything, but you want to look good. You primp a little. It's like you just wanted to be liked, no matter by who."

"That's bent, is what that is." Jack said.

"No," I said. "It's just everybody's vanity."

"See," Barry said. "He knows. Him too."

Jack had frozen all but his eyes, as people do when they can't believe their ears.

"You too," Barry said to me. "If Gail only knew."

I believed at the time that Gail and I, though together, were far less serious than they all presumed. But we must have looked devoted—the bank held us in a mild reverence, the kind commonly exhausted on the corridor royalty at junior high. Our branch was the bank's least desirable; the work area walled by high security glass, transfer there declined by all with seniority. I knew that this population of young tellers gave Gail and me most of what we had in common. For the longest time we began every night in their company, drinking where Peggy moonlighted: a far-off hotel cocktail lounge for people twice our age. The tellers showed up every night on Peggy's station to ridicule the music and force tips on her. Gail and I stayed late with them, until we were ready for privacy.

When we found Pauline Street, Peggy was watching from her dark porch. Jack stopped the car near the flagstones.

"Hit the horn," Barry said.

"She knows it's us," I said.

In the kitchen windows, the younger brothers and sisters cleared the table and loaded the dishwasher. As Peggy moved toward the car I was thinking about how, when it got cooler and darker at mealtimes, a bright oven-warm kitchen was precious again. Supper began tasting better right after the clocks were turned back.

Peggy took her hand from her pocket and turned a tight circle with it. Jack rolled his window.

"Hi," she said, leaning to see inside. "Where's everybody?"

"What you see," Barry said.

"We called the Cahill twins,"I said. Then I waggled my fingers toward the front. "Rather, these guys did. The grandmother said they went drinking."

Peggy's wide ponytail hung at her throat. She flicked it back. "I though Gail at least," she said, looking at me.

I shrugged. "Not her scene." Then I said, "But I think she'd have a good time."

"Mark was coming," Jack said. "But then he said he got his period."

Peggy smiled a little. She straightened some, and her head

went out of my view. "I don't know," she said, "I didn't think such a small group. I though maybe another carload. Two cars at least."

The porch light came on behind her. It glared on a pumpkin hollowed by one of her little brothers. Her father, looking as amiable as he could, watched for a minute from behind the storm door. Thursday was Peggy's only night off. She was working two full-time jobs for a year, to stockpile money and finish college. For assurance she looked into me, the attached one.

"Nobody else answered their phone," I said.

"I just thought everybody would be going," Peggy said.

"Turns out just the regulars," Jack said.

"Come on," Barry said. "It's nicer than the dogs, if you've ever been."

"Haven't, no," Peggy said.

"Well jai alai's a lot cleaner," Barry said. "And you get more than thirty seconds of action for your money." Barry opened his door and stood, talking to Peggy across the roof. "Listen. If somebody spotless like you comes back with good reviews, then they'll all want to go."

"Spotless," Peggy said.

A neighbor and his five retrievers passed behind Peggy on the sidewalk. He had all the leashes in one fist. He nodded to Peggy, who said hello back over a tilted shoulder. If they knew names, I was thinking, then they'd use them.

"We never said the whole bank was coming," Barry said.

"Everybody makes money their first time down," Jack said. "It's a rule."

"Be a pioneer," Barry said. He pulled the passenger seat

forward. "It took us forever to find your house." He called in to me, "Slide over, buddy."

"It's all right," she said. "I'll sit in back."

On the highway Jack's car jerked into its upper reaches, somewhere near sixty-five. Though sealed tight, the window glass rattled. But there was something too loud from Barry's door, and as we moved he opened it to inspect. He even leaned out a ways, for a better look, but nobody said anything.

Finally, I did. "This is his peculiar way of convincing you that you haven't made a mistake."

When Barry slammed his door the clattering did not resume. "No harm done," he said. "It was stuffy in here. The air's still dead—somebody talk."

I asked Peggy what was for dinner, and she said pork chops. I mentioned how supper weather began near November, when the kitchen's a fortress. Then there was a polite pause.

"How you like this boy's haircut?" Barry said.

"I like it fine," she said. "So you guys do this all the time?"

"All the time so far," Jack said. "It's only been four weeks."

"You didn't know each other before this branch?"

"Right," I said.

"I didn't know that," she said. Then her eyes followed the carom of words around the closed car. Her face looked wide and well scrubbed. She stopped short of chubby, but no tendons showed in her neck, no vein-threads or bones near the temples. She was all skin. She worked her second job in a cocktail uniform, but managed to look wholesome.

We approached a car in the right lane. We could see hung

shirts on a pole across the back seat. "Bet it's Florida plates," Jack said.

"Beat me to it," Barry said. "I was just about to say that."

Peggy looked at me, and I shrugged. Barry hadn't turned his head, but he knew to answer us anyway. "Every car with stuff hung like that is old duffers from Florida. They pamper their Ban-lon down there. Watch and see next time."

I began the survey of money supply. Barry brought sixty-five, far more than either Jack or me.

"If you win some," Barry said to Peggy, "and there's these little pen marks across the 'U' in United States, then those were Jack's once. He marks 'em up when he handles them." He rapped Jack's shoulder. "Don't go blushing about it, pal—it's legitimate experimentation. I'd be curious how much I've handled, off the job. Did you bring money to bet?"

"Of course she did," Jack said.

Peggy said, "I guess I've got about a hundred dollars."

"Jesus," Barry said. "We had you wrong."

"Well good luck to you," I said.

"I doubt I'll bet all of it."

"You will," Barry said. "If it's not left in the car, you bet it."

"The more you bring the less you come back with," Jack said. "It's the law. Last time we all came down loaded, with a plan to crush 'em. We came out with change. With coins, I'm saying. We got the car home on fumes."

"Thanks to the system," I said, knocking Barry between the shoulders.

"It's a good system," he said. "You just need deep pockets and some big balls. Stay with it and it works."

"Only it kept saying to play Larrinaga," I said.

"Larrinaga and Altuna," Jack said.

"And Aramendi," Barry said. He turned to Peggy. "You'll like the names. Except for two-three local clods, they're all Basque."

"Suarez," I said.

"Churruca," Jack said. "Azcarte. Miguel."

"Miguel I and Miguel II," Barry said.

"How many do you bet on?" Peggy said.

"Two at a time," Jack said. "It's like doubles handball with eight rotating teams. Seven points wins."

"They've Americanized the hell out of the rules," Barry said. "It's all fast action here. In Basque country one match lasts all day."

I reached under Jack's seat and found an old program. I read more players' names aloud. The car was dark, but I made do with just the shadows of letters; I knew the names.

Jack eased the car onto the exit ramp. In the low distance, past the tall roadside grass, stood two long bridges.

"Twenty more minutes to the fronton," Jack said. "Fronton. It's another language. *Cesta*, *pelota*, *rebote*. Look at the bridges all lit up."

"I'm getting to know a guy down there." Barry talked directly to Peggy now. He held his head straight as he turned in the front seat. "He seems to know what's up. But I'm not sure he knows the players. Outsiders aren't supposed to talk to them—they're locked in the dressing room something like ten hours a day."

"Fifteen hours on matinee days," Jack said. "So this guy claims."

"You've seen him?" I said to Jack. "I've still never seen this guy."

Jack said, "He looks kind of Spanish, the one big eyebrow

type." In those days Jack and Barry seemed especially close. I was always hearing late about records they'd borrowed or dinners they'd pooled.

At the state line Barry reached for the dashboard. He crammed his hand in as far as it would go. "I'm there first. Rhode Island."

"Tell her about the players," Jack said.

"My guy talks all about these players," Barry said. "They're competitive as hell with each other. But since they don't speak word one of English, they stick together like you wouldn't believe."

"Well they're vacuum-packed all day," I said.

"That's how they like it," Barry said. "At home, the inbreeding is vicious. Highest RH percentage anywhere, Basques have. They marry girls from their own village *exclusively*. Another world, my man says. A time machine."

"The Pyrenees," Peggy said.

"Where's that at, exactly?" Jack said. "Gibraltar?"

"No," Peggy said. "It's southeast France and northwest Spain."

"It's great," Jack said, "people walking around with that kind of stuff in their heads." He turned from the road to look at her. "I'm not making fun of you. It really is."

"Jai alai means joyous festival." This was something Barry liked to say. He turned to Peggy. "Maybe for the bettors and the yankee players, Steve I and Steve II. But those hombres don't look joyous to me."

We went big-time, bought box seats. There were plenty left. Once inside, Barry broke away for the windows. "I've got one to cash," he said.

"Why'd you wait?" I said, following him. "We could have put it in the gas tank."

"No." He grinned, embarrassed. "It's from night before last. I came down by myself." He went off, sneakers chirping against the floor.

The fronton, at first sight, dazzled—the cool crack of the pelota on marble, the green mammoth walls, the stout, casual Basques with the cestas laced to their arms. Peggy perked up right away. She seemed glad to have come. She sat between Jack and me. Barry paid for his seat but hardly used it; he roamed around the building. After that first game he appeared briefly, a round of beer in his arms. His first ticket was a quiniela winner, for $57.60.

"It's such an easy game," he said.

"Quit now," Jack said. "Go sit outside. We'll lock you in the car."

"You'd enjoy that," Barry said.

An usherette appeared and asked us to take our feet off the seats. Then Barry spent a moment repeating to Peggy what I'd just explained, the rules of the game. Then he stood again, pointing at the tote board.

"They insist on betting the gringo. Steve II, the spastic *yanqui*. No matter. It just helps my prices."

Peggy looked to me. "The Americans are no good, I take it."

"They suck." Jack leaned our way. "They don't belong."

"He exaggerates," I said. "They can hang with these guys, but barely."

We sat near floor-level, close to the wire mesh that screened the open side of the three-walled court. We could see through the glass partitions and far into the player's waiting area.

Before each game the lights went down, a canned march

played. The referees and the eight pairs of players paraded to the middle of the court. On signal they raised their basket arms. Some people saluted back; Barry always did. Then the players went behind glass to wait their turn. When it came they played until they lost a point, then they moved to the end of the line. When a team collected seven points it was over, barring ties for second or third—in which event came playoffs meaning everything to the bettors and nothing to the Basques, who muffed shots and walked away under gentle jeers. For our part, we rooted modestly and under our breath. We'd learned to mimic the fatalism and mild disgust of the heavier gamblers, and to use and pronounce correctly, with the shouts of "Let's go, four!" all around us, each exacting Basque name.

Consciously or not, Jack and I never made duplicate selections. Both of us cashed the odd ticket but were losers overall. Barry seemed to be facing grand and constant reversals of fortune, but rarely in our view. Her feet elevated, her knees at eye-level, Peggy could support without hands her unmarked program, which she kept open to the page with the player pictures, a page full of head shots.

"My yearbook," Peggy said. "*Journeys*, '78. All crammed in like that, I mean, but with white faces. I went to a huge high school."

Jack nudged her with his shoulder. "Here comes that girlie in the Burger King suit."

The usherette used precisely the same words as before. We pulled back our overhung legs.

Peggy said, "Those players must love this game not to get sick of it."

"It's in the blood over there," I said.

"In the Pyrenees," Jack said.

"The Pyrenees," I said. "Over there people will watch all day without betting on it."

After the ninth game a lucky ticket holder stood to win one thousand dollars if he could throw the ball to the front wall without a bounce. A man in a vinyl jacket trudged to mid-court, wicker crescent strapped to his arm. His ball skipped twice and was rolling when it reached.

"Closest we've seen yet," Jack said to Peggy.

"It's much harder than it looks," I said.

Barry startled me with a knock on the shoulder. He'd dropped into the row behind us. He hadn't seen his foreign friend, but it didn't seem to matter. The money was wound thick as a cast around one finger.

"Did you have Suarez and Barrena?" he said. "Neither of you?" He leaned forward to squint at the scribbling on Jack's program. "How we all doing here? Anybody making money? Minus twenty-one sixty, Jackson, does that count this last race?" He had a hand on Jack's shoulder and a hand on Peggy's. "I should go find my man, then. Bring a winner back. Everybody should be making money." He slipped the cylinder from his finger and began to examine the bills. "Don't seem to have any of yours, Jack. The cashier next to the information window's paying with brand new tens."

I looked around as I spoke. "Never seen a bank teller so fired up about money."

"That's not money we work with, cheesehead." Barry tapped my skull with his encased finger. "This is money."

Peggy, Jack, and I kept our seats. Jack and I each gave

Barry five dollars and instructions for the next game. Barry struck up a short conversation with the usherette, then he was gone.

"Is he always like this?" Peggy asked.

I started to speak, then yielded to Jack. He looked over to Peggy. "How would we know?" he said.

I needed to talk. "It's the way betting is," I said. "When you lose you should have won, when you win you should have won more."

Barry returned ten minutes after the next game. He had a cardboard tray with four cups of beer. Peggy declined hers.

"Christ," Barry said. "I was going to buy hard drinks, but I thought you'd want this instead." Some sweaty hair clung to Barry's forehead. He seemed to breathe from the roof of his mouth.

"You found the man," Jack said.

Barry shook his head no. He kept two beers for himself and dropped into a chair. "What I found was Amos 'n' Andy. I found these two old-timers downstairs. It was insane, but I listened to them."

"Listened to what?" I said.

"They said the three. Two black guys did. The three horse is ready, they said. There was no information or anything, they'd just been watching the guy." Barry took a small sip of beer.

"How big?" Jack said.

He stretched his legs forward and reached into his jeans. "I played it fifty to win and wheeled it in the quinielas. Two black guys in Newport, Rhode Island. I just made like four hundred dollars. I'm completely serious."

"Nobody said you weren't," Peggy said.

"I'm not kidding." Barry stood and dug his hand deeper. The sight of big money unbound, outside glass, made us stare.

"Go find them," I said. "Say thanks a lot and give them a twenty and be their best friend. Really. They must know something."

"They know shit," Barry said. "That's the whole point." When he sat again he knocked his cup over. Beer went gliding down the concrete steps.

Barry touched Peggy's arm and spoke in a forced air of humor and confidence. "The lady asks how you want it. I took twenties. I almost asked for fives and singles."

"Tuck it away somewhere," Jack said. We all stared at the electric numbers above us. In a minute Jack's arithmetic was done. "I get a profit of three-eleven and forty cents," he said. When we looked back Barry had left again, and Jack said what I was about to. "Somebody should have gone with him."

We sat through the next game, the feature singles match. Peggy asked me what Gail thought about gambling. Nobody went to find Barry. Later, on the concourse to cash a show ticket from three games back, I saw him sloped against a pillar below the TV monitor, reading the program. The liquor he drank came from two plastic cups, one inside the other.

"Winner?" he said.

I half-nodded solemnly. "You?"

He showed me a two-hundred-dollar win ticket. "A week's pay, and this Bedia was never in it. Now what fun is that?"

We were ready to leave. Barry was still considerably ahead. Jack, who kept accounts, lost $27.40. I was somewhere in the negative teens. Peggy'd lost nearly half her money. She couldn't imagine how so much had disappeared. "Well it's gone now," she said.

"You fit right in," I told her. "With our group fifty seems to be about the limit. You lose less than that and you can manage to talk about other things on the way home."

Jack studied Barry's big losing ticket—he braced it with both hands. At the car, Barry held the front seat forward for Peggy. After she slid in, he followed. He said to me, "Only fair you get the front, long legs."

"Maybe Peggy wanted to sit up front with Jack," I said.

"Never mind," Peggy said. "Forget it."

As I sat down, buzzers went off. "Sit more to the left," Barry said. "You won't trigger it."

"Or you could buckle the belt," Peggy said.

Traffic clotted at the parking lot exits. Jack kept a safe margin off tailgates, so others kept cutting in front of him.

"Do you realize how much Bedia would have made me?" Barry said. "It boggles. Nearly two dimes. I could have gone to the islands this winter. And cross country next summer. Met some different people. But that fat little Basque—if you bet the one-horse or the two-horse and they lose the first point, then you're out of it. A week's pay gone because Bedia can't serve. The fat guy can't throw a ball off the biggest wall in Rhode Island."

I laughed a little.

"Yeah, he's happy," Barry said. "He just cashed. You're always as happy as your last bet, the rest doesn't matter."

"Which islands?" Peggy said, and now Jack laughed a little.

"Go ahead," Barry said. "I could have quit the bank. I might have explained my last MoneyNow account."

"You'd be a bank teller on vacation," Jack said. "That simple."

"You sound like Gail," I said to Jack.

Traffic was lighter on the two-lane highway. I was turned to face the back seat. The shoulder harness made this difficult. Peggy had moved over against her window, where the rattling glass might have been all she heard.

"You know," Barry said, "the only guy there tonight fatter than Bedia was the regular with the meatball subs. You catch him? When he loses big he eats more, when he wins big he eats more. Some guys just can't take the pressure. Having fun is too much for them."

Now, with no other cars visible, Jack used his high beams.

"When we were fifteen," Barry said, "we all piled in a car and went to the Marshfield Fair. We weren't ready. The guy with the learner's permit drove. We had beer in the cooler and the six of us giggled like hell all the way down. Plow horses run at Marshfield for ten days every summer—pigs, rejects from Narragansett, which was as rinky as tracks ever got. At Marshfield the jockeys were younger than us. We drank and rode some rides and lost two dollar show bets on plow horses. One guy fell clean out of the car on the way home. We were completely unready. We were ill-prepared. Before they'd *touched* a beer guys were dry-heaving, just from the giggling. Guys didn't know not to pour their beer over ice. The kid driving went sixty and talked about smokies all the way down. Broad daylight, luckily—that much fun after dark might have killed us. We weren't ready in any way, shape, or form. Everybody's cheeks hurt. Old jokes, jokes running since seventh grade. Plays on the first part of 'country,' the usual. Jokes that just ran and ran. If we'd actually won money they'd have needed to hose us down, like at Japanese riots. On the way home the kid driving takes a rotary at forty-five or fifty, and the back door swings open and a guy falls out. Nasty scrape. To this day he's got a purple back. But that's not the point. The point is that we're all grown up here, we're all fully developed. We can enjoy ourselves. We should go someplace for room service. Really, let's turn around and get a room with a view and order six dollar sundaes. Come on, I'm still way ahead. Anybody who doesn't want to sleep there can leave."

I heard money crackling behind me. We were on a four-lane road now. Jack dodged an animal corpse—though I was belted, his right hand shot out instinctively, as a barrier.

"Come on," Barry said. "Everybody does only what they want to. He can call Gail if he wants. Why the hell not? Getting and spending. What's the point if you don't have any fun? Nobody forces anything. Who'd want to do what wasn't fun for everybody?"

We crossed the state line. "Mandatory one-year sentence for firearms possession," I read aloud. "We're home."

"What now," Barry said. "Nobody looks at me, is that the deal? Am I a disappointment to you all?"

Jack looked into the mirror. "You should put that stuff away." I heard Barry jam money into his shirt.

"Crash away, buddy," he said. "Or push me out the door. I got better than an airbag."

"That was the turn, I think," Peggy said.

"It was," Barry said. "Stop the car."

"I'm past it," Jack said.

"Stop the car," Barry said.

Jack applied the brake firmly and evenly. No one was thrown forward, but the harness tightened around me. We sat well past the off-ramp, maybe three-fourths of the way toward where entering traffic merged. A car blew by, spitting light gravel on our closed windows and swaying the tall grass off the shoulder.

"All clear now," Barry said. Suddenly he sounded grateful for a chance to help. "You can back it up."

"Did you see a sign?" Jack said.

Barry snorted. "I know that's the road."

"I was going to say something," Peggy said. "But I thought you saw it."

"Got a map?" I said.

"That's the damn road," Barry said. "Just roll back there and see."

"Do the next exit," Peggy said. "Then swing back around and get it from that side."

"Piss on that," Barry said. "That's lame."

"The exits don't always work that way," I said to Peggy. She stared at me.

"Just back up the car," Barry said.

"You're the lame one," she said quietly.

Jack sent retaliatory high beams to an offending car across the way. Nobody spoke for a while.

"If we lived here, we'd be home by now," I said.

Calmly, Barry said, "There's nobody coming, Jack. Just get your stale car into reverse, please."

Jack opened his window and craned his head out. "I can't see far enough back."

"We'll all help you," Barry said.

"Look." I felt pressure to say something rational and precise. "We're coming off a peninsula. If we keep going and don't get wet, then we're bound to be headed home."

"I have to be up at ten past six," Jack said. He slumped like an accident victim over the wheel. "Let's do something."

"You're driving the car!" Barry threw himself against the seat. We rocked in the wake of a chartered bus.

"My father's two commandments," Peggy said. "Don't fetch toast with a fork, and never back up on the highway."

"Rinse the match after you light the pilot light," Jack said.

The punch on my shoulder. "Let me out."

Jack straightened and turned to face Barry. "You going to be sick?"

I unharnessed myself and stepped out. Barry walked around the car to the driver's side, stood six feet from Peggy's closed window, and undid his pants. He shot for the hubcap. He had to raise his voice to be heard.

"I could go out and wash the white line if I wanted. There's nobody on this road. I swear to you, you can back this car up. I'll meet you there."

As this happened I got into the back seat. I blocked Peggy's gaze, which was aimed out over the grass triangle. It was the sort of stoicism for which, after that night, she had small use. There was little in the world to try her patience; she went back for her degree, fell into a life with Jack, and moved into a smooth, self-contained apartment complex a toll-call away from us. They had a baby right away, and that was the official reason why, when we visited, it was Gail and I who did the traveling. But mostly, it was hard to bring Jack out of his new house on weekends.

When Barry was done he passed behind the car. He

stomped through the high weeds—we watched him lift his legs as he went.

"Hope he tucked that money away," Jack said.

Peggy cleared her throat. "Let's circle around, then come back for him."

"Let's not come back," I said.

Jack rolled his window tight. Then he reached across the seat and closed the passenger door. He said, "Wear mittens below zero and gloves above."

"Don't stifle sneezes," Peggy said. "Don't send cash in the mail."

We could only think of a handful more. "How long's he going to wait there?" Jack said. "An hour?"

"All night," I said.

"Ten minutes," Peggy said, and of course she was close.

OURS

Greta knew she'd been talking in her sleep again.

"Well rested?" was all Danny had to say.

It was the weekend and they'd both slept too long. After showering, Greta stood in their bedroom and fumbled through the underwear drawer for something of hers. She thought she remembered the sleeptalking. A dream set at work, at the restaurant. She thought she remembered wanting to pull it back, to unsay it, as soon as it was out. Hearing Danny's infrequent sleeptalking made her uneasy—it was hard not to talk back—but still nothing, she knew, like what hers did for him. It upset his whole order of things. He came out of the shower as she finished with the hair dryer. She pulled on her sweater as he pulled on his.

"Did you dream about a riot or something?" he said.

She had no clean underpants. Danny's side had half a

dozen clean, and she stepped into one of his older, skimpier pairs. For their closet Danny had found a box so large that laundry never spilled over, which precluded judging at a distance how full it ever was. Danny reckoned by his underwear. When he was out he'd say "We need clean clothes" and leave for the laundry room. She'd lived there seven months, had arrived under something near to the grandest inelo-quence, love at first sight. Greta belted her jeans as Danny located his. It was so unilateral; she guessed that's what unsettled him. Sleeptalk was a one-way mirror. It was like contact with the dead. It was an exchange that could never be closed.

He looked more like a Dan. A Dan would carve methodically his half of grapefruit, a Danny wouldn't.

"Can we please watch one thing all the way through," he said to Greta, and she released the selector box. "It doesn't matter what."

He was Danny, even to his ex-wife, even to their daughter, who was eleven now. That he looked his full age was something else to belie the name. Greta wasn't hungry and she went to load the dishwasher. Danny's polite sigh said please sit down, we're not done yet, no meal, not even breakfast, can be eaten amid movement all over the place. Greta moved clear behind him in the kitchen and Danny ate again. The sunlight hit his scrubbed, just-shaven face, and Greta thought about their smooth choreography, about how their fights evolved as ordered as in the old westerns, where the card slips to the floor, and there follows the shove, the punch ducked, the one landed, the rebound, the toss onto the bar, the leap and crash through the card table, the duck of the breakaway bottle, the hit with the breakaway chair. They perfected their unspoken blocking, braced by the danger of a slip, as can happen, the punch un-pulled so it hurts. Danny was the one to lead them through it. In the marriage he'd quit on, he said, the fights were real and brutal and were their only communication. Nothing else happened. He spooned his clean grapefruit sections. At the end he wrung the husk three ways, for the juice, then threw his head far back to drain the bowl's last.

Greta needed to tell Danny, it couldn't wait, it wouldn't seem complete until she did. She found him on the bed facing away, wearing headphones in the dark. Impossible to avoid startling him—but she tried to figure how. Hearing her might be less jarring than seeing or feeling her; not perfect she knew, but the best of bad choices. She stole slowly across to flick the power switch. Even better, she thought, drop the sound lingeringly, over minutes if need be. Up close, Greta squinted for the proper dial. Two hands seized her from behind. She stood deaf with the shock until he kissed her and pulled her down.

After, when she told him what a scare she'd gotten, Danny kept apologizing. She forgave him several times. An hour passed, then he went out to watch the news. His insomnia was no better and no worse since she'd moved in. In bed, as after meals, Greta was often left to herself. When Danny finished eating he cleared his plates and moved, he couldn't help himself. At dinner it was often to catch the start of "World News Tonight." He watched several hours of news every day. He'd leave CNN running until the staff went home and the news began replaying itself. After four Greta would half-hear him beside her, where he'd stay for only three hours, then groom for work with "Today" or the Weather Channel running.

Greta heard the refrigerator suck shut. She remembered what she'd come in to tell him, but she was too tired to move. She sung the sentence over and over in her head. Not speaking it aloud bothered her for a time, but soon enough she drifted, and sleep made all that stop.

At last night's pre-meal the head hostess had ordered all long hair tightly bunned and netted from now on. She declared the Suzanne Sommers fad dead, no more halfhearted binding.

"They're not just bringing their own glass shards now," said the manager, who came to pre-meal the next night. "They're plucking hairs out of their salads, too, and that's harder for me to disprove. I can't turn your tables as fast when we're dickering over free meals."

Then Bob A. interrupted to suggest once again a dollar raise in the prime rib price, since as it was now John Q. Dacron could bring the Mrs. for two prime rib, unlimited salad bar, and two bottomless coffees at $18.65, tax included, which tempted him to drop a twenty on the table and waddle away, leaving exactly seven-point-two percent for the waiter. The manager cut him off midsentence to say his own hands were tied, and to make the main announcement: a new carpet, same tartan pattern, was going down soon, and once it did waitresses were responsible for trailing the sweeper behind each under-12 on their station.

Greta had waited until pre-meal to wind her hair tightly behind her, doing it blind, unable to bear her silly reflection that way, the coiled mound behind her head like dogshit pinned at forty-five degrees. When pre-meal adjourned she hadn't quite finished, so she fiddled with it while they equipped and organized their service areas and waited for the rush. This anticipatory rite made no sense to her; it was folly to try banking a nightly reserve of order for later use—by eight o'clock, if not sooner, the action would wipe out all planning.

Tonight it was sooner. By six-thirty they were swamped. Chef shouted to Greta to speak up when she ordered. By seven-thirty Chef had peeled down to his black "What Do You Want?" T-shirt. Greta's first party on the round table wanted seven different broiler items. Chef cleared some fire for them. Ordering was verbal only; Chef kept it all in his head. When his grill overloaded like this he talked nonstop gibberish, but never forgot an order.

When busy Greta moved, methodless, from one urgency to the next. At the most her design took in the next three things to be done. Three was as many as she could keep straight. And though her whole station often filled at once, it never came to where she could order all drinks or pick up all dinners simultaneously and be done with them.

At the service bar she sucked ice in the line for cocktails; her own Coke sat unfinished and unreachable in the break room. Milt was seated at the bar already. Milt had retired, but from exactly what no one knew. "Now we can see your face," he said to Greta. Milt said little, but whenever she walked back to the dining room Greta felt he wasn't quite finished. Milt sat next to the service area drinking rye every night but Sunday. "Finally out from the hair—how would you fancy being on the television?" was what Milt said tonight.

Greta revised and revised her next three tasks until two hours had passed. For the thousandth time she squeezed through the shuffling herd near the salad bar. Later she had a moment while her sundaes were made. But in the break room the new dishwasher drained a Mountain Dew; he was tall and older, near fifty, and looked half-witted, with fingernails dyed crimson and some kind of lettering on his teeth, which he didn't often show. He wore a severe crewcut and appeared to have applied light mascara. Greta turned right around. Chef came toward this new dishwasher, patting Greta as he passed. As she collected her desserts Greta heard Chef get a slurred explanation of the difference between a break and a breather.

It slowed some. The busboys drew area assignments in pre-meal, but they preferred to race through all the dining rooms, covering for each other. They were a group; they drank together after work. Greta overtipped them, partly because she knew that Bob A., for one, was practically stiffing them, but mostly she just liked them—they worked hard and were friendly and had asked her along a couple of times when she'd already phoned Danny for a ride and couldn't go.

With her last parties still eating Greta did her sidework, pulled her sweater from her small locker, untied her hair, and punched out. She'd collect her late tips in an envelope tomorrow. Those who didn't close the place rarely saw their night through to the finish. She called Danny from the kitchen pay phone. She gave the busboys $7 on the $34 she'd already made—an average night. She waited against one of the thick front pillars outside. The December wind numbed her and whipped her unbound hair. She moved around the pillar but couldn't seem to get clear of it, the wind came from everywhere. She still sought the calm side as Danny pulled up.

Back from a visitation, Danny checked the mailbox while Greta unlocked the lobby door. "GMAC," he said, "they're starting." He opened it on the elevator.

Greta dropped the K-Mart bag on the table, then went to the TV. Danny, coat still on, spread the car finance papers across the breakfast bar. Greta opened the new hairnets, just to see how bad it would be. Danny went to the chest of drawers for the calculator. She told him she would need a ride home tonight.

"But we can't tell just when," he said from over the papers. He hadn't undone a button yet. "You ring, I have five minutes. I mean I understand and all, but still, I'd like something close to the same time every night. You know?"

He reached for the checkbook. They had fifteen days, but Danny wouldn't sit until the records and figures were checked, the papers signed, the customer copy filed, the check written, the checkbook balanced, the envelope stuffed and sealed, the stamp applied. "Now," he said when he was done. "Groceries?"

Greta had an hour before she'd begin grooming for work. Danny enjoyed shopping and did it capably. Greta saw her function as regulatory—to stop him from stocking them so thoroughly with staples that their storage spaces overflowed.

"Where's the late mailbox on Central Avenue?" he asked her. Danny jangled his keys a little, twitched the TV dial, waited for Greta. Greta gathered her coat and told him she had no idea.

Greta entered to find him jolly and relaxed in the armchair, finishing that day's *News*. Regular delivery people knew their morning doormat easily, the missing tooth, the only unit not to take the *Times*. Danny hadn't read it since he'd left home for college. They've come around, Greta told him, down to six columns, more modular, less of a jumble. He said the *News* was their paper forever. Tabloids made easier stacking and bundling, too; he could bear up to two weeks' accumulation in the living room. At work Greta could scan the *Times* occasionally.

He sprang up to kiss her. "Read Herman. When you get a sec."

She knew about layout from the electives she'd taken her senior year in college. She'd considered quitting until—she listened so hard then, just last year—Danny urged her to finish what she'd started. He had a master's. Greta graduated three weeks after she moved in with him. So far her degree meant nothing: jobs were scarce, she was waitressing at the place where she'd checked coats through high school.

She was half undressed before she noticed the neat piles on the bed. He'd done all the Christmas shopping that day. A ribbon and a bow for each, all tape concealed under folds, the boxes strung tight and addressed in handsome capitals.

"So see them when we give them," he called back. He smiled when he saw her. "Our work's done before Pearl Harbor Day, that's the incredible part." He brushed away the last of her clothing. He stepped behind and enclosed her in his arms. "And I can tell you what's in each. I can list what every one contains."

He talked long-distance with someone Greta had never heard of, an old male friend. She took comfort from knowing that he got just as uneasy, worse even, when he found her that way, talking to a name she'd never mentioned. It was silly, but real. Seven months was time enough for full history, everyone of significance should have come up. Greta did her best not to listen. She sat on the armless sofa and began another of the endless, map-sized crossword puzzles.

"We get two hundred a week from the waitressing," Danny said in his summing-up tone "Hardly taxed. And it's all going great for me. In my field it's all anticipation . . . I work one project at a time . . . Everything's fine, no repos for quite a while . . . They're super, I was just back for turkey . . . Greta . . . No, flew."

It had been brutal. When not numbly self-conscious, she'd noticed his full exasperation with his family. He still seemed to expect of them all a shared reality. He'd gone back for fourteen Thanksgivings, but hadn't stopped resenting that they no longer led parallel lives, that so much required explanation. In Greta's own family each visit meant new variations. She had seven brothers and sisters, all older. Each had broken free and coupled, and some had fragmented beyond that, and were single.

"I have offers," Danny was saying. "For the right one we could pack our tent." He sat at one end of the living room, in the large armchair. "No, not really . . . I want to see this project through to the end."

Forty-five minutes for a table. Greta half-overheard that several times in passing fragments. Or thought she did—talk scraps registered with her only in some estranged and secondary way; all night she trained mainly on her internal recital of where and what came next—steady as pulse: drinks on 41, water on 50, check on 52. At the service bar she stole a brief look around, and forty-five minutes seemed right. Customers spilled in from the front desk. The taped music had been overwhelmed. The standees made passage impossible, so the head hostess drew a breath and bellowed her pages at large. Out of ice ten minutes now, Bob G. the bartender paused to mount his aluminum sink and flag a busboy. In a corner used glassware threatened to crowd itself from the tray, and might have, had not drunken optimists improvised a precarious second deck.

Greta's station of 40–41–50–52 sounded orderly but wasn't. Table numbers here conformed to no known pattern; Bob A.'s neighboring 22–42–53 was actually a neater, more adjacent station. Greta's 52 paid cash and as she wormed toward the cashier she saw Bob A. for what seemed like the first time all night. The rush had yet to take his calm smirk. His side towel hung tidily from his bent wrist.

"I know these four scrods are next," he said to her. "Right by the rail. Don't let her stick them on 52. You'll be sorry. Stall a minute for something better." Greta smiled at her exiting party as they tottered past and patted their bellies for her. Bob A. waved toward the two busboys who'd pounced on the table. "I'm telling you. Slow those apes down, else it's four scrods and lots of coffee and an hour of talk about capital gains."

But at 52 Greta said nothing; in fact she helped two busboys clear and set. One's bow tie, the genuine kind, came unwound as he leaned over to slap clean the booth seats. Greta liked the six of them—all aged eighteen or close to it, they worked hard and very well together. Waitresses vanished when a birthday cake left the freezer, but the busboys stormed every dreaded table as a group, and sang low and lustily, and eased the whole witless business for everybody. They drank in their parked cars every night except Saturday, when they played cards through to the brunch shift. Off the job they seemed to talk little except music and sports, and while on it they'd invented a new vocational tongue, a dozen words so far and growing. Watching their reckless teamwork did something for Greta; she admired them. The two resetting 52 thanked her for the help and charged off for the kitchen, and the head hostess brought the four from the rail right over.

"I know it's full moon," said somebody in the kitchen.

Greta waited to order her four scrods. She heard porcelain fragments scrape under her feet. A moment later a junior dishwasher was sweeping there. "In China," Chef blurted, "there's a billion people don't want a thing from me." Greta's chant went order on 52, appetizers on 41, coffee on 40.

"I'm trying to help you out," Bob A. said at the soup station, where the overslopped chowder and the cream of asparagus had run together and burned brown.

Greta half heard him. "Thanks," she said.

Bob A. talked while he ladled chowder. He told Greta how

he could tell drinkers from non-drinkers, and how selling drinks was ten times more urgent than selling desserts.

"I'm telling you. With a big table like 16 you had last night, you have to turn it three times. Whatever you can do. Sneak the thermostat down while they're on coffee if you have to. The third turn makes all the difference." Since Bob S. had returned to law school, Bob A. was the lone waiter among waitresses. His moustache was finally filling out. He squatted below his tray of soup bowls, then lifted. Unlike the busboys he used his shoulder to balance it.

"I know it's easy to spot the only waiter." Bob A. turned back to her. "But you need something distinctive. It helps make money. You girls all blend together." With his free hand Bob A. reached behind his head. "Especially now."

Appetizers on 41, coffee on 40, pick-up on 50. Greta reached behind her own head and realized that, though busy, she hadn't fully forgotten the strange bun, had not gotten used to it, and knew that all she could hope for was getting used to the idea that she never would. People walked through the kitchen in every direction, random as a kaleidoscope, Greta thought, and through it now she saw the older dishwasher across the kitchen, walking straight at her. Tonight he wore a Walkman, which Greta couldn't believe was rightfully his. His throaty squeaks to the missing music sounded like someone enduring a bad but sometimes funny dream. The headphones didn't muss his hair, which was shaved short as a putting green. She stepped aside as he loped closer, stack of soup bowls shifting in his tattooed arms; they all slid dangerously, but only one fell and broke. The obliged kitchen hurrah stopped mid-course, when the help saw who had done it. From the side Greta saw his new blue sideburns, mutton chops, inked on heavily with Magic Marker.

"It never ends," she heard some waitress moan, but didn't turn in time to catch a face. Greta stood fourth in line at the service bar. Drinks on 50, refill coffee on 52, order on 50. It was as far as she ever got. Others seemed to have better arrangements, a system even. Drinks on 50, refill coffee on 52, order on 50. Greta looked down at her scuffed shoes, which were identically untied.

"Hey," Milt said through his cigarette. "Meet Chet. Like I said, he'll put you on the television."

Greta looked up into a face as craggy as Milt's. "You're perfect," Chet said. "Milt, she's perfect."

Chet looked like he'd be a friend of Milt's. Milt had abused his wife and kids before they left him, but he felt redeemed by the fact that this was long ago and before the vogue, before the exposés cluttered every Sunday feature section in the country. Chet looked like somebody Milt had found wherever he drank on Sundays. Chet's face sagged but his slicked hair protested youth, it shone bright yellow, with a single stiff wave at the top of the skull. Chet did not look TV. He nodded while Milt spoke rapidly. Clearly this wasn't the night's first stop.

"You couldn't see it with how her hair used to be," Milt said.

"You don't believe I can do it," Chet said to her. That's right, Greta thought as she kept her inner chant going. Chet smiled what he must have considered his charmer. "Well believe it. You've got the face. We've still got other places to look, but you've got the face. The open-endedness is there."

"The open-endedness," she said, without losing the chant.

Pick-up on 41, drinks on 40, pick-up on 50. "Gentlemen, I require a mop around front," Chef called to the potscrubbers behind him. Greta was next to skid on the wet tiles. She collected her big order, with a busboy right there to help. Chef had a talent for tossing and sliding things that didn't tip. He filled vegetable dishes carelessly, then flipped them under the heat lamps—but they held the right portion, looked carefully done, stayed upright. Chef hated slower nights like Tuesday and Wednesday, he said everybody worked best when they didn't anticipate. The knuckles of his spine showed through his third shirt of the night. He drank wine spritzers and nibbled when he could at some of his mistakes, which Greta suspected were largely pretend, forged errors, quick energy for the kitchen help.

"Six minutes on your swordfish," he said to her. "And tell them don't start breaking down the salad bar yet."

When the rush abated and it got late enough the help broke things down. It was a restaurant term Greta had trouble with; she found the busboy nonsense words, even, easier to accept. But it was universal. Soon busy restaurants throughout the East would begin breaking down. The break rooms would fill. Conversation fragments would lengthen. Things would slow enough so thousands of floor help could finally feel the night's work in their ankles and spines. Things hadn't finished, but the pace slowed. In the kitchen it was finally observed that the garbage disposal had earlier quit, and that the dishwashers were wrist-deep in a coffee-colored ooze. Two guys coming to work all night on the new carpet arrived early. They stood in the kitchen and looked around. Bob A., still hustling, nearly ran them over. "I'm having a night," Bob A. said. "I'm selling drinks and drinks." He drummed on his tray. "Ordering!" he called to Chef, who told him that a billion Chinese could give fuck-all how many drinks he sold.

Soon Greta began her sidework, filling salt shakers and ketchup bottles. "Where's the zipperhead?" asked one of the underage dishwashers, and Greta noticed that the half-wit with the Magic Marker had disappeared. She reached to count her money. Eleven crumpled dollars came free. Greta felt liquid panic through her legs—but there was more in the other pocket, and some in her apron. Wadded bills fell and change rolled away. At last she corralled it all on the steam table, forty-three and a quarter. She began to unwrinkle and order it, but then saw no point and stopped, and settled for having it all in the same pocket.

"Our Christmas present to us," Danny said. They sat together on the sofa while Greta turned pages in a swank mail-order catalogue. They would select a single extravagance, to be all they'd give to each other, or to themselves. Danny looked over Greta's shoulder. "Hour Magazine" played on TV.

"I'm hungry," Danny said. "Are you hungry?"

Greta leaned over the catalogue. She shook her head no.

"That's right out," Danny said of the unfinished wood table she noticed. "Let's keep looking." Greta flipped quickly past the electronic gear.

"How can you not be hungry?" He bent to see her face. She smiled and shrugged. "Hour Magazine" ended and Danny stood. "I'll make us some chicken."

He kept his recipes in a metal filing box behind the first cabinet door. He pulled a single typed card. He skinned, split, and boned the chicken breast. Before he diced, he trimmed the edges and pulled the long white tendons from either side. He sprinkled flour over a saucer and rolled the pieces there. He set water boiling for rice. He chopped a tomato. He tore lettuce gently and washed it under a soft cold spray. He simmered butter in a small skillet, poured the floured chicken cubes, and added salt, pepper, bay leaf, parsley, tomato, and sauterne. He hung a small towel in his back pocket. He rinsed his dishes as he went along. "Not long till it's done," he called back. "Fifteen minutes and we're eating. At the outside. Fifteen's the absolute limit."

"Sorry," he said, "I interrupted you—but what I meant was, I know I'm not done with it forever, but she's met somebody and it's serious. So many bad things will stop." He threw his head back in the armchair and took a loud breath. "It's about over," he said. Greta framed some remarks but held them. She was happy for him—thus for them, or so it should be—and she wouldn't ruin that.

Again she stripped bed linen, as she'd been doing when Danny hung up with his ex-wife. Down the hall she saw him at the front door, talking but not inviting in.

"Greta," he called after he'd closed it. "Can you bring out a spare Charmin?"

She reached into their closet stock. The first was ripped some, the top sheets folded back on themselves. "For the neighbor," Danny said, walking in. He caught the roll with both hands. "Look at this thing." He reached above her for a new 4-pak. She stared at his shirts, hung in their ten-day rotation.

"What're you thinking?" he said after a minute's silent scrutiny.

"That you're psychotic, mostly."

"At least," he said, "let's give the guy a normal roll of asswipes."

"I'm sure he won't care," Greta said, "and since I certainly don't. . ."

"But *we* do," Danny nearly shouted. He looked at her. Greta was reminded of her dorm years, when mood swings were competitive sport. "It does to me, to us it matters." She wanted to laugh but couldn't. She asked only if they had to go over and present it together, and was rewarded with an empty hug that forgave all.

You worked harder to get more work. On busy nights the reward for coping with chaos was more of it sooner. Get-'em-in-get-'em-out: the busboy chant smudged to a single word, and when two or more of them met in the kitchen they hollered it at each other, overdoing it until Chef told them enough. Saturday night, as if some thin whistle had blown in customers-only pitch, three-fourths of the front dining room paid and exited in a two-minute drove. The remaining strays squinted around and wondered what they'd missed. Busboys left chores elsewhere unfinished and converged on the scene, relishing the red alert while still feigning wonder at it, though when business was good it happened regularly.

At that moment, the back room where Greta worked was near empty too—the customers, heeding some secret command, went to the salad bar as one. The huge lettuce bowls at either end encouraged them to move in any direction they pleased. The two girls in striped aprons had to muscle through with fresh feed. Greta, chanting silently, stood blocked behind all this, tray of hot dinners balanced on a shoulder, steam heating the newly bared skin behind her ear.

Ahead an obese man lisped to someone he called Daddy to don't snatch up all the scallions. Women clutched their purses along with their plates, then failed to keep it all steady—romaine spilled into three-bean salad, croutons sank in sour cream, dressings dripped to paint the shaved ice below, vegetables were crushed into the hours-old carpeting, the laying of which had not been finished, the head hostess warned, so keep one eye down for the deadly seams. Dinners on 72, check on 85, pick-up on 60. An hour and ten, Greta thought she heard for the wait. "All friends are," a person at the lettuce bowl said near Greta's other, colder, ear, "are people in the same place going through the same phases at the same time you are."

For the second time that night Greta was unhappy with Chef; she saw that the crewcut hadn't been terminated for his vanishing act the night before. Tonight he scowled, not showing teeth, and stood at the end of the big machine, pulling clean plates off the plastic-spiked conveyor—the best position, it belonged formerly to the Cuban who stood now up front scraping unfinished food from what the busboys hustled in. The underage was in the pit, rinsing the dishes, disposing the garbage, feeding the steamy machine. The crewcut wore pink rubber gloves. The inky blue mutton chops held unfaded, and he still groaned along to the Walkman's silent command.

One busboy lobbed used cloth napkins, the other finished them off with a stuff into the laundry bag. They laughed hard at something. Going out they feinted incoming traffic: no acting there, people years on the job still moved uneasily in a kitchen too big for established paths. The Saturday night kitchen was made especially perilous by the engaging blonde salad runner, whose hair swung fleecy and free in defiance of the new rules, and who worked only Saturdays, causing busboys and kitchen help to stop short at every chance and chat her up. As Greta moved along the kitchen wall and out a cheer greeted the blast of emergency alarm. At the back door the new potscrubber wrestling garbage barrels had pushed the lever rather than wait for someone with a key.

Dessert on 72, drinks on 60, check on 85. Chef had first displeased her that night when she arrived in her big hoop earrings. "No chance," Chef said. "Sorry." Undaunted and still on retainer, Bob A. was advising. "I don't look at my drink tray," he said as he waited on the phone for credit-card clearance. "I carry it out here, waist-level. But don't stiffen up, and don't ever look down—when you watch the stuff you spill it."

At the bar Greta noticed Milt wasn't in. A busboy fought through the herd and dumped two buckets of new ice. Bob C. the bartender needed a new Tab tank connected downstairs, but the busboy, fighting his way out already, shouted back something about a billion Chinese. The cubes came from the kitchen machine together, in gridded chunks, but tonight the heat was such that they'd shrunk and separated in the buckets, before they reached the bar.

Greta wondered if she wasn't just not seeing Milt. Only the deranged would squeeze in here on a Saturday night just to drink weak drinks, but Milt hadn't missed a Saturday since Greta was the coat-check girl. Behind Greta the head hostess had intercepted the Sinophile busboy and was chewing him out as quietly as she could. Then the manager interrupted her with something urgent.

"I wouldn't get my hopes up," Bob A. said to Greta, who

slid an $18.65 check and a $100 bill across to Clovilla the cashier. "Most Guidos that flash that stuff, they tip lousy." Bob A. reached around her for a doggie bag. "He goes over ten percent, you come tell me."

Rare prime rib was out already. With a blue marker, the sauté cook posted the news—RARE RIB 86—on his paper hat. Officially, Clovilla the cashier was information officer, but on nights like this, as if wasted with vertigo, she glued her eyes on her till and her paperwork and refused even a glance at the swarming kitchen. In front of her bowed head the manager now collected the six busboys and gave them a coin. The loser won the ladies room and its vomit-spattered wall. The busboys were uneasy, but joked hard when the loser set off for the job. The swell of bunned waitresses at the broiler grew while Chef explored the walk-in for something he claimed only he could find. He'd been talking nonstop since six-thirty. Greta stood last in the line, chanting fast, noticing the subtly looser hair behind all heads.

She ran for another solid hour, then had a minute to wash her face. The door to her small locker hung open. Only the earrings, which had been sitting on top, were gone. An older waitress came in, splashed herself with cold water, and squinted the latest rumor Greta's way: IRS audits of everybody, beginning the week after Christmas. Alone again, Greta sat on a closed toilet and tried to relax. She breathed deeply, then worked her chant back up to two tasks before she returned to the floor.

Then, approaching the service bar, she lost the chant completely. She knew it was legitimate, the third guy with Milt and Chet was real. As soon as she saw: thirtyish, a Singapore Sling and a baseball cap on the bar in front of him, awful posture, a white Goodwill shirt and drab olive pants, a beard, hair combed straight back.

"Greta," Chet said. "My son Steve."

"Yes," Steve said. Then after a moment, "Hi, I suppose Chet's told you all. It's a Waring's, silent vignette, with a little girl, yours is, runs two and a quarter seconds at the most. I think you'd be perfect, but everybody on the project needs a look." Steve handed her a card. "C'mon downtown a week from Monday."

Greta still must have looked like she felt in the bathroom. Milt touched her lightly on the forearm.

"I told you open-endedness," Chet said to his son.

Milt said to Greta, "They owe me a favor and you're it. No lines though, kid. The theme song plays all through. The sharing-caring people of Waring's Restaurants. Fast food's not the competition, strictly speaking. But I'll square it with the warden here just to be sure. I'm your agent by the way, which means nothing, except be nice to me. I'm not taking a dime."

"It's Milt's only motto," Chet said, elbowing him. "Be nice to me."

"A week from Monday," said Steve.

Greta had to pick up. Another minute and Chef would throw the filets at her. And after that she had to clear 60, and ask sweetly about coffee or maybe some dessert. One of the newer girls had a walk-out on a seventy-two-dollar check, just now. The manager and two busboys dashed to the parking lot but came back empty. The new girl sobbed softly over Clovilla's desk; she tried to stop herself but couldn't. Word got around, and at four dollars a head the floor help had it covered in fifteen minutes. Bob A. paid his share in quarters and dimes. He said a walk-out's your own fault, no matter how busy you are.

But there was no time to consider any of it. It was the busiest night in months. "I sold three hundred ribs last night," said the sauté cook, "I may be there again already." Clovilla ran out of tip trays—they were all in use, or stolen. The manager couldn't find any in stock. Checks went to the tables on saucers and on bread plates, and the head hostess fumed. Greta passed Bob A. in the flock at the salad bar. "I heard some guy just had a coronary right outside the door," Bob A. said, as softly as he could. "I'll finish telling you later." There was a kid in a coat and tie, somebody's nephew with a heaping salad plate, and he asked Bob A. "Was he coming in or out?" but the waiter was off for the service bar. Nearby a body went sprawling over a carpet seam.

In the kitchen the main dishwashing machine went down. They were using the smaller silverware washer for everything. Plates piled up, the stacks made shaky by unfinished food. Back on the floor, Greta heard Bob A. bellow "I'm out of rare rib!" into a hearing aid. She went into the kitchen to retrieve three things she'd forgotten, but could remember only two.

The pretty blonde salad runner sliced off the very tip of her finger cutting date-nut bread. Greta was standing six feet away. Chef rushed the fragment into ice from a passing shrimp cocktail, and the assistant manager drove it all to the hospital. The girl's face was blank as she hurried past. Greta's chant got simpler and faster—she told herself only what to do next. The head hostess toured the floor screaming license numbers from three different states, cars with headlights burning. A minute later Greta ran out into the cold with four doggie bags she'd just packed, chasing the people who'd walked off and forgotten. When she came back inside she heard the rumor about the salad girl's finger begin its way around the lounge. And for the first time all night, Greta noticed the red fuzz on everyone's feet, from the sections of new carpet.

Though there was no time, she needed a minute. Her chant shrunk to a single, personal chore—sitting down. They would all have to wait. At the service bar she broke all the rules, made herself an ice water in plain view, and carried it back to the kitchen by hand. She sat in the empty break room. There was no moon, and the window overlooking the golf course was fullest black. In it the bright kitchen reflected clearly. Greta stared down into the free floating ice. In a moment she became conscious again of her foolish bunned hair. She looked up, and she saw the sharp reflection of the older dishwasher standing just behind her. He was in focus. She could see the new ink, a lopsided blue moustache that clipped nostril on one side and smudged lip on the other. In the kitchen's backlighting she could see stray crewcut bristles, could see the tattooed wrist, and, because of the slight angle, could see the pink-rubbered hand that twisted her bound hair like the stubborn lid of a glass jar. Even the teeth reflected sharply. In the smile she recognized now the shadings of decay centered in each tooth; no message, no lettering. If he prevented her from pivoting, or if she just didn't, she couldn't tell. She thought of nothing while he was there. She guessed he never reached the roots: it wasn't particularly painful. At any rate it didn't last long. Soon he stopped and turned his back, and his reflection receded into the kitchen again.

Greta left the break room. She came diagonally across the

kitchen and cracked head-on into a charging busboy. It happened near the threshold of the dining rooms, and near Clovilla, who finally looked up. It was Greta's fault. She, the busboy, and his two tiers of bar glasses scattered. All the restaurant hushed for seconds afterward: it was a horrible crash. On the floor Greta drew in her legs and pushed back so she could lean against the coffee machine. She rested there, declining hands offered down. Chef came over and looked at her. He told the head hostess to send her home.

She felt better a few minutes later, but didn't contest leaving the night unfinished. They sat her in the manager's office with ice for her forehead. The dishwasher seemed to have vanished again. A junior hostess tied her hair back and took part of Greta's station. Bob A. volunteered for the other part. The busboy had bloodied both hands, neither seriously. Through the office's glass panel Greta could see the busboys making chatter as they charged in and out of the kitchen. She couldn't hear, but knew that they mimicked the sound, they mimed the explosion. It occurred then to Greta that the busboy coda, the only justification for their slang and jokes and rituals and hard camaraderie, for all their elaborate behavior, was a maxim brief enough to print on their T-shirts or glue across the bumpers of their prized cars. All they did and said, all anyone ever seemed to do and say, could be stripped to four words: Be More Like Me. But maybe that was right, and as good as any other.

Clovilla offered to call for Greta's ride but Greta did it herself, from the manager's phone. She told Danny only that she needed to be picked up. He said he'd come when the documentary ended, fifteen minutes at the most. Greta fetched her sweater, and out in front of the restaurant she untied her hair. The four-sided wind gusted again. Greta stood out in it, she let it whip her skirt and lash her hair around her jaws. She hoped it might blow away some of that tenacious restaurant smell. While she waited a cab pulled up, and after a while Milt and his two friends came down the steps and piled in, chattering. Off to scout more vignette talent, Milt said. "Monday," Steve said, and shook a finger at her. Chet crooned half of the caring-sharing jingle before the cab rolled away.

The throbbing in her forehead became her only sensation, all Greta chose to recognize. She could pull her whole self up into her head, bathe in the dull ache, shut out the cold and ubiquitous wind. Greta thought idly about her parents and her seven brothers and sisters, and then she culled from nowhere the names of people she'd lost track of in high school or before. She wondered how many people she had known, as one said "Sure, I know him" of acquaintances, and wondered how many hundreds of names she could list if required. She thought briefly about her name, her voice, her looks, herself, and about all the night's events. The car rolled to a stop by the front steps and she lowered herself in. "Hi," he said. Then an exaggerated shiver, and without malice Danny said, "Close the door." She said hello and was quiet a minute, holding all her news. And Danny did speak first, did have a story to tell, and as they rode home Greta suspected it wouldn't be at all difficult, as time passed it might in fact become dismally easy, to stay silent about all that had happened, to leave it unfinished, and to keep it hers.

AGENCY

For my one hundredth day at the employment agency, Coleman announced he was springing for lunch someplace nice. Precisely at twelve, he threw my down jacket over the phone I was using. "Let's roll," he said.

Outside, it was raining harder than our tinted windows showed. I straightened my necktie and moved toward the parking lot, but Coleman said we could walk; he'd picked Guillermo's, right there in the plaza complex, a place I didn't consider all that nice—certainly never as nice as it was crowded. A hostess led us to a converted cocktail lounge, and a small table about eighteen inches from the next one. Coleman refused it. "We'd like something civil," he said. We sat on a purple bench by the reservations desk. "We don't look sharp enough," Coleman said to me. We waited to what seemed clearly beyond our turn. Then Coleman stood up.

"Easy," I said. He let the hostess pass, but pursued a waiter leading two young gray suits toward the Tampico Room. One of Coleman's hands grabbed the waiter's collar, the other flailed at the menus. The restaurant help converged faster than you'd expect. In no time a busboy had Coleman by the legs, and down they went, near the wooden plank for the nighttime guitarists. I found myself standing between tables with the two gray suits; we all watched Coleman flail like a nasty fish, with the waiters on haunches or knees all around him, looking to grab a piece that wouldn't hurt them. They finally got him quieter, and vertical—but then he was bucking again, shouting things, and backpedaling unassisted for the door.

We stood in the hard drizzle. "Half my age, some of them." He struggled to breathe normally. "And built. I had no case." He was panting and smiling. In a minute he was being funny about it, plotting to phone a series of fake reservations whose first letters would spell out vicious, hateful messages, and though I still felt humiliated I found myself smiling at this, and at him. On the way to his car I suggested a quick deli that sold beer, but he drove through at Burger King and returned to the same parking spot. His car smelled musty, and a little rank. Our building—four stories, new brick, brown glass—filled the driver's side windows. Coleman was calmer now. His deep voice had come back. Almost daintily, he pulled things from the big white bag.

"I had a backache last time I hit that deli," he said. "Then with their heartburn I had it in stereo. All afternoon I felt like I was impaled."

He studied the wide computerized receipt for a long time.

He opened his burger carton, poured his fries into the empty half. He squeezed his ketchup into a corner. I'd moved to the back seat, so we could stretch out. Coleman folded the white bag and tucked it in the glove compartment, whose open door held his Pepsi. Settled, he hoisted his cup.

"To your hundredth day."

"Thanks," I said, hoisting mine. "To your ninth."

We'd eaten together only a couple of times so far. The office had no lunch room, and Mrs. Roy banned eating at the desks. I skipped lunch completely or I went out for something. Coleman ate lunch in his car. I talked to him enough in the office. He'd told all about himself, his layoff, his jobs before that one, his court adventures, his ex-wife's career as a caterer, his aborted second engagement, the two-thousand-dollar teeth in his head. I had no complaints, though; he asked questions as often as he explained about himself.

Today he'd made a job placement and wanted to talk business. How many days did I take to make my first placement? How long had it taken the woman before him on the Secretarial desk? Did I think he coached his girls too much: was it better to let them interview dumb and natural? Had I seen who he asked out this morning, sweet little farm girl typed just twenty-two words a minute but with no mistakes? Did I do as much cold-calling for job orders as when I started? How long did it take to get rolling, make real money? What sort of commission could we talk, realistically, in a fair-to-good month? I fudged some answers—I thought it fairer to report what I could have been doing, had I been working harder.

Coleman was a little overweight. I guessed that he'd never been handsome, but was no less so now than he used to be.

He grew his hair long at the sides, but instead of combing it over his thinning top he let it cover his ears to the lobes. His lunch was gone in something under three minutes. He removed the straw and plastic cover to get at the last of his drink. Now he seemed fully relaxed. When he spoke slowly his voice dropped still deeper.

"How old do I sound on the phone?"

"Don't think I've ever heard," I said. "That's what you mean, right, through the wires? Not across the office."

His digital watch beeped once, on the hour.

"We're due," I said.

"Take some time," Coleman said. "Finish your drink. The old girl can wait. You give her way too much credit for being sharp."

Mrs. Roy, who'd been there three years, was our supervisor. She was short and she wore sweaters year round. Coleman was disappointed—working for a woman in a place called One Plaza Center hadn't been anything like he'd imagined, sexy and high tech. Already I'd heard variations on this.

"I was hoping," he said today, "for a boss in completely unsensible shoes. And those camisole things, which I just found out the name of yesterday. You know the things I mean?"

"I do."

"They wear them under silk blouses. I had my heart set on silk blouses, too. And hair that looks great if they'd wear it down. Somebody driven, Ms. Somethington, looking a little drawn, like she needs a rest."

"Scary," I said. "The new woman."

"I didn't expect sweaters with snaps," he said. "Or hats like this person wears. Or a purse like a gym bag. Doesn't do it. I expected Ms. Somethingdale, ruthless in seven-dollar nylons."

"Seven-dollar nylons would frighten me," I said.

"Seven-dollar nylons would be great," Coleman said. "And they shouldn't scare you at all, Gil, you could thrive in there. Let's face it, they're your peers. You're thirty?"

"Twenty-six," I said.

"Twenty-six, even," Coleman said. "I like your chances to mine."

The next day Nona came to work for Plaza Temporaries, our sister firm, with offices two floors below us in One Plaza Center. She had first come upstairs to us, looking for secretarial work. Coleman took her application. Then he had some stories for her. They all featured a younger Coleman doing business abroad, stroking men of means and haggling with the service sector, having it his way in a brand-new language. He'd been talking to her for a long time when Mrs. Roy came back from lunch. One look—Nona was older, well groomed, friendly—and Mrs. Roy offered her the receptionist's job downstairs.

Nona did the job well enough. But she improved Plaza just by being there. Though their office space was identical to ours, modern and severe, it always seemed to me a disorganized, lethargic place. The frumpy young office girls were like the parade past Coleman's Secretarial desk; among them only Nona seemed aware that she was out in the world every day, and that it meant something. Nona knew how to apply makeup. She wore pearl earrings and looped strands of pearls around her neck and around one wrist. She had an overbite that looked somehow adult. I didn't know ages, but I figured

Coleman had a dozen years on me, and Nona had a few years more. She had a husband who died in '72, and a son gone from home last month to join the navy.

After Guillermo's that week fell into repetitiveness. I had some out-of-town employers in the office interviewing every afternoon, and I prepared my unworldly clients every morning. We had no facilities—they interviewed at my desk while I tried to stay out of sight. I'd wander toward Coleman. If he wasn't with a prospective secretary he probably had one on the phone.

"I'd ask only that you not share this job information with anybody," Coleman said to every one of them. "It's all I have, this information, it's how I make my living. Please keep it confidential."

One time I had my printed business cards, finally, to show off. One time I had some news article for him—just a blurb really, seven paragraphs. He put it flat on his desk and leaned on his elbows. Though I couldn't believe it, I thought I saw Nona's name, with the hands of a clock adjacent, written in a couple of spots on his Weekly Minder. I framed a remark or two about this news article, which Coleman should have finished reading by then. I looked at Nona's name again and tried to make out the times, which were probably either 6:00 or 12:30. I looked back at Coleman, and he was still reading.

Quite often I'd walk down two flights to Plaza, where Nona always looked glad to see me. If she was busy she was too polite to say. She forwarded calls and took messages, and then in the same soft voice went back to talking about her only child and the navy, about my fuzzy career plans, about her new job, about my little bouts of depression just sitting around at night by myself. I waited for mention of Coleman. I hadn't seen them together since their first day, and the image grew harder to recall.

One day I sat on the painted cement wall in the lobby, fingering the cedar chips under the rubber trees. Coleman came down.

"Smoke break," he said.

"Your hire guy still up there?"

"Yup, and if my chickie can just watch her little mouth five more minutes, I think she's got a job. I'd like to call time-out and tell her how close she is. I don't think she knows." Coleman lighted his cigarette. "Three placements, this'll be. Her fee makes this month's draw, and the next one starts *co*-mission."

"The fee employer-paid?"

"No sir."

"Stay after these girls," I said. "They want payment dragged out, a zillion installments. That may help you later, but it hurts you now."

"But we have collection people."

"At six months delinquent," I said. "Till then you're on your own."

"Gil," Coleman said. "Is it the same on the Management desk, or is it different? Is it like these girls come in and sit down and act civil for an hour so you can give them a job? You know? Little girls think it's all handed out somewhere, it's all in one bin or another, you grab your tray and get in line and walk it on through. They shouldn't earn something, or be told something, or have to make impressions. They come in for a job like they're signing up for free cheese, that type thing."

"That's why I like Plaza," I said. "The temps seem to take it more seriously, they're more mature about it. And there's something relaxed about that whole place."

"No commission down there."

"Yeah," I said. "Commission's a bitch."

Coleman looked at me. "Things get done on commission. Commission's how the whole world should run." He ground out his cigarette. "God knows I need a commission check and soon. An expensive week, this has been."

"Not much Spamming it in the car lately, I've noticed."

"No sir," Coleman said. He patted his pockets for the pack, then for the lighter. His watch beeped once.

"Three o'clock," he said. "Don't panic—only two hours to go. It beeps once no matter what the hour."

When Coleman spoke again his voice seemed deeper. "Nona likes you, Gil."

"You too, it would seem." Until that moment I'd kept some doubts about his Weekly Minder.

Coleman smiled, and after another beat he laughed. "Sort of silly, and excuse my asking. But what's the gossip on us?"

"I'm nobody to ask," I said. "I really don't know. I don't think any. I haven't heard a whisper." I talked some more, but Coleman seemed uncomfortable and he cut me off.

"Anyhow," he said, "I'm supposed to ask you over to dinner sometime soon. That's my assignment. We'd like to have you."

"You've moved in?" I said. He took it as a joke and laughed heartily. "No, no," he said. The new shirt he was wearing looked good on him, classy and comfortable. It was clean, but he seemed to be wearing it all the time now, almost every day.

What he said next seemed unreal to me. It wasn't that I didn't know what he was talking about. It wasn't even that I didn't believe him, really.

"You forget what it's like," Coleman said. "How it makes a difference how somebody else's day is going. This goes back many many years for me. You know, having it be important. Wondering what mood somebody else is in, right now, how their day is going, at this exact moment."

Then Coleman acted embarrassed. "At any rate," he said.

As it turned out we ate in a restaurant, the dining room of a two-star hotel. Nona and Coleman were there ahead of me. They sat in the back of the cocktail lounge, talking. He wore a navy blue blazer and white turtleneck, and he'd gotten his hair trimmed. Nona's pink dress had a wide bow at the waist and a neckline wider than it was deep, showing a trail of freckles from the throat off toward each shoulder. They looked comfortable but not intimate. She had to push closer to Coleman to make room for me on the end.

"You both look very nice," Nona said.

We were in the Castaways Lounge of the Piper Inn. People sat in the orange curved chairs alone or in pairs, looking tired. Some small kids ran wild in the lobby, the restaurant, even the bar. Their parents lacked the energy to control them.

"This is kind of nice," I said to Coleman, after I'd adjusted to the surroundings, and to the sight of the two of them. "An interesting choice."

"Nona's suggestion," he said.

"I worked here once," she said. "On the reservations desk,

back before my son Jeffrey became a full-time job." Nona smiled and looked around. "I thought I'd still know people here."

"It's a chain," Coleman said, tapping his cocktail napkin. "I had no idea there were other Piper Inns until a few minutes ago."

We had drinks. A hostess came and lifted our third round onto her cork tray. We followed her to our table, a booth. Coleman had the bar check, and he tapped my shoulder with it. "This is mine tonight. Touch your wallet, I'll strangle you."

The booth was curved and heavily padded. The table wasn't as close to me as I would have liked. Immediately, Coleman got up for more cigarettes.

"Order whatever you want," he said.

When he was gone I held Nona gently on her wrist. I said, "He's only making his draw. He's six weeks away from any commission."

We looked the menu over. Nona said, "Just come up two or three from the bottom, Gil." She smiled at me. "You've never heard that? Really? Well I'll be the one to teach you. It's manners I learned early. When a peer treats, or anyone on a budget, you go about three dishes up from the lowest."

"The sole, then. Eight-fifty."

"That's it," she said.

"You look quite nice by the way. Terrific."

"Thanks," Nona smiled again. "I've had this one. The working wardrobe is what'll kill my first check. My first checks."

When Coleman came back she took a cigarette, the first

I'd known that she smoked. Our waitress looked new, and a little nervous. She stuttered some over the specials, which sounded good to me, but which were priced below everything else. We all ordered for ourselves, Nona returning her menu with a small smile as soon as she was done. Coleman studied his for a long time. The girl stood and waited. She could have been nineteen or twenty-nine, plump, arms swirled in fine hair, complexion dotted light red. Coleman grilled her on the specials again. She was unsure, and went to double-check in the kitchen. When she came back Coleman ordered from the menu, the fourteen-dollar lobster.

After we were seated the restaurant filled up. The food was subpar, but it came right away.

"I'm sorry that fish is so skimpy," Nona said to me. "You're welcome to some of this."

"No, no," I said. "No thank you. There's enough here for me."

Coleman disdained the lobster bib when the waitress offered it. "Does he know your tricks?" he said to Nona. "What you used to do?"

"What do you mean?" Nona said.

"With feeding your kid."

"Oh," she said. "No I never told. It worked on Jeffrey for eleven years." She turned to me. "Once I was widowed we didn't spend much on groceries, so I always put less on his plate to start and more on mine. Plus a little left in the pot. There have to be seconds, psychologically. And after he cleaned the pot he could have some of mine, which was more than I wanted."

"Isn't that amazing?" Coleman said, cracking shell. "The

kid felt full after every meal. Eleven years." He had that tiny lobster fork in the air to make his point. "As long as there's kids, folks with some experience can really do business."

"How does he like the navy?" I said to Nona.

"I think he'll like it fine," she said. "Right now he's got a thousand complaints. In his first letter he sent me these crazy charts they gave out, Rube Goldberg stuff."

They both looked at the expression on my face.

"Rube Goldberg," Coleman said. "Rube Goldberg."

"He was a cartoonist," Nona said.

"We're here with an infant," Coleman said. "A toddler."

"Yeah," I said. I had that same unreal feeling, and my pulse was picking up. "It's not *my* tantrums I'm worried about."

"Hey fella," Coleman said. He altered his voice. He made it sound purposely silly. "You don't lay off I'll put out your lights, I'll ring your bell, I'll clean your clock."

Nona laughed, she thought it very funny. I tried to relax, beginning with the muscles in my toes. I wondered how well they knew each other and I decided not very well, certainly not as Coleman had hinted to me. A week and a half, they'd shared a meal or two. I pictured them in his car, Coleman cursing the traffic, Nona breathing through her mouth.

Coleman made us sample the lobster. He flagged the waitress and asked for more drawn butter.

"I came back here two weeks ago," Nona said. "Before I went to the agency. They wouldn't have me, though." She looked at both of us and smiled. "Probably just as well."

Coleman held her wrist a moment. "What are the rooms like here?" he said.

There was quiet. I didn't look to see what Nona was doing. I sipped my drink. More quiet. "Expensive," I finally said.

"Not what I meant," Coleman said. "I meant are they nice."

"They're quite large," Nona said.

We were done sooner than I'd expected. Our waitress didn't ask how things were until Nona and I were finishing and Coleman was done. In a few minutes she cleared our plates and offered coffee, which we all declined. Soon Coleman was wondering where the check was.

"I guess we look pretty settled here," Nona said.

"Which one's ours now?" Coleman was turned in his seat. "Fun is goddamn fun, and all, but let's go. Where did that chickie run off to? Nona's got a cat to feed."

"Oh he'll be fine," she said. "Let's sit a while longer."

"But this girl makes no sense," Coleman said. "We're done—we're not buying anything else. How can she not put the goddamn check down?"

"You scared her off," I said.

Coleman drank his water glass dry. "They have parties waiting out there."

"It's all right," Nona said.

"Go tackle her," I said. "That gets us noticed."

Nona gasped and laughed. "I know you didn't tackle a waitress."

"A waiter," I said.

"I exercised bad judgment," Coleman said.

I excused myself. On my way to the men's room I spoke to the hostess. When I came back the check was there, and Coleman was helping Nona out of the booth. Then he held a dollar out to me. "Would you get her coat?"

"Sure thing."

"Take it," he said. The dollar stuck between my fingers.

Her coat was some kind of fur. I couldn't tell if it was real. As I retrieved it she came up behind me.

"He's trouble sometimes, Nona," I said. "He can be one hateful son of a bitch."

I helped her on with it, and she wrapped herself tight. When she was done she looked up at me.

"I remember I hit Jeffrey once. It was in a public place, at the town pool—all the more amazing for me. I had my bathing suit on. That always made him uncomfortable. He was with the kid who drove him there and he was acting like a jerk, so I called him over. It shamed him to be seen with me, much less obey. He was fifteen then, learning things. He said something, it was unbelievably foul, and I hit him in the face. He looked so embarrassed for me. He wished I was stronger, I think."

We found Coleman in the lobby. He stood with a bearded guy, about my age: an army jacket folded over his elbow, some rumpled fives and tens in his free hand. He was in line at the reservations desk, where at the front a customer was dickering with a young employee. Nona wanted to stay where she was. I went over, and I could hear them before I got there.

"This is unreal," the man said. "I'm Earl Hasty's nephew. I remember you from Fourth of Julys."

"You're going back a long ways," Coleman said.

"What're you doing here, anyway?"

"Don't know," Coleman said. "Being out on the town. Being half in the bag, mostly. You're getting a room here?"

"All-night poker."

"Gil," Coleman said to me. Then he tapped the guy, who'd turned back toward the reservations desk. "Meet my friend,"

Coleman said to him. "Meet Gil, a guy I like a lot. Gil, this is a seven-year-old kid used to loiter in my old, old circles."

Now Nona was coming over. Behind her our waitress stood in the restaurant doorway, looking out at Coleman.

"What's her problem?" said Earl Hasty's nephew.

"She's stupid, is what," Coleman said. "She's running around, not looking out, and it cost her."

"You didn't stiff her," I said.

"She earned every penny," he said.

"Coleman you did not," Nona said. "I can't believe you did. Hear me now, that just isn't right."

He gave us a brief, one-shouldered shrug, and was through the door.

Outside, his voice grew louder and higher. "Do you know what tip means?" he said. "What it *means*?" He walked backwards in the parking lot. "To Insure Promptness, that's where it comes from. Common goddamn sense—you put the check on the table. She cries and quits tonight, she's lucky." He half staggered, half danced. "You put the check down. You turn the table over. You get new customers in there."

A few steps behind him, Nona reached and hugged me, as best she could with one arm. I moved in closer.

Coleman shouted, "How fair to a real waitress, tip that chickie?"

"You have a car?" Nona said to me.

"Yes," I said. She'd relaxed her arm, but I held her with mine. "It's not far, just around the other side."

She froze for a moment. "No, no," she said. "I meant you didn't take a bus, someone hadn't driven you. We can't drop you anywhere?"

At his car, Coleman opened the passenger side, pulled the

front seat forward, moved his small traveling bag from the back seat to the floor. "Climb in, kid," he said. "We can run you over to yours."

I refused with a motion. He let the seat swing upright. Nona kissed me and got in.

"Gil," Coleman said. "That kid, he's playing cards all night. Believe me Gil, he's just like that waitress. And like all my chickies. Go in and make some money. He's from a lazy, losing family. Believe me, play hard ninety minutes and you'll clean him out. Go ahead, have fun, see you Monday. Go ahead."

WAIT

Sometimes, our phone gives a hollow first ricochet as warning. This time it just rang. My brother had received a promotion and a substantial raise, to $41,000. He called from Kansas City and this was his subject. We went on about the dead pennant hopes of his Royals and my Pirates and our native Red Sox, and about coming summer vacations (and about cars, too—I had acquired an appalling long-distance habit of asking after people's cars, elaborately, as you would of a relative, though I could not have cared less about them), but it was Jerry's raise, even more than the promotion, that powered his voice along the wires and restored its Rhode Island harshness.

"People are saying," Jerry said, "my friends here are saying: 'I wouldn't know what to do with it all.' Stupid. I know exactly how I'm starting."

The line crackled for several seconds.

"Hello?" I finally said.

"Where'd you think? And don't say invest."

"I don't know Jerry, a car bar?" Jerry was my only brother. He was the tougher of us; I was considered less dangerous. Jerry had needed the bulk of his teens and twenties to brood and find weapons for making his way in the world. He built office space now and I knew little about him. Only what he called to tell me.

"You've got to come out, Glen Paul. I'm going to buy a bass boat."

"That's excellent."

"And the bass boat that I buy is going to have an outboard in the back, and it's going to have an electric motor in front, with foot pedals. I'm really doing it. So make some time. By Labor Day weekend, I'll have one."

"Bring Daddy out there."

"I will. I'm thinking I want to get a tackle box roughly the size of a golf bag, and a ridiculous big spread of lures. I'm getting rod holders, and I'm rigging the bitch with a custom bait well and I'm going to rug the bottom and pad the seats. And then next year, a sonar fish finder."

I whistled for him.

"I hope all this shit's available out here. I may need catalogs, keep an eye out, if you would. I've been running to gear shops nonstop since my boss told me today. It blew me away. It's finally through my thick head that the good things just happen, you can't be ready."

"Well, congratulations."

"I don't think I can sleep. I wanted to find somebody to

share it with right here, you know, but it's slim pickings at Andre's Sportsworld or wherever. Tomorrow night I'll get that going."

"Where's Barbara?"

"Somebody has to tell me. I haven't gotten a smile since Memorial Day. From anybody, come to think of it. It's been bad times. Bad, bad. Sorry to complain, but I'm a tad overripe here. It's near the point now, I hear dress heels clicking out the window, just crossing the parking lot, and boom I've got a handful."

"But," he said. "Enough. Changing the subject here. How's things, you working?"

I told him about my job for the week; I'd been hired by a man named Bevis Kelvar to photograph a big meeting of district credit managers. My wife, who'd known Kelvar on business since the year before, got me the job.

"How's that wife holding up?" Jerry said. "She's been busting it for that outfit two years now, at least."

"It's a little tense sometimes," I said. "A lot of things are kind of adding up at once."

"She's maybe due for a little breather then."

"I guess so."

"Nothing like a little bass fishing," Jerry said. "You need to see how I get along out here, both of you."

We had been making love when the call came. As it continued Nancy rolled over and when I hung up, long after midnight, she stirred. She was warm. She reached along her jaw for a tangle of hair that wasn't there.

"That was your brother?" she said.

"Uh-huh. I thought you were asleep."

"Mostly I was," Nancy said. "But with Jerry you get the tune of it pretty quick. Your voice goes all Rhody and blunt and on guard."

"I apologize," I said. "I shouldn't have answered."

Nancy is of the sort who can say "Come back later" to someone's face. She is stronger than I am. Eager to please and quick to answer, jumpy when offense might be taken—these traits govern my life to its smallest corners. Nancy holds her tongue, ignores the inadequate, lets telephones ring themselves dead, refuses to participate in surveys. She is embarrassed for herself rarely, and for others never at all—their problems are their own.

Usually she withheld opinion on my brother. If this implied she thought him beneath it, fine. When they met over Rhode Island holidays Nancy ignored him without seeming to. Now she listened without a twitch to my description of Jerry and his new raise.

"This is your brother," she said.

"So he crows a little."

"Oh a little," she said. "He loves to be loved from below. He likes a fixed game. He'll only compete where there's no competition."

"I'm outfucking him," I said. "We talked about that."

Nancy gave a tired laugh. She groped for the lamp.

"Raises always happen out of the blue," I said, squinting. I had worked at nothing but freelance photography since graduation, and my last real raise was from the Shell station at home, but still I imagined that I understood. "You know that. Even for someone like you who has the guts to ask and ask. It comes unexpectedly. You can't think about much else for a few hours."

"And you can't wait for the next." She stood and found her nightgown among the lower sheets. "Right away you want another."

"That's right."

"And since you can't have another one the alternative is to run this ego trip again and again and call up everybody you know. And certain people resist the impulse, and the Jerrys don't."

"Jobs matter to him. They make news. He doesn't want to be my brother on a schedule. This stuff's something real to tell, and that's worth a dozen of these Christmas deals to him."

The wrinkled nightgown fell over her. "Glen Paul, please."

"What please? It's all true. He does what he feels like doing. I'm not saying he's somebody you can like, objectively."

"Your brother likes himself," she said. "A lot. *That's* why he gives lousy Christmas presents."

She was off to the bathroom. She had wanted to conceive our first baby by last month, August, at the latest. Her mother told her don't be pregnant in the summer: carry in the fall, winter, and spring. Our failure over recent weeks and a false alarm last year had frustrated her unusually, and past trusting herself. She thought she might have conceived. I believed it true, and told myself so. We would know the next day—her appointment was for ten-thirty in the morning. We'd had sex on more than half the nights of the month. Even so, she had undressed me in front of the television fifteen minutes before my brother called. She'd looked tired in the blue glow, and tireder now. My fondling now was tentative, of the defensive variety.

"I can't stay up," Nancy said. "It's one-something already."

"Sorry about stopping."

"Don't apologize so much. It's pointless to cram. If we can't pass by now, then we won't."

Nancy drifted off. I had to wait for sleep. I had rusty methods from old acting classes, tricks to clear my mind, but they were sure to fail on these hardest nights, which came months apart and found me unprepared. There is little way to describe these occasions other than to call them mawkish. In the morning they're mawkish; at the time, in the dark, they seem important and new. I brought myself near tears one night by imagined success at recollecting doors: the feel, the tension, the sound, of dozens opened regularly—to schools, apartments, cars, sheds, offices, safes, deep freezes, garages, cupboards, closets, bathrooms, lockers, bedrooms, a 767 once in a comic traveler's nightmare—and then forgot about it completely until I went to the refrigerator in the morning.

These flashes didn't require the dark; they came also when I was in the car, and alone. My freelance work was mostly outside the city, but when I drove downtown there was an element in emerging from the Fort Pitt tunnel that—if I did it rarely enough—gave the same quick delusion of clarity. It involved turning out. Not that I'd done it poorly or well, but a low-level joy that I had, in fact, turned out. In the opening-credits scenery and the traffic I remembered that I was here in a city my family had never even seen, working a newly mastered stick shift, a back seat heavy with photographer's gear, a low sun highlighting in the windshield mirror one side of a face I hadn't much looked at in ten years, a new face with tiny craters and a ten-hour beard and a dry, adult shine to the jaw.

These moments came unpatterned as the worst weather; I could never keep them waiting for the proper intervals of ceremony. On I-279 East I thought about time and love, age and family. Rhode Island every Christmas, church when I attended, couldn't do the same.

And I suspected a raise held the same sort of mirror for Jerry. That was why he called. Something had become, was becoming, of him. He turned out—how well was secondary. As vague as those feelings were, we both saw that they involved permanence, and permanence was all tied up in family, always, even as we moved into a future where we meant even less to each other than we did now.

It was 1:58. On my back in bed, with my wife asleep beside me, I tried blowing myself up, as they'd called it in drama class. A good session should take an hour. Imagine each breath inflating you, filling you with air, slowly, starting at the smallest end of the farthest toe.

Nancy slept. In another exercise, you took your chin in your hand and worked the jaw until, so they said, it let go completely and all muscles went slack. My drama teacher did it every day without full success, but she knew someone who knew someone who'd made it, and reported that the sensation put orgasm in the shade. In our summer sessions we worked at it thirty minutes a day, without any winners.

It was true that I had always been poor at the exercises. And that I couldn't act besides. A month after I got to college I gave it up completely. I couldn't even be low-key on cue, never mind giggly or enraged. Jerry was a better actor but by high school he'd abandoned all supervised extracurriculars.

We'd turned adult before it was apparent to me that Jerry had been a thug, and a pretty fair teenage alcoholic. He was a year older but a double stay-back, and so always one grade behind. We haven't seen each other more than two days running for thirteen years. I was still trying to act the last time our being in one house didn't mean a holiday or an occasion. I do not think about my brother at all regularly. In my everyday life, bad as it sounds, I don't know that I have a brother, or a father either.

But while we were in school, and while bells were going off, I thought of him. At two in the morning this is strange but a breakthrough—remembering my remembering Jerry as bells sounded. He was always in another part of the building, removed; our experiences as we advertised them to each other at day's end (and never at formal supper-table recitals; always dribbled out across the evening, during commercials), these did not connect. There was no evidence that they happened to brothers, or within the same institution.

Without much effort, I was the superior student—the sort awarded assignments that freed me of the classroom—and I remembered helping the tired grammar school janitor by the furnace, and judging drama auditions in the junior high auditorium, and that ring then producing an odd pull (four hundred others—but not you—summoned) and a small longing for what I would miss (junior high especially, four-minute spells in the halls like dense abrupt block parties), and inevitably a stubborn image of Jerry, somewhere in the building, collecting anecdotes that would sound foreign to me.

He ran a bank in second grade, collecting play investments from the smart kids and currency from the others. He talked about sex to them. His claim of experience dates from as far back as I remember. In a group his age or younger the subject came around naturally; Jerry was the casual hero in his stories, which featured sex episodes of several hours, and other intervals, also prolonged and usually occurring first, in which the partners performed a detailed and formal visual inspection, with commentary. I was never sure where he came up with this stuff. His seated audience was silent and looked at the sky, most times, or at their crossed ankles.

I felt the urge to roll to my right side and I hesitated, because the first move always brought several more, each triggered by an unpleasant thought, six or seven heaving turns, a half-hour cycle. Our bed was uncomfortable; we bought it in another city and it had gone soft. It was on a night like this one the year before that I'd noticed this, and then had amused myself by imagining that the bed's sprung tension over the nights had been lost upward, spilled into me.

I was a morning person failing at sleep. I was up late. The thrill, like that of swimming in the dark or playing past the bell, had worn off when I was fourteen, or about the time Jerry could be counted on to be out every night and sometimes, rarely enough to surprise with it, bringing a girlfriend back, through the cellar, loudly, well after midnight.

My father had been legally deaf more or less since his twenties. He knew he couldn't catch Jerry and he didn't wait up for him. For a couple of years in there Jerry was cruel, talking very softly in front of him, and then a bit louder once he'd swung his head from my father's view. What he said didn't matter. Some of it wasn't insulting, most was: nothing could delight him like my appalled face. Often I faked it—but he knew when, and he pursued the pure reaction.

My father has always looked old. We saw him gray and in hearing aids at forty, in his TV chair after dinner, arms at chest-level, one knuckle caressed by all the fingers of the other hand. He had four older sisters who came one at a time to give him some help with us. Five years ago he married a woman who has redecorated with vigor, down to puffy home-sewn placemats like compressed quilts.

The worst was when he hollered with his hearing aids out. There is a dramatic wail, of the radio-theater sort, that underscores my father's voice when he can't hear himself. He refused to bring the things fishing; his clumsiness and inattention got them wet enough around the house. Jerry, at the bow of the rented boat, found those summer weekends ideal for murmuring toward my father at the stern. The family's worst at fishing, I always took boat's middle, and my incompetence—I am thirty-one and I have never felt something potent and alive take the line—tempered Jerry's triumph, since I was concentrating too hard on the lake to react purely to whatever he was doing. I spent those afternoons not awaiting the sudden tug, but still expecting myself to be ready for it, and so irresolutely I cast and recast from the center of the boat, snarling lines semi-regularly, as my father's advice started coming in his worst voice. To this Jerry's reaction was anything but pure, it was the forged delight, the righteous snort, the hard cackle of teenagers, and of brothers. And it was loud as he could make it, because then he needed for the whole boat to hear.

I need to keep making one thing clear. These thoughts came to me waiting for sleep. It was not as though in my everyday memories I had sorted and discarded the family unpleasantness. I had discarded the family, period. Weeks passed, easily, between times when I thought, for a second, about either one of them. There was no patterned suppression. My father and I had entered a sizable local raffle and won; and Jerry and I had prevented or at least abbreviated a sexual assault; and we had talked our way into a police helicopter once; and we had snorted, once the unspoiled shock faded, after we saw a neighbor we both hated get careless and lose a thumb in a lawnmower. These too escape my head for the same chain of days: they wait for the sudden blanks, the waking nights and the world's random episodes of delay.

Phone nerves, for the caller, begin with the third or fourth ring. Nothing's expected on the first ring, little more on the second. But the third ring and especially the fourth—twenty seconds now since the connection, twenty-five or thirty since the dialing began—these let the caller model and remodel words, tone, mood, and decide how badly he wants, or doesn't want, an answer. Even with calls not openly dreaded, the telephone can intimidate, and it's hard to root against the chance—good now at the fourth ring—to be free of it in just twenty, ten, five more seconds.

I was in a downtown hotel. The meeting I'd been working was in its last day, and the awards ceremony ran well behind. The plush phone stall was wide enough for three. I was calling home to see if we were expecting. The back of my throat was pounding, which I should have anticipated, but don't think I did. They said once on "Hollywood Squares" that twelve rings is the etiquette ideal, and though I knew that past the fifth ring there was no harm in letting it go and go, I broke it off in the middle of the sixth.

Kelvar came steaming down the corridor, looking ready to chew me out, but then something in my face may have softened him, at least a little. Still he locked me with his eyes.

"Glen Paul. You got a life, I know. And also I know that you don't slack on me much more than most guys, and a lot less than some. But for now pal, tough shit." He looked as though he wanted to grab my cheek or my ear, half playfully, but had reconsidered. "I need a salable shot of each award winner. I need everything that happens in there. We can't take it easy yet."

Ten minutes later Nancy came up behind me in the main ballroom. Her voice startled me past where I could guage my own anxiety, or even think of the question to be asked, before she answered it.

"Nobody knows yet," she said. "I never made it there. Actually I made it there twice, but there were mix-ups and I didn't see her. One of those things. So, Monday."

"What do you mean?" I said. "What are you talking about?"

Nancy smiled at me. She didn't look good. "It's so involved I may not even remember it all. It takes awhile to tell." She reached for a copy of the events schedule and looked it over.

"I have to get all these guys and their plaques. Maybe a half-hour more, if they pick up the pace. I can get a lift home, though."

"It's okay."

"If you want go ahead," I said. "You look wiped out."

"No not really. I'll poke around. I'll meet you here in an hour. I like hotels."

"Don't wear yourself out."

"Big hotels are lots of fun," she said. "More fun than cities. Lookit here. Altman In Focus group, third floor. Whoops, Thursday at eight-fifteen. Oh well. They don't show his stuff as much anymore, you know? You probably won't see *Thieves Like Us* again until right after the guy dies. Terrible way to think."

Nancy wanted to drive us home. She could not bear my city driving, especially at this hour, and on Friday. And I do get impatient, and tense, and say things about other people I never say anywhere else, and let it ruin much of the rest of my night. But this time I protested. It was her body, more than her voice or anything she said, that made me think she was fighting to keep control. Her body looked like it wanted to scream. And her hair looked out of place and uncommonly oily, with the front bangs in a bell curve, where she'd been running her hand.

But she had the keys and she wanted to drive. The garage was clogged and full of fumes, and we were ten minutes escaping. Nancy began talking once we hit fresher air.

"After I dropped you off this morning I had two hours till the doctor so I drove up to the office, even though I'd taken it off as a personal day. Well there was all this unscheduled work the city dumped on us that had to be done before the weekend—so I pitched in for a little over an hour and then I drove back down to the doctor's, but the chain on my watch gave out this week, and the whole world was making left turns, so I was forty-five minutes late. And the two women with appointments after me were already there and if the doctor took me she'd make them late and this one black lady was very pregnant and sort of sniveling about a personal emergency. So I volunteered to come back. The black woman made a big show of thanking me and the doctor told the girl to try to squeeze me in later. So we settled on two-thirty, and that gave me the bright idea to stop back at the office and maybe with luck this could count as a working day and I'd save my personal day for sometime later like the Friday before we go to Florida. When I got to the car I decided to walk, since that would be relaxing and it wasn't all that far, a mile maybe. Shorter than I used to walk to school. I forgot all about these heels I have on. I stood there for a minute at the car and I thought I heard thunder, or I did hear thunder, but the sky looked pretty clear. The garage was all-day. I thought about it and I left the car. I thought the place might be full later, and more than that I couldn't stand the thought of paying twice. And that lot is much quicker for getting you at the hotel in rush hour, and I was short on cash. So I left the car."

"And it rained," I said. "I hadn't even noticed."

"Three blocks I got, and the big drops started. The first time in two years I have any use for a bus and they're on strike. It wasn't that heavy yet, but just to be safe I detoured over to the parkway, figuring it might even be quicker and in any case I'll have the trees to walk under. About halfway over to the parkway it opened up. I stood there and watched it for a while, and I felt pretty good, but that can bore you after a while, so before it let up I sprinted over to this laundromat to wait it out. But instead of letting up it rained harder, which I didn't think was possible, not at all. I waited and waited, and that laundromat was steaming. Then I wanted to call the office. And the change is all in the ashtray. And I had no singles either for the dollar changer, and I'm all alone in there. I almost sent a five into the goddamn machine, but I just couldn't make myself push the tray, and then I stopped for a minute and it dawned on me that I could charge a call to our home phone. So I call and Mary's swamped and all bitchy and she tells me that if I get back by noon, and not after, then she wouldn't count it as my personal day. So I ran over to the parkway."

"You must have been going crazy. Five would have got you a cab."

"I know. I swear it didn't occur to me. All I can think is get to the parkway, walk under the trees. So it's still pouring and I run over there but there's no sidewalk on the edge with the trees. My glasses got fogged up so now I can't see with them on or with them off. I don't want to exaggerate this part, but really, with anything faster than a walk I was stumbling over rocks and cans and roots of trees. And then it stops. Or at least it's very light. Once I wipe my glasses on my shirt I can see that I was less than halfway there—it's longer than it looks by car. So I kept going but the trees are dripping nearly as hard as the rain was. I moved out onto the side of the road with cars going forty miles an hour and they're still dripping on me, the trees are. So I stopped to think. Right under this goddamned bus stop. There was a dog—without a leash, and not really close to me, but he was still mangy and nasty-looking and I got a little silly and decided I couldn't think with this attack dog in my sight. And I walk some more in my heels and get wet and I decide that I'd try the Lettuce Patch, since by now some office people might be there for lunch, and I'd calm down and get some food and go back with them to see if Mary was happier and if she wouldn't work something out. And so, I go all the way to the veggie place. Nothing, none of them there. I sat for a while and nobody came, and my ankle was nagging me so I sat longer. Finally I saw them going by on the other side of the street and after maybe a block and a half I caught up to them."

Nancy stopped talking and turned up the traffic news coming over the radio. We were trying to make a left turn through a big intersection with a broken traffic light. There was no pattern or procedure established. It would take minutes for even the brief chance to be aggressive to arrive.

"Two people from the office agreed to staying out for a

quick cup of coffee, and the first thing I did in the coffee shop was get change and call the doctor's office and tell them I couldn't make two-thirty, but how about later, at the end of the day. The girl had me on hold twice but finally she said fine. So I relaxed a little then. I went back to the office and I got some of my clothes dry. I worked until four-thirty, then I called a cab and waited fifteen minutes and then downstairs it took me another, or it seemed like another, fifteen minutes flagging one. But the traffic was snarled so I got out and walked. The traffic wasn't as bad as this stuff here, but the weather was worse right after the rain. It was steamy and miserable. But I felt better—I don't know, I felt as good as I had all day. Things were all right. So I'm trying to tidy myself up as I'm walking along, and after a while I don't feel quite so repulsive, and I guess I'm swaggering a little up to the doctor's office, and then they're closed—I don't know if I was too late, or the girl didn't understand me or what. And like an idiot I'm there pulling on this locked door and there's a security guard, this hideous-looking kid, leaned against the elevators staring me down."

I thought as she went on that I should have comforted her right then, in the only way that she could be comforted, with talk that wasn't cosseting, or even very soft. The words didn't come immediately, so instead I looked at the traffic knot and its sturdy, patient regulars and my mind was on her muddled doctor's office and on how messy and immodest and trying it will be making and expecting children, leave alone having them, leave alone raising them, and whether we were up to it.

"Walking on the parkway," Nancy said, "I knew I could have flagged a cab. Or I could have called one. And borrowed money at the office or made Greg or somebody stop at the bank machine. But I guess I didn't think of it then, not enough to do it. It's so strange. Like this absurd situation can't be spoiled, or at least it shouldn't. And you realize that. Not anywhere in your head where you can say it, or even where you can really think it, but still you sort of know. But I'm going down there Monday when the doors open. And I won't move without an answer."

Nancy got us through the intersection, over the bridge, and onto the roads home. A few miles out water sloshed in the streets and traffic was heavy but it moved. It was two-lane road now, plain territory, the scenery of fifty states.

A minute later the wheels on my side slipped from the pavement to the gravel shoulder. I looked over. Nancy was shaking.

"Nancy," I said.

And she was crying. One car squeezed by us on the left. She kept our speed up to thirty or thirty-five, but she couldn't return the right-side wheels to the road. Her lips out and her neck cord taut, she looked like it hurt. It was silent crying. In my surprise at this sudden sight I reached one hand for her shoulders and one for the side of the wheel but I couldn't say what I was saying—"Pull over, Nancy"—with any force at all.

"Foot cramp," she said in a rushed voice. "These goddamned heels."

I had never seen her in total collapse, but once the pain passed she looked ready for it. "Pull over," I said, more audibly. But with the right words came, from nowhere, thoughts. I thought I wanted her stretched under me across the front seat, quickly, as she dissolved.

By the time we exchanged places, at a gas station ten minutes from home, the pain was all gone. "Stupid to walk three miles in those shoes," Nancy said, collected. "Then hold down the brake pedal half an hour."

"That'll do it," I said.

"Since Greg called my other ones come-fuck-me shoes I've worn these right out." She winced. "Oh oh oh. Coming back again." She locked her fingers at the back of her head and shut her eyes. "What a stupid day this is. Common sense is just out of stock. When I go, I really go."

Our evening lacked further surprise, though we both seemed willing to pretend that the sex came without warning. Afterward Nancy was in bed asleep and I was on the couch feeling a familiar mix, more exhaustion than relaxation, when the burst of telephone noise brought a similar spasm in me. I was on it before it could ring again.

"Glen Paul." I was late to recognize the voice, since it belonged to the last person I expected that night.

"Jerry."

"Hey. What's up, what news? I'm guessing it's good. We in that family way, or what?"

"Nope, not yet."

"Aw, Glen. I'm sorry."

"Well we don't know yet. Nancy missed her test. Still we might be expecting."

This made Jerry laugh through his nose first, then from his throat as a kind of afterthought. He sounded loose. "That sort of sums up everything, no?" Jerry said. "Think about that phrase, 'might be expecting.' The human condition, whatnot. Whatever. But that'll be good, new generation. I'm rooting for you, grandkid for Dad, and all."

I wished the years had helped my sense of when Jerry was drunk and when he wasn't. But I had never known.

"Yeah," I said to Jerry.

"Yeah," Jerry said.

On my end could be heard the electronic summoning of other numbers, and a sound like tape through my cassette player in the moment before it runs out. It was the first time I'd ever gotten it on the line with Jerry.

"So, otherwise?" Jerry said.

"Same as it was going last night, I suppose. I'm shooting this huge pep-rally for Region Three, whatever that may be."

"Uh-huh. That easy?"

"Near what I figured. Today wasn't bad but yesterday they had their outing, two hundred guys dressed like football coaches, out in the heat—Jesus, Jerry you don't want to hear this."

"No, I'm interested."

"You're not and I'm not wild about telling it. I just talked to you last night. We're not about to start with how our days went, that won't last."

"It *is* interesting," Jerry said. "I really don't know what you're doing. I should know what you're doing."

"I'm sitting on the edge of the coffee table," I said. "I'm trying to soften the bell on this phone. Before that I was lying next to Nancy."

"I still don't have myself a woman," Jerry said. "I envy you that, brother. Right there when you want it. The friendship, I mean."

"Sure you do," I said. My impatience gave me a tremor of good feeling. "Jerry what's the agenda here? Let's get to it."

I think he knew I liked my own aggressiveness, and to

fight it he faked a laugh, or so I thought—a breathy, too-long series of short grunts, like something heavy falling down carpeted stairs.

"Look," I said. "I'm really wiped out,"

"Let's just talk awhile?" Jerry said.

"I can't see it," I said. "You're drunk, I'm not, what's to talk about?"

"I don't really know," Jerry said quickly. "I called home tonight."

"Uh-huh. How'd Dad handle 40K?"

"That's the thing," Jerry said. Then silence, and more of the breathy sounds. "He's not working anymore, Glen Paul. Not even half-time. He's stopped."

"Well they've got disability. Noreen's got money coming in." I'd known about his full retirement since right after it happened in the spring, but it was news to me that they'd kept it from Jerry.

"It was just depressing," Jerry said. "I was joking with him and nothing was coming back. It's been a lot of years since I can't get a laugh."

"Lighter on the drama, Jerry. He probably couldn't hear you. What'd you say?"

"Oh I don't know. I was trying little stuff. He had the pension physical so I asked what the pre-mortem found."

"Well Christ, Jerry, of course not."

"Well *not* of course not. You lived with him, Glen. It's just the thing he'd laugh at and pitch in, especially since we've grown up. But he's sort of past that now, or past something—I don't know, I'm not making any sense. I keep thinking when will we see him again."

"Christmas, don't be an idiot."

"No, *see* him. Not like that. I don't know, not live with him again but something, you know?" Jerry's voice was cracking. "You must know. It's just hard to think of Daddy not working."

"Christ almighty, he's fifty-nine years old. His blood pressure's half mine. I gotta say good night, Jerry. I'll call you sometime."

In the bedroom, the small breeze through the open windows had quit. Nancy had kept her nightgown off. She was on her back, sweating under the sheet. Her voice sounded snapped awake from sleep.

"That was Jerry?"

"Yeah," I said. "Noreen didn't tell him Daddy gave up the part-time until tonight. I was kind of short with him."

"Good for you," she said.

"No," I said. "Last night would have been better, I was feeling right with him. All he means is my father's had his last raise, and he's remarried. There won't be much news from him."

"That's ridiculous," she said.

"It isn't," I said. "Last night I was right there too. Jerry's drunk tonight, or he isn't drunk. He's thinking that maybe there's no reason left to hear from Dad without warning. He'd pretty much have to die for that."

Nancy raised a small distance from the pillow, showing that I'd have to say more before she could understand. I stood over the bed, thinking. A minute later she had dropped far into sleep.

At the phone, I called Jerry. It rang twenty times before I reasoned that this didn't have to mean he'd stormed out of his apartment after I cut him off. He could have been calling from anywhere at all.

I slid in next to Nancy and tried to sleep, went to use the bathroom, and tried again. Then I got up and watched an hour of videos, which put me once more onto childhood and how much it must matter, since as soon as we feel ourselves through with it we're anxious to scramble off and make substitutes to send over the same terrain. Which looked, on the small screen, like hell itself. I sat through the failed music and the tales of powerlessness, revenge and victimization, stylish denial. The hour passed quickly. In the bedroom, Nancy had kept her position—she was exhausted and hadn't shifted a muscle. When I lifted the sheet I caught our scent in the bedding. I hung a leg over hers, and rubbed her shoulder and her breast after I settled in.

I did some breathing. Sleep should have come easier. Unlike some other times, there were now avenues of my world that were clear. There was the job: Kelvar's little scold aside, the day of work was good, *felt* good—an uncommon absence of any physical pressure at all, in my head or my bladder or my ankles or wrists, or my neck from the swerving and the camera straps. There were the Steelers, marching crisply through the preseason, avoiding injuries, setting up for a big year.

But I couldn't hold these in focus. And I couldn't rest. My wife lay thick and warm at my right side. I pulled the sheet to her knees, and she didn't move. It was a damp, bottomless sleep. "My girl," I said aloud, burrowing one arm into the junky mattress and under her back, resting my other hand at the slope of her thigh. With time my night vision improved. I could make out the glint on her belly and the slices of shadow around her closed eyes. I sucked at her a little.

"What is it?" she said suddenly.

"I love you."

"I love you," she said. She was asleep, and her weight felt heavy and good on my arm. I went to gather her in but she was rooted, and I pressed up as close as I could and tried to freeze myself that way, to hold her and feel content. I closed my eyes. Her breath was hard to hear. I nuzzled her, but the texture I felt was my own, beard rub and the features of the ear. Then I slipped my arm away and rose up to my knees. From above she looked handsome and patient in her sleep. I felt myself rushing, but I worked as gently as I knew how. At the first pain Nancy opened her eyes, and saw the love and panic in mine.

"No?" Nancy said, a question, a small voice full of pitch. She tipped herself away to one side. I told her I loved her and kissed her neck, once.

I went onto my back. I took care that no body part large or small overlapped another. I commanded myself to relax, to make time lighter, but it was as futile as striving to levitate, or striving to die on the spot.

I tried making myself fantasize, for a change.

TEAMWORK

Mrs. Fair lives with her six daughters; Janet is twenty-two, Andrea is nineteen, Donna is eighteen, Jill is seventeen, Chris is sixteen, and Ellen is fifteen. Experts say don't dote on your kids and she doesn't really, but she will take the time to rattle off names and ages like that, and add some data on each, because she wants them to exist for everyone as individuals, which they are, rather than as just her kids. She calls from work no more than once a day, more from habit than from worry. Mrs. Fair is a secretary at a clinic where it is always a dull kind of busy. This morning she calls an hour before lunch, and Andrea tells her that Lew is on the side steps waiting for Ellen to get home from summer school.

Ellen had refused to sign up, but Mrs. Fair got help from her two oldest girls and forced Ellen's agreement. That nasty strict scene last April was exceptional for Mrs. Fair, who in this advanced age usually lets things slide—but none of her daughters has ever stayed back, and the school's counseling specialists say promotion denials as late as tenth grade are threatened only in extremes like this, so Mrs. Fair is satisfied that she isn't being too severe. She's making it up to her littlest one by accepting Ellen's mangy twenty-five-year-old boyfriend without comment, except to Kit McGovern, the doctor's wife two blocks farther up the hill. Kit agreed about summer school, in this case, and she advised flexibility on the boyfriend. "Sometimes," Kit McGovern says, "they have to run before they can walk."

Ninety and humid before noon, extreme for New England, but Lew wears long pants because he may need them. Ellen told him to get her at home right after summer school, and they would go to lunch someplace nice before the Cape. Ellen shouldn't be too much longer, especially if she's getting a ride. Lew knows better than to turn up early, but on his day off there's little else to do.

Facing downhill from his spot below the kitchen window, Lew sees approaching traffic long before it arrives. What little there is. Most shoppers in the plaza below don't use the shortcut through here, and they barely notice the neighborhood—from the parking lot below this hill is pure background. The Fairs' is the smallest house in sight, an odd lot bordered by streets on all sides but the back. A few houses farther up the hill look nice but most, like the Fairs', don't quite.

Lew's head at least is in the scarce noontime shade. He reclines against the house's gray shingles, arm's length from the kitchen door. In the Fairs' backyard a manual lawnmower ticks through the shaggy grass. Jill mows in a pattern, a perpetually shrinking square, and as instructed she walks forward with the mower, she never pulls it back toward her—Mrs. Fair has schooled her daughters in the menace of machines. For protection Jill wears solid black shoes, nun's shoes—they look silly with her loose tank top and shorts, and Jill is the first to laugh about them. She plows up a small rise and into a corner of the yard. They never use the motorized mower; Ellen tells Lew it's been in the garage for seven years, gas tank full. Mr. Fair once shattered a car window by mowing a rock with it.

The screen door opens and Chris steps out, in her one-piece bathing suit. After Ellen, Chris is next youngest. A dull, scratchy beachtowel, wrapped from waist to calves, has the Pepsi label across it.

"You can go in if you want." Chris steps over Lew's feet. "They're having lunch soon. There's nothing to eat now, so somebody goes to the store and buys all sorts of stuff. You're welcome to it."

"Ellen said something about eating out." Lew squints up at her more than he has to.

Ellen talks about Chris a lot. Chris's retainer can finally come out next week. They have a new woman dentist, an angel—she grants gas and Novocain both, liberally, on even the slightest of fillings. Mrs. McGovern found her. Before her the Fairs, Chris especially, suffered under Dr. Carr. Hairy hands and heavy breath, he asked which one were you now, what grade in school now, how many older sisters how many younger; then he revved his brutal machinery. Janet, the oldest girl, lost six teeth in an hour under token Novocain; at the magazine rack she stabbed him with a pencil. And it infuriated Janet that he couldn't learn their names. But Chris withheld all complaint. Even when her mouth moved freely, Chris came home from Dr. Carr with nothing to say. The brace that straightened her back came off, after four years, about a month before Ellen met Lew. At Mr. Fair's funeral the relatives marveled; Chris nine years old and as much help as Janet, more. Mr. Fair spanked Chris least, even in the last two years, the only two Ellen can remember, always one sister screaming and another recovering.

But Lew does not know quite this much, though Ellen may mention it. They talk, they live, in his car, into the night, with the radio going, and he follows the music. To Ellen he half-listens. Of her family he knows names and a little more, he can tell them apart without help but that's all; they're still a group, the sisters.

Tall as a tropical bird, Chris walks away up the hill, where the McGoverns have a pool. Ellen says they chlorinate to death, and they make you wash your feet first, in soapy water. Mrs. McGovern invites Mrs. Fair often. Mrs. Fair comes back with books. Together they've done some political work and taken two night classes, each claiming they could never do it alone. Ellen likes Kit McGovern in small doses, she says. Lew watches Chris walk with perfect posture and on her toes, gingerly across hot pavement, cooling her feet in grass where she can.

"Hi again," Mrs. Fair says on her second call. "How's everybody?"

"No different. I think the problem with this fan is just a wire."

"Andrea please don't monkey with that thing."

"It won't take much doing, I don't think. Just some black tape. This kitchen is a sauna."

"Please don't fool with it," Mrs. Fair says. "We'll call somebody qualified. I'm going to come home for lunch. That's what I called to say."

"Oh," Andrea says. "Suit yourself. There's absolutely nothing to eat."

"Oh. Have you got money?"

"No cars," Andrea says.

"No cars. Heaven forbid anybody walks or rides a bike. I assume that means Janet hasn't turned up yet."

"Nobody will get on that bike we have," Andrea says.

"And Ellen's come and gone already."

"Ellen's not back yet. Whatsis is still here. That's the only car, Mom."

"Lew's."

"He waits and waits. I don't know what he sees in her."

"Well don't go asking him," says Mrs. Fair.

"He sits and sits. Maybe he knows wiring. Maybe he can monkey with it."

"Don't stereotype, Andrea. We'll get the thing to a repairman tomorrow. I'm going to call this afternoon."

The Fairs own a cat, a huge orange male, husky and well scarred, old enough to be named G. Gordon Liddy. Janet named him from current events way back, and nobody much cares for the name anymore, but it's too late to give him another one. Ellen says that as a kitten he'd dash halfway up a tree trunk, stop, and hold his grip that way for as long as he had the will. Near mealtimes Liddy is expelled from the cool kitchen linoleum, and he usually waits sullenly by the side door. That space taken, he rests now in the garage's shade, his eyes half open and his matted fur rising and falling. He's not nearly as cute as he used to be, Ellen says.

Lew shifts his weight from the top of his back to a new spot near the middle. He doesn't wear a watch. Twice in the month he's known her Ellen has turned up absurdly late, both times with a pretty good explanation. He can't imagine that she'll be much longer. He knows for fact that she's running on four hours' sleep and has only change in her pocket. She has to be back soon.

He can hear just enough low notes from Donna's upstairs radio to recognize Siouxsie and the Banshees. Late last night in the car "Tenderness on the Block" came on the radio for the first time in three years. Lew relished the news—Warren Zevon was dried out and ready to make another record. Ellen never heard of him; she nearly turned it. When they're parked she always has a hand on the dial. Or, when involved, a foot. It breaks both of them up, the music change right in the middle: at that point each lyric has implications. Ellen is small-breasted and she wears the sleeveless white undershirts Lew connects with girls in subtitled movies. They use the front seat always. In every car, save for buckets, it is wider and more comfortable. Sometimes Lew wants to expose the back-seat myth, but he knows that twenty-five is a little old for that kind of explaining.

Andrea brings a plastic bag of trash around to the side of the house, past the kitchen door.

"That wasn't Ellen, was it?" Lew says politely. "I heard the phone."

"Sorry."

At Ellen's suggestion Lew is growing a beard. He wore one briefly seven years ago in his first and only semester of college. Crazy as it may be to grow a beard in July, here he is. Lew's fingers probe it as much as Ellen's do—mostly they wander past the knob at the base of the jaw and farther back because Lew finds that an astonishing place for man to have hair, growing wild. Lew hasn't touched a razor in the month since they met. If he tried a trim he'd do it unevenly and then have to shave the whole thing. And Ellen says she likes it this way better.

What happened between the first and second beards, Lew couldn't say. He walked into Sears one day, began work the next, and spent most of four years at the Brockton store in power tools. Before that three years slicing deli in the city, at the big grocery in the Pru. Same thing: he applied on Tuesday and punched the clock Thursday morning. The most frozen food space per square foot of any major store in the country. On Saturday nights he left the deli section to ring a register, for the career girls buying seven days' worth of Stouffer's and brie. At least the gays cooked; the city girls just boiled water. If they didn't stock up weekly they were in every night at ten before six, with the corporate up-and-comers delayed until seven or later. Most would hardly look at him, taking their half-pound of sliced jarlsberg, but a few smiled like the shampoo commercials. Yes, an act, but Lew never caught them in it with others on the floor. Maybe that chest-high deli counter gave them their nerve. In his worst moods Lew wanted to vault the counter and grab them, and see if they kept smiling.

■

Home for lunch, Mrs. Fair parks the station wagon in the driveway behind Lew's car. She doesn't step over him at the kitchen door—instead she comes around front and passes through the empty living room.

"Is anybody watching this?" Mrs. Fair touches the television.

"I am," Donna calls from the bathroom.

Mrs. Fair hands the car keys to Andrea. Andrea opens the kitchen door, steps over Lew's legs, and asks if there is anything he needs. Lew says there isn't.

Jill has finished the lawn; she lifts the old mower over G. Gordon Liddy and then wheels it deep into the garage, which stands separate from the house. "Get something good," she calls to Andrea. Jill smiles toward Lew, and, with the cat at her heels, she walks inside.

Andrea drives away down the hill, flipping the dial away from the all-news station.

"Where's Ellen?" Mrs. Fair asks Donna, who is out of the bathroom.

"School still." Donna shrugs.

Jill kicks off her nun's shoes. She pours three glasses of Tab. "Maybe it's an extra-long class."

"I doubt that," Donna says. She looks at Mrs. Fair. "She's kept him waiting half an hour already."

"More," Jill says.

"I'll get those Mom," says Donna.

"It's hotter here than it is outside," Jill says.

"Chris is swimming?" asks Mrs. Fair.

"Right," Jill says.

"It's too hot to eat," Donna says. "It's way past eating weather."

"Today's the worst yet," Mrs. Fair says.

"The grass is loud," Jill says. "You can tell it's super-hot. It's just noisy out there."

"You'd never know this cat ate four hours ago," Mrs. Fair says.

"Sit down and relax, Mom," Donna says.

"Toss him out," Mrs. Fair says. She reaches for the mail, which is always placed, by the first to spot the mailman, in the pantry atop the stack of eight high school yearbooks, '75 to '82. Chris's *Sports Illustrated*, a letter from their congressman, and a bank statement, that's all. Donna is already into the *Psychology Today*.

In the living room the television plays to no one. At some point years ago the family moved into the kitchen. Now rarely all together, as they might have been in the living room, Sunday nights especially. Mrs. Fair had liked that crowded sight, regressive as that may sound; she cursed the vanished chances for photos of her daughters all together, or in their many other combinations. These, by her careful count, number sixty-one; the thought of that hidden list makes her feel silly but rich. Without many pictures, Mrs. Fair finds herself envisioning her daughters as a tight package, a kind of ball, with the ends—Ellen and Janet—fraying just a little. In her first year as a widow Mrs. Fair sat at the kitchen table writing checks one Sunday night when Ellen, she was seven or eight, came in from the living room and asked if they were poor. Mrs. Fair said no but Ellen cried anyway, she made herself cereal and would not leave. Mrs. Fair corked over what used to be the kitchen art wall, and with bright plastic pins she tacks notices of who must sign what and register where to keep up all the brown envelopes with the government checks. It's too bad, but that's how it must be done. The older girls register for community college and then drop out the first week, and they are paid off the books where they work. Except for Janet's crusade to buy herself a new car they've all been saints, and the family manages; they don't talk about it much.

Lew sees Janet's red Celica on the approaching streets for a good minute before it finally pulls in. The car rattles to a stop behind Lew's. Fresh dents on both sides. On the driver's side it's the whole door. On the passenger side the parking light and the sweet curve of metal above the front tire. Janet is furious. She scrambles out from behind the wheel, and she flips open the passenger door on her way into the kitchen. Scott climbs out slowly—he wanders for a moment, then stands in the cut grass and leans against a rusty clothesline pole. Scott is only seventeen. He's carrying a camera, which seems out of place on him. Some people don't look right with cameras. Scott looks to Lew like the new stockboy the market hires every three weeks, the low man who draws frozen food duty, the one who learns about gloves the first day and then forgets them all the next three weeks, who stocks hundreds of viscid numbing frozen juices without complaint, who would rather take a wrong guess than ask you something, but who is not without value, who you're wary of at first but who might be interesting, a friend, if after three weeks he hasn't vanished and the next one already punched in. But Lew has never seen a stockboy with a nice camera around his neck.

■

"Have I had this car a month yet even?" Janet asks. "We hit a moving car and a parked car at the same time. A fucking Japanese sandwich, sushi, Jesus God." She storms past Mrs. Fair and straight to the telephone. "Fucking how about it? From both sides. I can't believe it. Nobody saw anybody. God fucking bless us every one."

But Janet talks sweetly on the phone, and Mrs. Fair walks to the screen door. It is her policy to stay out of earshot of all phone calls, no matter, to provide full freedom for everyone. Donna and Jill are outside circling the wrecked car and avoiding each other's eyes. Both say hello to Scott. Scott mumbles back. Jill is still without shoes; in rhythm she lifts each foot off the hot cement, then touches it down again. Ellen's boyfriend stretches out just below Mrs. Fair. From her angle Mrs. Fair can see only Lew's corduroy pants. The cat, perturbed, is prowling nothing. For a moment Mrs. Fair forgets to consider what it is she should do, in this situation. But the answer is nothing, she has no duty, so she rests a little and looks outside without really watching.

"I talked to my boss," Janet says, "and she knows somebody. Really good, supposedly. And fast."

"Nobody was hurt at all?"

"Nope. Excuse me." Janet squeezes by and walks back to the car, where she rummages in the glove compartment. Janet's boyfriend has wandered into the garage; he appears amused by the old manual mower, the two-handed saw, the bike with its white wicker basket, the big hedge trimmers. Janet, much calmer now, comes back to the phone. She has had the car for a month and the boyfriend for not much longer. She has five and a half years on him. On the morning after Janet signed the papers at Toyota, Mrs. Fair rose at six-twenty for work, and she bumped into Janet on the stairs. That was fine, she's an adult, but when Mrs. Fair stepped out of an unusually weak shower, and when the foggy window cleared, she saw Janet's boyfriend washing the new car, scrubbing and hosing it down, and he was still finishing with a rag when Mrs. Fair silently left the house. Andrea said it was another half-hour before he finally walked home.

Now Janet is off the phone again and out the door. "Back in a while," she calls to Mrs. Fair, and then the same words, softer, to Scott her boyfriend in the garage. But under the words she's glaring at him. Janet is frequently intolerant; she explodes often and calms quickly, just like her father, and just like all of them when they were babies. But more of Mr. Fair survives in Janet than in any of the others. Mrs. Fair watches her back out half carefully, the loose metal scraping over bumps.

Lew jerks his shirt from his chest a few times to commiserate about the heat. Without seeming to notice the connection Scott threads the front of his own shirt through the camera straps and up to his face. The shirt is short enough for Dixie college football anyway, and now Lew can see that the middle of Scott's firm belly is as lush with hair as the bottom. The clothesline pole has branded a streak of rust down one shoulder. Scott's camera hangs ready around his neck. It looks as though Janet and Scott were planning travel, too. Scott looks around and then at Lew again. He steps out of the garage. He groans, and he throws his arms open.

"I never saw him coming," Scott says.

Scott is Jill's age. In September they will be seniors. Jill tells Ellen that in China Studies this year Scott looked exhausted—he tried not to fall asleep but he always did, for about a minute at a time. Jill tells Ellen that it was pretty funny to watch. For the first time Lew realizes how tired he is. It's not something he usually notices. He has at least four hours driving today—two down two back—once Ellen turns up. She must have a ride, or be waiting for one. He should have suggested picking her up at school, though so far she's nixed that idea every time. A warm vertical halo rings Lew's face. He can feel the heat coming off it. A beard does that. Soon comes the first dull electric charge in his stomach, hunger. A strange thought occurs, one so irrelevant he doesn't think it anymore: he doesn't much want to go.

Mrs. Fair's younger brother parks on the street. He enters through the front door. He is thirty-four years old and a captain in the air force. He is an angel: thoughtful, respectful, fair-minded, considerate. Her daughters fuss over him some—they are polite, they don't exactly swarm, but they perk up and show off whenever he visits, which is about once a week. He is always in uniform. He knows about the social security, the off-the-books, the college registration; he understands. Mrs. Fair told him about Scott, and he lectured her some. She hasn't mentioned Lew. In the living room, before they see her daughters, he hands Mrs. Fair an envelope. Mrs. Fair's brother has money saved up; he spends nothing on himself. Without him she couldn't have done nearly as much for Chris, the new woman dentist and the orthopedist. The counseling would have been impossible, both for the family as a group and for herself. Her brother has Mrs. Fair's private counseling bills sent to the base. Mrs. Fair is grateful for the chance to talk, alone, with professionals.

Even in her less thoughtful years, Mrs. Fair knew that her husband was not exactly the love of her life. She was trained to do all that simple women are trained to do for their men. They met through a cousin when he was seventeen and she was nineteen, and they were married a year to the day later. She sees that their courtship, such as it was, was typical lower middle class. Married, they did not spend much time together. They got along, but Mr. Fair knew nothing of children or of the most basic psychology, and he refused to learn. During those bleak provincial years she really had no clue. Though not happy she did not feel unhappy either, and of course she probably wasn't, technically, since she was ignorant of her confinement until near the end.

The last year was a trial. In Mr. Fair's house, experts were not consulted and the common sense they spread for free was ignored. It was the dark ages. Doctors yes, but only GPs and a dentist for the kids, no specialists. When his bosses and a few smarter friends began listening to the femtalk, his phrase, from their wives and books, from talk shows and doctors, he would have none of it. Once Mrs. Fair discovered her dissatisfaction she was on her own, there was no working with him, and things became worse fast. It was truly unbearable after a while; she found coping difficult. Each time she spoke out he got tougher and more dogmatic. He was taking a belt to the kids when she finally convinced him that violence wasn't the way. Then Janet's new high school friend, Annie, ran from her dreadful parents. Mrs. Fair took her in, protected her, and Mr. Fair hit the roof.

He was moving out, and they had agreed on separation, when he died in an industrial accident that took three lives. This was seven years ago. A belt snapped. Technically there existed no basis for lawsuit, qualified people told Mrs. Fair. The company paid his salary through the year, which helped, and they provided for some crisis counseling at the hospital. But it was probably Kit McGovern who most helped Mrs. Fair get through her rage, as Kit insisted on putting it. And at the hospital Mrs. Fair made the connections that led to her job.

Lew's posture is terrible. His shoulders are sore, and a shingle advances slowly into the back of his neck. But he doesn't move. He is not sure that he could. Scott emerges from behind the garage—still walking, always moving—camera bouncing off his chest.

"You can go in if you want," Lew says, and it comes out smug. He wonders why he is sounding so much the insider.

For the first time Scott stands still. He looks into the kitchen. "Who's this guy?"

"Their uncle," Lew says right back.

"That his car?"

"That's mine."

"I thought the Pontiac was yours."

"I don't know whose that is. Across the street's maybe." Lew points to his own car. "That's been here since you pulled in."

"What's the engine?" Scott asks.

"In mine?"

"Yeah."

"I don't know. I'm not much on the grease. The vroom-vroom. I'm not much on the hard-guy stuff."

Lew regrets it right away. A peculiar look comes over Scott's face; the jaw tightens and all the other muscles relax.

Scott takes a long breath. He sits down on the step, very close to Lew. With his head still back against the house, Lew moves only his eyes. He has to look hard to the side; the sort of maneuver that brings a headache before long.

"Which one you waiting on?" Scott asks. He is beginning to grin.

From higher up the hill comes the sound of water. A cannonball with a full running start. A deep plush healthy plunge, then the lighter splash across the redwood deck.

"Ellen," Lew says.

There is a pause. Scott does not know them by name. Lew fights a desire to call him on it.

"She's at summer school now," Lew explains.

"With the short short hair?" Scott smiles again. "The little one?"

"Right."

"How long?" Scott asks.

"Have I known her?"

"Right."

Lew considers. "Four weeks I guess."

"I think I've got you, but it's close."

They are touching from the hip to the knee. Scott plucks some weedy grass from a crack in the cement and he puts a blade between his lips.

"Been waiting long?" Scott grabs Lew's knee. "Don't have to say, buddy. It shows. You been here about all day. Right as rain, you are full-out pussy-*whipped*. She's making you suffer, little girl is. She sweats you for it."

Scott absolutely beams at him.

"I know," he says. "I understand. Too much bed not enough sleep, as we used to say." Scott stretches his fingers around the meat of Lew's arm. "They fuck like a dream these girls, don't they? Weren't a cherry made it through seventh grade, I'm betting."

Lew can't seem to move. He wants to motion that they might hear in the kitchen, through the screen door.

"Oh. A nice tight fit. Tell me I'm wrong. And delicious. A tasty family, right? You want to eat till you die. You want to suffocate. You want to absolutely swallow every bit. Am I right?"

Scott squeezes Lew's arm harder—his long fingers reach most of the way around. Lew's neck and all below has gone numb. He can't feel, he could be floating.

"Now I'm only seventeen. But I have never, never had my cock sucked like this before. You know? And all the time, and anywhere: they'll do it, they don't care. Oh, sweet Lord." Scott lets go. "You need your rest." He taps his camera. "With this at least I can get away to across the room."

He slaps Lew's leg and gets up. Concentrating, Lew pushes off with his tingling neck and thrusts his rump back flat against the house, where it can support weight again. He reaches into his shirt pocket for cigarettes.

In a pile of grass cuttings the cat hunkers down. He sits and sits, he waits and waits, then he wiggles his back legs like a golfer addressing a tee shot, then he pounces, and a squirrel darts up a maple. At the base of the tree Liddy stops and turns back slowly.

"I'm stranded here all day I bet," Scott says. He keeps the blade of grass in his mouth. Lew's sleeve is damp from his grip. Scott is a busboy where Janet works, and he has huge hands, enormous. Ellen told Lew what Janet told her, that clearing a function room Scott can carry seven water glasses in one hand, a glass under every finger with room for two more in the middle. In the cocktail lounge he does nine with highball glasses, and eight with rocks. Ellen seemed as fascinated as she said Janet was. Scott has seniority among the buses. The lady manager, according to Janet, can't get him to keep the top button of his coolie bus jacket buttoned. Lew thinks his last name might be Kelliher.

They watch Andrea climb the hill and pull into the driveway. Before the engine finally dies she is out of the car and trailing a paper bag in one hand. In one motion it is swung to her chest. The cat, persistent, climbs out of the grass and falls in behind her

"Not back yet?" she says to Lew on the stairs.

"No."

"Unreal. They're done an hour ago. Has she called?"

Lew shrugs.

"I'll tell you if she did, or if she does," Andrea says as she steps over Lew's feet. Lew is ready to tell Scott which she is, but he doesn't ask.

With both feet Andrea tries to block Liddy, but she fails, so cat and daughter come stumbling through the door. "Getting warmer by the minute," Andrea says, and then, to her uncle, "Howdy." Mrs. Fair's brother perches by the sink and dangles his legs off the formica counter, sharing, Mrs. Fair thinks, the male preference for any seat that is not a chair. If they'd make a study, Mrs. Fair would read it.

Donna walks out of the bathroom. "You missed some fun," she says to Andrea, who plants the bag in the center of the kitchen table. Andrea is told about Janet's accident, and there are amazed looks all around. In front of her brother Mrs. Fair's daughters are as primed-yet-measured as the great stage actresses. Everything seems very very lightly contrived.

Jill has Liddy half-lifted, wobbling, on her bare ankle. "Those ears look hideous," she says.

"He's got an appointment," Andrea says.

"Shanga or Carpenter?" Jill says.

"Shanga," Andrea says.

"I hate that place," Donna says.

"She's the least expensive," says Mrs. Fair.

"It smells even worse than Carpenter's," Donna says.

"Carpenter closes Monday nights," Andrea says.

"We have to coordinate these things," Mrs. Fair says to her brother. "It takes about five of them to get this cat off to the vet's. They hide all around with blankets to throw over him. You wouldn't think the place was so big."

"Liddy sees that little kennel, he just freaks," Jill says.

"Hide it," says their uncle.

"Yeah," Jill says, "but now if there's a blanket out of place, then he smells a rat. Don't you, Gordo?"

A package of jumbo hot dogs comes out first; they are dumped in water set to boil. Donna unpacks the relish and a box of popsicles. Andrea pulls out Nature's Organics Plus Jojoba Conditioning Shampoo. A half-gallon of Hood's Nu-Form; six frozen burritos; a bottle of Baco-Bits; Seven Seas Creamy Italian Dressing; a Charmin Four-pak, white. "All the provisions," says Mrs. Fair's brother. "Andrea the great provider," Jill says, "she brings home the Baco-Bits." Jill must be content as a voice out of the picture—they all realize that three at the table unpacking would look silly. Donna holds a package of sixteen Lite Line Slices. Andrea takes out the hot dog buns. A two-liter Tab; a bag of Cain's No-Salt potato chips; a box of Entenmann's chocolate chip cookies; *People*; two heads of lettuce; a tomato; a cucumber.

"Ninety-nine cents a head," Donna says.

"Where'd you go?" Mrs. Fair asks.

"Christy's."

"Andrea."

"Mom you're not having to pay for it," Andrea says. "You said you only had half an hour. I figured you didn't want me stuck at the supermarket behind some lady's week's shopping."

Mrs. Fair stops herself from suggesting that men shop for groceries, too.

Jill reaches into the cupboard for the plates. "Andy we have cookies already," she says. "Chris baked them last night."

"She's all over the place lately," Donna says.

"Happy as a clam," Jill says.

"That's a stupid expression," Donna says.

"Who bakes cookies in this weather?" Andrea says.

Soon the hot dogs boil in the white water. The cat rubs around legs, begging. Now Andrea kicks him gently, pins him between her feet, and after Jill sets everyone's place she puts him out.

"Shouldn't we ask those guys in?" Jill says.

"I already did, kind of," says Andrea.

With a fork Jill spears hot dogs and puts them into buns.

"What do you *say* to them?" says Donna.

Mrs. Fair reaches for a large bowl and a head of lettuce. "No more hot dogs for a while after this, all right?" she says. "They're not doing anybody any good."

"They look awful," Jill says.

"Who are these two?" asks Mrs. Fair's brother.

Donna points. "Janet's, Ellen's."

He puts his plate down gently, but it clangs on the rim of the porcelain sink. It's the first he's heard of a boyfriend for little Ellen. Mrs. Fair keeps him seated with a look, a look with reinforcements, a look that grows sterner from necessity every few seconds, because each time he thinks again her brother is propelled forward, almost automatically. Yet she keeps him still, her little brother.

"Jill." Mrs. Fair begins conversation. "There's no reason to keep the garage door open like that for just anybody to see."

"The cat likes it," Jill says.

"That door's only got a few closes left before it gives, Mom," Donna says.

"There's nothing anybody would want to steal," Andrea says.

Donna laughs. "Or could even stand to look at."

"Unless they're Pennsylvania Dutch," Jill says. "Or serfs."

They all laugh. Mrs. Fair's brother smiles.

"No money and no science past the wheel," Jill says. "We're crime proof."

"We'll just point them up the block," Donna says. "Send them to McGovern's."

"Have you seen their new shower?" Jill asks, putting her food down.

"The car wash!" Her daughters are laughing, guilelessly.

"What is it?" asks her brother.

"You should get a tour someday," Andrea says. "It's a panic."

"Water comes out of the shower walls in six different places," Donna says.

"Not that many," says Mrs. Fair.

"From every side," Donna says. "It's wild, it's just like a car wash."

"But you never have to *turn*, you see," Jill says mockingly. "That's the beauty. It cuts down on mishaps."

"And it's so progressive," Andrea says. "So extremely today."

"Easy," says Mrs. Fair.

Jill says, "And it doesn't violate the rights of women, for which we've all been struggling."

Her daughters laugh. Mrs. Fair looks at Jill, who doesn't see. In another moment Mrs. Fair will have to leave, only halfway through her salad. Her brother wants a word privately, and her daughters hear this and make small faces at each other. In the living room he says he can't believe what his sister lets Ellen do. Mrs. Fair says she's late, she'll call tonight, promise. Just don't do anything. Her brother kisses her and walks back to the kitchen. As always, Mrs. Fair glances into the hall's curved mirror while she goes to the front door. The image is distorted, but she can see Jill going down to the cellar, can hear Andrea calling "Take out my uniform, please," can see Donna salting the no-salt potato chips. Her brother is back on the formica counter, drinking milk from the carton.

The sweat climbs Scott's hair as up a rope, slowly. The curled ends flatten against his neck. While the heat darkens his hair at the bottom, higher up the sun turns it lighter.

"Murder," Lew says, tugging his shirt again.

"Not so bad, buddy. Try Texas sometime."

"That where you're from?"

Scott raises his bicep to his forehead to wipe sweat. "We were there three years. It is hell. My town it wasn't just linebackers shaved their heads. Bunch of us did arms and legs, too. An insect paradise—truly. They vacation there. They come for the humidity. They bus down from Tulsa for the weekend."

They hear laughter from the kitchen. Scott walks right up to the screen door and looks for a minute. "It's ten past one," he says to Lew. Then he prowls the grounds again. In a few minutes he's back.

"They keep it up good here—no surprise, I suppose." He sits differently this time, far across the cement step, elbows on knees and hands dangling in. He looks over the streets leading down the hill. He has placed his camera beside him. He's no enemy, Lew knows.

"You need to take charge," Scott says. "She'll use this. It's a weapon now, Scott's famous car wreck. It's like being married. More than a month and you're married. We can't even agree on what movie now."

Scott feeds himself another blade of grass. "I'm stranded all day, bet you. That car's out for a while, no matter who she knows. My walk home is fifty-five minutes—I went and did it a while back, at seven in the morning. Maybe I can catch a ride when you're ready."

"Maybe."

"Whenever that is. Whenever you stop waiting."

Lew is thinking of Ellen. It was the same with her, like with Sears or the supermarket. You just began, off the street, thrilled that someone not selling anything actually said yes, without strings. Two-ninety an hour or not, fifteen years old or not, you gratefully began. In no time you were an old-timer, an original. You bitched and maybe threatened, but you never gave your notice. You talked about butchers and cashiers and singers on the radio that nobody else remembered. Their names came right back to you. One of the vets, trusted, in charge of closing meat and deli, with a crew of three, but still doing the dirty work yourself, to get finished faster. Cleaning the deli slicer yourself, the shortcut way, the risky way, running a sponge over it at full speed. Pressing the spinning blade firmly, making the wet brown film. The quick way to do it. Watching your rolled-up sleeves carefully, keeping them clear, picking the thickest sponge you could find or if the coast was clear pulling a new pack from the shelf. Checking yourself a dozen times a second, and running it until the thing was clean enough, close enough. They met at an outdoor party in Walpole in June, that was all he could say. In bed Ellen was solemn at first, now she is active but still solemn, and still says "Thank you" at the strangest times.

"It should be my car," Scott says. "This is ridiculous. I should have the car. You got it right buddy, a younger one. You need somebody younger."

"That leaves you only Ellen and Chris in this family," Lew hears himself say.

"I used to force it into every conversation, a girlfriend six years older. Seventeen and twenty-three. I was a big man for a while. But you have to be in charge." Scott wraps the camera strap around one huge finger. "The fucking is like the arms race, up and up and up, and you can't de-escalate. It's like taking a test." He looks straight at Lew. His face is red from the heat. "Tell me if I'm crazy. Really, I want your opinion. When you were little were you sure you'd marry a younger girl? I mean as sure of that as anything. My dad was older, and that was that. They had friends, you couldn't tell to look, the lady was something like thirty-nine and the man thirty-six. But to me it was like she married a midget. Now am I the only one?"

"Will you believe me?" Lew says.

Scott is looking straight at him.

"I know exactly what you're talking about," Lew says. "To the word. You're reading my mind. You could not have said it any better."

In the clinic parking lot Mrs. Fair idles and waits for the man to vacate the parking space, while he waits for her. She hits the horn. Her brother might leave the house quietly, but tonight he'll be demanding Ellen's boyfriend's address. She's going to have to tangle with him about Ellen's rights. And she can't call him tonight. Dumb. That was why she came home for lunch, she'd be late tonight, the Pierces were giving dinner for friends of Betty's campaign. She beeps again. She's in his blind spot—he's got to be all blind spot. So she reverses a few feet. As best she can while sitting down, Mrs. Fair makes a sweeping after-you gesture to the old fool in the Buick Regal.

As the front door is pushed open by less experienced hands, the cat darts from his place near Lew and Scott; he tears around the corner of the house and inside to be fed, finally, from a can. The air force uncle comes into view. He carries his hat and an envelope. He opens his car door slowly and lowers himself in at straight angles. From the other side they hear a high yell. Chris waves with one hand, slips through the crack in the hedge, and runs past them to the car. The other hand holds the Pepsi towel around her waist. She makes gentle straight-legged leaps over the oil spots in the driveway. Shards of cut grass flash on the bottom of her feet. She's still wet; her straight straight hair has waves and curls.

"Look," says Scott.

She leans far forward, trying to keep her feet on grass and still reach her elbows to the driver's side window. It is too far, and while Chris talks to the air force uncle she steps delicately onto hot pavement. She puts one foot down at a time, and cools the other against her calf.

It is weirdly wholesome. The soldier takes leave and the young girl says breathless goodbye. The air force uncle can't see them for Chris's face, and they can't see him for her back. She drops the towel and stands on it for relief, wiggling her toes in it. A one-piece paisley bathing suit, not shabby or torn but still a relic.

Lew has been at least two hours here, outside this women's house, sweating and waiting. Lew and Scott both look at the car and at the girl. They don't speak. Lew has no questions, though he can't yet name what he knows. That something here needs fixing, maybe. He knows he's not waiting anymore.

Chris's legs are thin and straight and bruised delicately, inconsequentially, the small bruises that fade in a week. Scott snaps a picture. She leans at a hard angle, elbows out and back straight, feet tight together as if a doctor were checking posture.

The air force uncle's engine starts. "We'll go now," Lew says.

Teamwork. With teamwork anything's can-do, it's all possible. Alone and wheeling produce or power tools through a crowded aisle you felt silly and demeaned, the gruntwork. But in tandem there's a world of difference. Coming through. You have right on your side. You want to be noticed—the crew. Coming through, please.

When the military man finally pulls away Scott moves first and Lew lifts himself to follow, or rather to join. It is odd to be walking again.

At first Chris smiles, turning to see them. Scott's huge hands settle gently on her shoulders, She comes along soundlessly. She sits between them on the front seat.

Lew doesn't notice right away, but his face fills both mirrors. He'd turned them on himself hours ago, sitting parked at the Fairs' house, in his first minutes of confinement.

Lew starts his car. He doesn't know what he's doing, but then he never does. He just walks in off the street and begins. He tells himself it will be nothing to regret. When he sees the mirrors it's the face in his wallet, on all his ID. Squinty, frozen, maybe dormant, maybe unprepared. Now with a beard.

The girl sits between them, and she wears a cautious smile. She has nothing to say.

It takes a full minute, but at last they are downhill and out of sight of the house.

LOCK

1

It's a Monday. In the football season. Hub and me, we've run our ads in the gambling rags and on the smaller-time scorephone reports. We've bought our updated mailing list and sent our bogus flyers. Promotion. Hub's part, or Hub's fraction, of the operation. And he's not half bad at it when he feels like doing it right. Since I've known him Hub's been good with words, and a pen. Two years back we were Seismic Sports Selections. His best logo: a naked girl in an easy chair, plugged in like the suckers are, transistor in one hand ghettoblaster in the other, three TVs going, rumpled notebooks and magazines high as her tits, and this real look of ecstasy and confusion on her face, which anyone who ever bet a game can recognize. We're opening the season as Solid Seventy Sports. We're claiming seventy percent winners, documented, every year since 1979. I picked '79; I figured it says track record, without saying geezers who don't fathom computer stats or the new pass-happy NFL. Plus, it's me at the library shagging old scores and getting queasy on microfilm.

Mondays Hub's lady Beverly and I hold down the fort. He plays basketball at this little college a few miles in toward the city. Hub gets on me about my physical condition. He's in great shape from playing with these teachers and artists, new acquaintances out here. They go full court, all day, up and down, in a brand-new gym. Hub calls all his fouls and gets into scuffles. He won't ever miss a chance to play.

So it's Bev and me on Mondays. We work out of the house they rent, off their breakfast bar. Let's use the best example: opening week, this year. I'm killing time with this fat book about Vietnam. When the business phone rings Bev's in the backyard sunning herself. In a chime and a half she sets down this sweater thing she's knitting Hub for Christmas, and tosses a bogus robe, an old dress shirt of Hub's, over her two-piece. In she comes, a touch stiff-legged but still looking good.

"Solid Seventy Sports," she says into the phone. "Yes sir, we certainly do. And what is your name? Well yes we do need it." Bev's left-handed. She writes like they do, hooking their arm, attacking the page from the top. "Great, Ed, where you calling from today? Uh-huh. How's your weather in Duluth, Ed? Right. What? Oh you bet, been hot here all summer long. Brutally so. That's right. Of course we get dry heat, though, the kind that makes you feel pure. I see. Well Ed, I don't have the information, I just work here, you know, I'm just one of the operators. But let me take your phone and address, all right, so one of our consultants can get right back to you. Ed? Well, we'd like it for mailing purposes. We'd like to keep all our clients updated, through the mails. Well sure, just the phone's fine for now. Terrific."

Bev tilts her head when she writes. She and Hub hail from South Carolina—she can work her accent like a hammerlock: hard, soft, not at all. When she's done she says to me, "Edward O. Dragich, Hermantown, Minnesota. Real name all the way." Which is right. People make them up—they go and flatter themselves, at least the downscales do, they can't seem to help but give you one from black-and-white TV. Douglas, Baxter, white picket fence names. Bev hands me the note gently, but with that little flourish, that may be cynical or not.

"Want a cooler?" she says.

"Thanks," I say. "How'd this sound?"

"Kind of young. Schoolkid, I'd say, mainly curious. Want lime?"

She fetches her glass from the yard, and ices one for me, and pours from the pitcher of pre-made drinks, and turns the radio up. She buttons Hub's shirt, out of a modesty I wish I can say I don't understand. When Hub and I roomed in college Bev was in high school. Hub's little brother's girl, at first. Since then she's been to college—with us at Clemson, then out here—and had her hair done sassy, where it used to be long and straight, and overall turned to looking both tireder and prettier. She's still extremely civil with Hub's little brother when he calls from Anderson or comes cross-country to visit. But she's crazy about Hub. They're not easy to take sometimes—all over each other, even in front of company.

"Dragich kind of sounds like money," I say to her. "As a name, I mean. But you think this guy's just playtime?"

"I got that impression."

"Didn't sound like a junkie either? Didn't need a get-even game?"

"Not badly, is my guess. If at all. He sounded green." Bev goes back outside. She strips the shirt and settles face-down on the chaise, reading her magazine through the cracks. She calls in: "And he seems to think we're out of Las Vegas, whatever that's worth."

With fifteen minutes before my turn, I get the fourth from the last chapter done. I try to do a book a week. I want to vary but find myself coming back to history. This football touting's all I've had going. Hub's a little better set up, he's brainier. He's still serious about law school, he's just taking his time getting here. He makes good money headwaitering in San Francisco, and works sixth and seventh nights when he can get them. He covers a lot of Sunday nights. Bev doesn't like him gone, and they must have tangled this weekend about taking overtime. She'd like to keep me in the dark when they fight—but it's no trick to see. There's never physical evidence, but she can't hide how restless she is, or how high she holds her jaw, or how much effort it seems to make good talk. I don't ever try to open her up on it. She won't talk about fighting him, not to me, not since the one time we had.

There's a comedy record on the radio. From outside Bev can still hear. We laugh at it and drink the strong drinks. When mine's gone, and the chapter done, I stop to rev up for the call. I do it all day on Mondays, and now minus the ethical tussles of old, but each call still takes some warmup.

I dial a wrong number. Always frustrating. To Minnesota before five, those minutes add up. Hub won't bitch about phone overhead. If a call goes twenty minutes and turns nothing, he understands. Misdialing, though, he may let me hear about. I'm bearing down the second time to get it right. As it connects I picture the hovering hand of Edward O. Dragich, wondering which ring will color him least like the anxious, pathetic loser.

"Yes, is Ed Dragich at home please?"

"Speaking."

"Ed it's John Pack, from Solid Seventy Sports. What's going on today?"

"Not much." Sub-thirty. Less than rich. Nervous. "How's it going out there?"

"Like you can't believe. We're swamped. It's unprecedented, Ed, and I'm sorry to be so long getting back to you. I know you got better things, and accept my apology. But the fact is we're bombed today, three guys aren't here, and the rest of us can only handle calls so fast. But again, forgive our keeping you waiting."

"No problem," Ed says. My other line I let slide. It goes: "We'd let these switchboard cunts help give out the picks, Ed, but that's not the personalized service big players come to us for, and fuck if we'll shaft customers to turn a dollar, it's not how we got to where we are."

Instead I move straight to: "Now I know you're anxious to get our Lock of the Year, Ed, but first allow me to fill you in about us, just a bit, so you get some sense of how it is we come up with seventy percent winners six years running. All right? You with me? You got a couple minutes?"

"All right."

"We figure you take our picks to the bank, Ed, *and* you understand them, how they're made, then you're likely to stay with us a long while."

Bev comes through the kitchen for a refill. I'm giving Ed

Dragich three and a half minutes on the outlaw line, the true line, the money movement, solid handicapping basics, yards-per-point ratios, sucker games, medical intelligence, computers, nationwide stringers, and team spirit loyalty at Solid Seventy Sports uncommon, and envied, in the industry. Hub wrote the riff when we were SportsAction, then refined it over time, figuring three minutes plus as the perfect length. The thing's just logical and fast-paced enough to whip anybody with the slightest mental hitch in their swing. It's a tower of jargon, all Hub could think of—but refined so it flows. Hub can't talk on the phone worth a shit, but he writes. I don't mess with the copy beyond loading the blanks. But this Monday, in the middle of it, I'm seeing the sports page left on the bathroom hamper. When Bev passes to refill the ice tray I get her attention with my boot, not hard and right below Hub's shirttail. With hand signals, I'm telling her.

"Ed, it breaks this way quite a bit, let me say. I've been on staff here for eight years and at least seven of those the best play, the absolute lock of the year, comes up in the first week. You've got to seize it now. It's always that way. We've done our work, Ed. We've seen enough tape to turn your eyeballs five kinds of crimson. At this point, right now, we're ahead of the goddamn linemakers. We can beat the line, right now. Believe me that's not easy. Those are pros Ed, those are sharp guys. But early on we can beat them like a fucking drum—we can. And tonight. Ed, tonight's play is so strong I've got five dimes on it myself—and I'm no Howard Hughes, Ed, I just work here, I'm just a two-hundred-dollar player. But five thousand and I'm not really worried, not at all. This play is so strong, it'll be over by the half. Five large ones and I've never felt more at peace in my life. Never more calm. All of us in my group—the Locksmiths, we go by—we feel very content right now, because we know, we *know*, that we'll all be working next to a lot of rich guys tomorrow morning. We had a good day yesterday," Beverly—taking it slow, for fun maybe—puts the *Chronicle* in my hands just in time, a tired, restless look on her face. "We hit five of six yesterday Eddie, we had the Jets and Frisco and New England and Seattle and Tampa Bay, all of them big winners as you know, but none, and Ed I swear this to you, none as easy as tonight. I'm down for five dimes tonight *so far*—I may go three or five extra before kickoff. In fact, that's why we're shorthanded here. Our guys not on the phones are off hunting more credit before the game goes off. They may be hocking things even, I don't know. The office is crazy, Ed, I really don't know what else I can tell you. How much can you get down for, do you think?"

"I don't know," Ed Dragich says. He stutters it out.

"Can you get down for a dime?"

"I don't think so," he says, flustered. He may be fourteen years old, an early bloomer, calling for fun. He may have never spoken to a bookmaker in his life.

"How about a nickel? Can you get down for five hundred?"

"Probably," Ed says. "I guess."

"OK Eduardo," I'm saying. "Here's the shot. Normally we . . . you been a player long?"

"No."

"How long?"

"It's . . . " Ed says. "This is my second year for football."

"Okay Ed. That's great. Everybody here loves to see new

guys get off strong. Toss a scare into their BMs first thing. Earn respect. Make that rat bastard fear *you*. How well you connected, Ed?"

"Say again?"

"I'm asking you, how many bookmakers can you get down with tonight?"

"Oh," he says. "Couple three." He sounds a little more confident, finding a rhythm. Hub should write in more pauses, maybe, let the caller talk more and sooner.

"Okay," I say. I run my mouth some more, and before long I'm noticing the hurry I'm in. I'm hooked up with Duluth seven minutes, eight minutes now. Too long for a low percentage kid like this. I'm feeling rushed and frustrated, and wanting to be outside. "So let's say you play our lock of the year with three books, nickel each. You'll clear fifteen hundred tonight. Fifteen hundred you'll make, my friend, and you do it so sweatless you'll be safe, you'll be *bored*, by the third quarter. Now normally we deal with bigger players, and for our lock of the year we charge four hundred dollars. And it's theft, at the price; you're stealing from us. But since you don't play for a big number, here's what I think I can do. Well, wait." Then I stammer a little, aping Ed, or Ed's earlier self. "Hang on here, Ed." I suck an ice cube and count to six. What I'm doing is not a career, it occurs to me. "No. No, Ed, fuck it, I don't need clearance for this. You're a young player starting out, I know the big man here would want this, and if he wouldn't . . . well fuck it, Ed, here it is: you get the game for half price. And *then* less fifty more because we want your business. One fifty. And with our full guarantee, meaning if this pick doesn't win, if you don't make money on tonight's

Green Bay–Giants game, then we'll give you free service for the rest of your natural life. Absolutely free, Ed, your natural life. Put a price on that, I don't know, it's dimes, it's in that district easy. But a hundred fifty to make a lock fifteen. That sounds beyond fair to you, does it not?"

"Thank you," Ed Dragich says. "I'll have to pass." Then that ratty tumbling, the sound of disconnection.

Ed would have gotten the Giants. His phone number goes into the file, along with the day—the next Monday—that I console him over missing the bonanza. The Lock of the Year can never lose for us. We have eleven customers on the hook already—I'd touted six guys the Packers, five the Giants. Among all the ways to make money at this, double-dealing's the safest, and I think the best. Twelve suckers is not strong trade. But the early season always crawls: they need a few Sundays to fall into the hole and get desperate. Even with twelve, dealing both sides, we're sure of six happy guys for next week's Monster Lock, and three jubilant guys for the following week. Most will pay extra with each successive lock. The losers with lifetime service Hub takes care of. He invents some picks Sunday mornings, purely blind, still in bed with Beverly. After a few weeks of fifty percent winners or worse they stop bothering us, unless somehow Hub finds a little hot streak, in which case the names find my A file again.

I read some pages, then Bev's back inside. "Ed took the gas," I say. "Ed didn't come through."

"Ed's a pest, then. Don't get hurt over it."

"I look hurt over it?"

Bev pauses and shakes her head. "You look like you look," she says. She'll never talk to me seriously, about anything that matters. She won't even get close. "Have seconds." She brings the pitcher my way. "Talk to somebody. Call Ernie Antonucci."

Ernie Antonucci was last year's lucky king of the hill. Pro-Action Sports double-dealt thirty-seven suckers, and more climbed on board during the season. When the pyramid played out in the ninth week, Ernie was 9–0, eternally grateful. He bought three cheap claimers in Florida and said he was betting only at the track. We gave Ernie my home number, as our boss's private line, but we haven't heard from him, or any of the friends we asked him to mention us to.

"Ed would square it out," I say to her. "He makes twelve."

"Eleven's hardly worth squaring out, even." Hub's shirt is damp and clingy in the tail. It gives her a flat-chested, round-bottomed look. She leans in to check the sheet. "Which side's out to the six?"

"Green Bay."

"So," Bev says. "Just root for them. Give you something to do tonight."

What I'm doing, after a while, is calling Ed Dragich again. Hub's not crazy about a money-back pitch; I just ad lib them since Hub won't write the script. It's strictly last resort—but with all the competition today, for a few guys it needs to be done. As it rings I see Ed doing the dishes, or his chemistry homework, thinking of who in the world it could possibly be except who he knows it is. And letting it ring.

"Eddie it's John from Vegas again," I would say, and do say, since Bev's back on the patio and I'm tired of my war book. Freelancing, I keep my voice down. "I want you to have this game. I do. The best ones always come right up front, before you really know what's going on. But I've said that already and Ed, I'll come to it direct. I'm not supposed to, but screw it: I'm going to offer you money back on this game. If it loses, and Christ knows how it could, but if somehow, if our side blows out a dozen knees before the half, then I do this for you. I make a special case here. I hold the charge slip till the game's in the clear. It's in my pocket till we're three touchdowns to the good. And if you don't get the cash with this game, I'll tear it up. It's a break you deserve and to hell with these other guys. You don't get the free picks for life, of course, but if that's the way you want to go, I can accommodate. Really, Ed, we both know it. This comes under something else, like revenge. You lose to the man a couple weeks running, and you can just feel the difference. This invisible thing. This grin coming through the phone, this arrogant smirk. To beat that . . . you know, it's not just the money. You want to dominate the *man*, give it back to him, it's human as can be. Force, we're selling here. But you've got to move. There won't be a better chance this season. Take hold of it. I can't do a thing more for you."

Then I'm hanging up the ringing phone. Slid under his couch by now, or unplugged. Five o'clock Pacific, which means the game in an hour and the chance, slim, of another call or two. I dial the tape in Vegas for the official pointspread, Green Bay by five. I hear the creak of the folding chaise. Bev moves past me toward the bedroom. It takes her awhile to dress, then she cases the kitchen, thinking about dinner.

"Have some supper with us?" she says.

"Okay, sure."

"Well." Her hands skipping gently over packages, around bottles in the refrigerator. "Omelettes, looks like. Unless I can talk you into running out for Chinese."

I'm short of cash and so's she. We try scrounging enough from jars and drawers, pants pockets in the hamper, the bottoms of large art objects. Bev's dotted the place with some Indian art bargains. I don't say it, but the look is very South-Carolina-girl goes to California. I would never say it. We're out of places to look when Hub comes stealing into the house, in that way he has. Except, like most Mondays, he limps in. Every week he breaks skin, plus queers an ankle or knee. Beverly is in his arms right away. The whole house changes, the instant he's there. You'd need to be a dead man not to feel it. Hub is tall and rugged. Very well cut, as the girls say, strong in the glutes. Today he looks seriously overheated, and below his eye a red spot stands out, off toward the ear.

"Hi," Hub says to her. "What's new?" he says to me.

"Nowheres near enough. For now we kick off with eleven fish. Three of them money-backs. I dealt Green Bay the extra time." Then I'm touching my cheek. "That come from an elbow?"

"That's from the ball," Hub says. "That's from listening to stories on the sideline. Not watching the action."

With looks, the two of them make up. They don't use words for it. Then Bev eases over that way and kisses the welt. "We're eating in a little bit," she says to him. "J.P.'s fetching chinks. You got twenty to shower up."

"I should have showered at the gym," Hub said. "But I was rushing on back here." He smiles, and they get all spoony right there in the kitchen. They fight, but it's stupid to think it's serious. This time she hadn't even quit knitting for him.

"Just one thing," I'm saying, while they can still hear me.

"Don't say it," Hub grins at me. "You're broke. You need twenty." Hub likes to get on me, in fun. Usually I don't mind. "Major sports consultant, big-talking handicapper," he says, walking back for his gym bag. "And he's Mr. Empty Pockets. You amaze, Packy." Hub grunts, not unpleasantly, each time he moves. "I know if I did the phone pitching, I'd need about two grand in my pocket just to fix my voice up proper. How you bluff like that, without a thing to back it. It's just past me."

To be at the wheel, in motion—it feels good enough that I ride past the big pagoda for a mile or so, then turn around. I'm from a glorious-looking part of the world. I take credit for it whenever I can, from Hub and from other people. Our first year rooming together, we rode out on our break, left Clemson on Friday and drove the weekend straight. A hysterical, buddy-buddy trip. Then we slept at my uncle's house for most of a day. Hub wasn't awake three hours before he'd seen enough and swore he'd settle here. Beverly didn't see California until moving day; she likes it too, but she misses home more, though she'd admit no such thing.

When I come back Hub still hasn't showered. I find them on the living room floor together, back-to-back watching some eyewitnessed news: a shootout. The timid cameraman makes us squint for the key players. Some minority newsgirl stands up and jabbers away. Hub knows me: right away he's got a hand up to deflect all my questions.

"They've got this welfare daddy trapped," Hub says. "They're shrinking his perimeter." He does an accent I can't make out. "We've got no angle, and this old gal won't even let us hear the gunplay. Blah blah blah. I'll bet they pre-empt the football with it."

I put bags and cartons on the coffee table. Bev busies herself in the kitchen with extra napkins, fresh drinks and things. Hub has an ice pack nearby on the floor, not in use.

"I can't eat smelling like this," he says. "Sorry. Save me some."

Hub leaves the room, and the look on her face—just a flash of it—when Bev turns the corner and sees only me.

"Now you look sad," I say.

But she catches herself in a jiffy. She comes back with this smile. Completely fake—and beautiful at the very last when it quits being dimply caricature, but still hangs there. Then Beverly drops her jaw a tiny bit, but stops short of speaking.

We're eating together for a couple of minutes. But when the shower goes, when the water hisses in the pipes, she's away down the hall.

On the box the shooting stops. The talking hairdos can't explain why, so they make way for football. The food sits out on the coffee table. Though Bev and Hub don't want it to, and though I slouch on the sofa with my war stories and the game, the sound of them travels. Substantially. Mostly Beverly. A lot of laughing, happy noise.

The Packers and Giants move the ball at will. I'm locking into a final drive to finish my book. The back hundred pages of something, there's that inner demand to make this the last sitting, read past normal comfort, and fast, hurrying through all the good stuff, the thought-out last pages.

The bedroom noises stop around halftime, but Bev and Hub leave the living room to me. I turn sleepy when I finish.

The sound of someone in the bedroom, then the bathroom, then back. Green Bay shanks a pair of extra points early on, and that puts the score right on five: 33–28, late third quarter. A tie bet being no good for us, the only way we lose all around, since it wastes a week of the season. The money-backs get their money back, and with no winners there's less chance to sell a bigger, second lock. The threat of a small crisis, and some more food, helps me fight away sleep. But I fail: before the finish there I am, big gut heaving, out cold in the glow.

I hear her gathering the greasy bags. Being her quietest. Ted Koppel goes round and round with bickering cancer doctors: I hear that, too. I'm keeping my eyes closed. There's a draft on the small of the back, but I don't want to move and cover. I wish I could be asleep, but still able to see her, see how she looks prowling along now, see what she wears.

We had a night in college, very early on. After that there was a look I tried to give her. A child's look. A wide-open face, but centered with eyes that flared. A why-not stare. Here, go ahead and play both sides. I went my senior year with that face on. And now I want to, but I can't always take it off.

It's no issue, though. We know, or pretend well, that we know where we stand. Hub hasn't a clue it happened. In a way neither does Bev anymore. For a while, I think, we've been to where it happened more to me than to her. It was very late April. Her freshman year, my junior. I'd known her five months. Hub was cramming at the library. A long night ending, about five-thirty, one more in the week of all-nighters, but the first without books. We had five or six hours of that talking. The real glorious stuff that, twelve years old, I imagined as college routine. As it came light we were kissing in my end of the room, then we were laid out the wrong way across Hub's bed. What I did, what I didn't do, I don't know. I may have been rough, I told myself not to be. I was in better condition then, but I was breathing hard, and I was throwing words down on top of her, talking all the way through it, through whatever in her face said not this much, not this hard, and past the little muscle twitches of caffeine exhaustion, and through the static that held her long hair magically to the wall behind the pillow, and past the ashtray and saliva smells and past my constant vision of the turning doorknob and through my wanting more than anything while I ran my mouth to say something good, and talented, something permanent which could completely, easily, without a sweat outlast the confusion and the disentangling and the joking and the long unchecked sleep that, once back in our places, we were both more than ready for.

2

Hub stirs first: six-thirty or seven. He comes into the living room raising shades. "That old couch monster grabbed you again." He fixes himself tea and peaches, then does his stretching in front of the TV, which ran straight through, talked in my sleep. I have to piss like a racehorse. It's a battle getting upright, and Hub's amused.

"Where'd the game land?"

I tell him I couldn't say, maybe five, maybe a problem for us. But Hub doesn't worry, he's smooth as ever. Which must be why, this morning, I say yes to basketball. He asks all the time, and I give excuses. But we're all three in the sunny kitchen, Bev and Hub gliding around operating all their appliances. Hub shows his top teeth when he asks me. Spur of the moment, I say sure, love to. Then I'm wishing I'd planned it better, worked my lines for top impact.

I go home to clean up and find some gear and get a full meal. We swap phone calls: I report Green Bay's late safety to win by seven; he tells me don't bother with a towel since his professor buddy has the run of the locker room. He uses his I'll-play-along voice, but we're on, I keep saying, so about noon Hub's copper Saab comes thumping into my complex, jungle music going strong. He drives a nice car, a handsome car. Those are just the words you need to use about it. It's pleasant to slouch down inside there and watch the controls and the scenery fill the windows, which is what I do, besides talking over the music, while we whip over to this small college where they're not in fall session yet, though the women's diving team, as we see at length, has training underway. Hub leans back from the wheel and folds his arms to watch them climb the tower, pull and tuck their swimsuits, throw themselves in again. Hub has his steering wheel rigged with clips for a pad and pen. He takes road notes from time to time, but not now. "What can you say," he says. "Agreed?"

Then he shows me this spanking gymnasium. We just poke our heads inside, on the way to the lockers. The light I can't describe, though some technical term probably does the job. It's yellowish, clean light; like there should be a taste to it. Netting and painted bars overhead, and rolling wall sections to give the place a dozen purposes, once the school year starts. This early, I'm figuring, only Hub's insider pals in the beards and wristbands and burning white high-tops know enough to take advantage.

"Hey, Bert," Hub says in the locker room. "Got a player, Bert." Already Hub wears his game face. Not a trace of Clemson twang. "This is John Pack. We're in business together. Packy, he goes by."

"Sir," Bert says, wrist tense for a hard shake.

"Here," Hub says. I get the quick tour: lockers in bright paint, the shower chamber, a sauna, a supply closet we're welcome to, an exercise bike. And of course there's the big platform Detecto, a whale scale. "Go ahead, Packy," Hub says. By now we're alone in the locker room. With me, he's still loose. "Mount it up here, let's get some before and after data." I wave him off. "Come on," he says. "Here, I won't peek. I'm off for the ballgame. My concern's not the totals, just differential. I'm only wondering how much a fellow can drop."

Upstairs we shoot warm-ups and don't talk and stand around while, slowly, teams get made.

They toss me in with the skin team—Hub, Bert, plus two bearded guys they all seem to know, though I'm not introduced. We all strip our shirts. Then we go squeaking along the new floor. Running. It hurts like the day after a car wreck—legs and ankles, kidneys, under the shoulder blades, deep in the gut. I feel the full benefit. My lungs are just on fire. I overlook this, to keep running. I'm doing nothing *but* running since they don't pass my way, and I can't outjump anyone to rebound what people heave at the rim.

Before long the guy covering me—a scholar, I think—figures he can cheat over to help guard the others. Especially Hub, playing our pivot. Hub shows none of his limp, bangs against the double-teaming, throws up little spin shots with either hand. He's dripping wet, too slick on his back to touch.

A stray elbow rattles his teeth, but he doesn't call time. Hub spits in his hand, checks it, and goes right back to blocking shots.

I'm a bad joke for a while: sprinting the court on special occasions, then falling back to that hurried walking. I show up near the action, at last, and somebody steals, or one guy calls another for traveling. About face. More race-walk, behind the play again.

Guys are hurting themselves every few minutes. Time out while they hobble and curse. There's physical stuff, too. Shoving goes back and forth, much bolder once peacemakers pile in. But the vocabulary, that's rough and tough without fail.

Miraculously we have a lead, as high as 9–3 at one point, though this is disputed. Litigated, near about. I use every delay for discussion to close my eyes and bend over, make sure everything on the inside settles near where it belongs.

One scuffle—a hard pick, a little open-hand swinging, Bert cussing one beard in a Dobie Gillis shirt—gives their side the lift they need, and right away they creep closer, outhustling us. Many two-on-ones and outright breakaways.

I'm trying first to ignore any news from below my neck, and second to stay outside and in motion, don't damage the team. But we give back our lead, and with the game at stake the action slows and most every play ends in a foul. A guy squares for a half-decent shot, he gets crunched—it's how pickup games get played, and nobody complains. Finally we finish at 18–16 when Bert makes a nice steal and pass to Hub, on the run, for the winning lefty layup. They're pointing at each other, Hub and Bert, and slapping hands.

We stagger into formation at the bubbler, except I'm seeing some spitters up ahead, and this just ruins it for me. I don't even bother drinking. When Bert's got his jersey back on, and the leather ball gripped two-hands at his chest, he comes my way to talk.

"I want you to tell me how you earn a living. I've heard Hub's side of it. I just can't believe it. I can't believe the business."

"Well," I tell him. "It's what we do."

"Who's that dense? They really pay you those figures?"

"I'm sure for them the fee's trivial."

Bert grins at me. "Trivial!"

"Yes it is," I say. "No question, adjusted for what's at stake." He may not follow me. But he teaches college, I'm not using the brakes for him. "Bookmakers collect on Tuesday, and they pay out on Wednesday. All right. Sunday, every so often on Sunday, you get scorched a little. Monday rolls around, and he's planning on you and a couple of your thousand the next afternoon. Well, you know. Monday Night Football, that ends the week. Make a small play, Tuesday comes win or lose. Tuesday is Tuesday. That's why I get heard. They need to hear me, because I'm talking about Wednesday, and on Wednesday you can look him direct in his beady, fucking eyes. It's hardly even the money—"

"Which is why we can sell a thousand-dollar pick. If it's a good one." Hub says this, over my shoulder.

Bert locks his brows. "So the games do win?"

"Well we don't get it right *every* time . . ." Hub says. I'm about set to faint. Hub's never mentioned the double-dealing here. He's selling these bearded people. Or holding out hope. Bert talks around me, to Hub. I hear Ernie Antonucci, Hialeah, classy allowance colts. I let Hub do his best, but he can't get far before we're out there again, as shirts now, taking on another bunch of guys that look alike. I cover a portly, headbanded guy with body hair. He enjoys flinging up twenty-footers and fouling, and I just let him.

We win again, and in the game that follows I break two barriers: I swing my elbows, for one, and I arrive at the far side of pig-tired, where it seems I can play my game, meaning nine parts chatter, one part hustling assist. Shirts, us, 15–10. A long water break. They drink, I boost myself up on a stack of gym mats; I spread out there and look around. They're straggling back from the bubbler, some of them. Others are packing it in. The holdovers—my count is nine—they shoot and squat and stretch. They all seem to stand tall, even in dribbling position. I don't mean they're erect all the time, not at all; but they do seem to have backbone and confidence, of the permanent kind. Their cars are parked together somewhere. I didn't see them on the way in, but I don't need to. That's what I'm thinking—besides breathe in, breathe out—watching these friends of Hub's circle around, shoot baskets, covet me as tenth man.

My family's nothing to brag about, but they taught me a few things, and I worked pretty hard and learned some more on my own. I had to cross the country to find a college. Still I got in, and got the degree in regulation time. But always there's more ahead, a couple higher levels visible, though murky, and past that more you can only imagine. I'm parked up there silent, taking my pulse, looking back when they looked, not saying a word. Some force for me there, small but clear. Maybe very small. Because they won't beg—these types return pressure hardly opening their own mouths. "What say." "You're the man." Like that. I'm up on those piled mats, damp and flushed. This will be me for a while, not much work to occupy me, keep me from sidekicking around Hub, betraying him on the odd day, doing what I do.

On the floor I'm a shirt again, running in a weary, rag-ass game. Fatigue makes Bert a better shooter, and he carries the load. We beat them 15–7 and Bert is the undisputed star. Nine players head for water, four return. The others vanish: no excuse made, no friendly signoff. The five of us look each other over. Bert, Hub, me, and two forgettable skins we just played against. Hub and Bert won't show any fatigue, not to each other. "I'll sit," I say. The others start a lazy game of two-on-two, me off to the side, when we hear a bouncing ball in the doorway. Three players. Teenagers, a touch swaggery, Afro-American.

"The community at large," Hub says.

They're dressed in heavy denim or corduroy pants, full belts and buckles, pullover shirts or sweaters, street sneakers, dark socks. They even wear rings and watches. They scuff toward the far basket. Hub lets them shoot a minute, then approaches. There's a boom box, too. I've seen bigger, but it has plenty of kick, or such is my guess, since the whole time it sits quiet on the sideline.

"Game?" Hub says.

"Sure."

"Four on four." Hub claps my shoulder, and calls to them: "Y'all draft yourself our secret weapon here. Let's get it started."

"Half or full?" one says.

"Half, man," says another.

"Full court," Hub says. "Got to."

After I'm down there, they keep shooting and stalling

around. Meanwhile Bert's bombing away at his basket, staying hot. Bert calls down to us: "Packy. You all go skin."

"Uh," Hub says, "we may encounter less confusion in this game, Bert, comparatively."

"Comedian." Bert throws his head at me. "I been passing him the ball two hours. We play shirts and skins, in this gym, winners' choice. These people, they go skin."

It's gametime again and, no surprise, the brothers freelance. They do nothing but. We have total team breakdown, every play, before one of them launches a fallaway prayer. It's not like this builds over time to offend the shirts. They're getting beat. They are promptly pissed off. On their side, I'd feel the same. But I'm jabbering away, whooping and pointing and patting asses.

Our side plays nothing recognizable as offense or defense. In all team principles, we are the abject illiterate. There's shaking and baking, hot-dogging, too much dribbling, gangly arms pumping the ball up and down. There's goofy eye-feints and wide-mouthed, floppy-tongued spin moves. Pass the ball, it's an upset if you get it back. I find I don't mind it even a little bit. These are long-legged kids, half our age, fuzzy hair on their heads and none anywhere else. We keep a lead—as I let everyone know. And just the idea of it boggles the shirts. Our team takes crazy shots, just the wildest shit, and something near half of them fall in. The shirt defense is still a dozen times more earnest than ours, but quieter now except for Hub's grunting and inbounding and barking for the score.

"Eight–three for the skin," I say, amazed I have lungs left to shout it out, and chatter at the brothers on our defense, such as it is. I'm feeling strong now, blood making the whole circuit, the crazy light in the place now speaking of health to me, legs taking me upcourt and downcourt until the end, which is hard-fought and prolonged. We bang underneath, which I must say I don't mind. Hub and Bert call ghost fouls, practically whenever they shoot. That this is even a contest, it nags at them, Hub especially, if Beverly saw it she'd be tickled, as she always is about what seems to matter to men. Her man Hub's in a frenzy now. Then I'm laughing right along, too, because the tallest kid, in the green corduroys, makes a game-winning shot that's just obscene, from near the sideline, practically on top of it and tottery as a logroller, Hub blitzing him and waving both drippy forearms in his face. A hard carom off the board and through.

None of the skins go for water afterward; they just keep firing up practice bombs. Hub stands under the shirt's basket between games in his Clemson T-shirt, laying test fingers along his fat lip. He hasn't grown a lick since we met across a poker table there—but he looms, he's plenty big. He elevates his game two notches in the rematch, yet still it goes tense, nip and tuck. My skins team bears down, too. One of the brothers climbs Hub's back a little for a freakish tip-in that gives us a lead, 10–8. The yell from the three skins, you could take it for rehearsed. Hub one-hands the ball out of the netting and when he fires it the thing whistles, it makes an insect noise, it moves along. I can hear it from where I am. The kid in the corduroys shuffles downcourt with plenty of swivel, much head and shoulder action. Lucky for him. What the ball misses by, I can't say except that it's a science word, some queer-sounding minor measurement.

"What's that garbage?" My own voice is saying this. Hub hadn't even bothered to target the kid who fouled him. "Explain that horseshit for us. Where'd you learn a fucking stunt like that?"

"Shut up," Bert says to me. The ball still kicking around the other end. "You people don't belong here," Bert says. "You're over the line. We don't notice, if things go nice and easy."

Well, it's a turning point. Hub knows he's way out of bounds, but he's smarter than letting it show. He backs down, he forfeits an edge that's useful. I know all this, while we're playing, but still I'm worthless to the skins, and I get to fuming at myself for it. My body can't help me with a single thing I have in mind. The shirts prevail. Hub is absolutely superb. Bert muscles me in the low post for the winning point. "Closing time," Bert says. The swank leather ball's his; he palms it, we file out, he locks the gym door.

Now the four shirts and me, we're in the locker room. I don't care to shower with these people. I don't think about why, at that point; I just sit on the floor until they're off for the tiled chamber. But first, they have to hang wet stuff over their open lockers and stall around bare-assed discussing one thing after the next—skiing and cocaine and landscapers and old service stations and the best pornography. Hub fits in a mention of the diving girls, and I back him up on it. Finally Bert's into the closet for everyone's towels.

"I like these things," Hub says. He handles a plastic tub that's big and square, multi-purpose. "Bev would go nutty for a few of these, no?"

"Possible," I say.

"I know she would," Hub says.

"Well," Bert says. "I need a long shower. Can't see myself eyeballing this closet all day. Checking what's in it or isn't."

When it's down to just me sitting there, Hub boosts one of these tubs, and tries cramming it into his locker. He's naked, all the while. The dorm showers, that far back, the last time I've seen this stuff, people moving uncovered in plain view. But Hub's in charge, even here, even buck naked and hunched over, ripping off trivial goods, fresh from losing his cool. He's happy and in control. It struck me as the most amazing, outrageous thing. I'm wearing cut-offs, a baseball shirt, sneakers and three pairs of socks. We work from Hub's lead, every time.

"Bert get you a towel?" he says.

"No." Hub's last shower is far, I think, from my mind. "Go ahead in," I say to him. "When I'm ready I'll grab one. I want to sit and breathe a little."

Do I hear it coming? At first I sit alone on the carpet, studying my newest pants in the open locker. A disgrace, my first size 40s, another sorry threshold cleared. I'm sitting there trying to make resolutions. I'm watching the sweat shine, feeling my forearms stick to my knees. Then, I'm stripped and in the sauna. More weird light. Pumpkin-colored. It's my first sauna all to myself, best as I can recall. Beverly's right about dry heat, the instant virtue. The box is soundproof, too, and I like how my voice bounces along the simple, ticking planks and over the toy stones in the corner. I had it in my head that saunas were foggy, blurry at least; but it's all heat and clarity.

The two dark heads I see through the door's window, after a moment, give me no surprise. They're standing tall together, facing the showers, fully dressed, and they have padlocks in each hand. I can't see the third kid, in charge of wallets and watches, and I can't see the shower foursome, either; I can't know what they see and don't see. I can't hear the running water. I can't hear that clack when the padlocks close in unison. But from the glance they swap I know it's impressive.

In the box I'm running my mouth nonstop. Nobody can hear me, but I'm talking to everybody. The thieves, Hub and the unseen beards, myself, telling them, us, all what to do. Disable Hub, he's the key; team up and rush them four on two; take keys and all the cars you can; shoot shampoo at their eyes; shut up, move out and do something. None of this happens. It's a blind standoff. And the skins don't spend their arsenal. Those are defensive weapons.

But finally, just before they run, the tallest one skitters the first padlock into the square shower, fires it like a flat rock. The other must feel my talk. He wheels around. He freezes to see me. I look right back. It seems I'm in proper position; his face takes the shading of a grin and an empty hand, his right, raises up, flashes pink underside, then closes, loosely, and points at me.

And that's what sticks in my mind, all week. Hub goes home to void credit cards and I lie to him, tell him I'm doing the same. But I sit at my window and wait. The night's quiet. Wednesday morning I'm on my little balcony, cursing the unseen mailman, willing him my way sooner. I believe my wallet's coming. I really do. I rehearse what to say when I show it off shipshape, full as ever. Thursday I feel much the same. Friday. Saturday morning—I've still got an eye peeled for that midget truck when Hub phones, reporting that Beverly judges his swelling's come down to condition green for new picture ID. Hub drives over there, Beverly sits in front for the ride, and I go, too.

THE HOLIDAYS

After supper Harlan sits in the good chair, picks up his library book, and begins. He's done nothing but read in the two weeks since he lost his job. What with no leads and the holidays coming, he takes the opportunity. They passed him through high school without making him finish a book. Ada keeps finding him reading in the good chair and saying she's surprised. She's not cynical, or enthusiastic, she's surprised is all. It's a college town, and Harlan's old installation partner at the cable TV enrolled full time for half a year and saved his ID. Harlan carries Paul Favolaro's card in his wallet now. He piles the books from University Library on the back of the couch, where the baby can't reach. Nothing written before 1976—Harlan doesn't care for things out of date. Borrowing is easy, since these aren't picture IDs here. It's such a cheap school. What they pay Ada for part-time secretarial is embarrassing, barely enough to cover in a squeeze like this.

The baby is by the heating unit and on the floor, where he won't fall. Fall is all he does at four months—crawling he won't go anywhere yet, the knees keep pumping but the arms are locked in place. Ada knits Christmas presents and sings him old Supremes numbers, which can make it tough to read. They have no spare room, just this living room and the one bedroom, which is too small for the good chair. It's a small apartment in an old building, but Ada's done a real job with it. When he installed the cable Harlan saw it all over town, dives kept up inside like the bridal suite, except in the student section where the only style was bedlam.

This place is just old. The bathroom is a terror—porcelain and painted cement, with an ancient four-pawed bathtub, a death trap for the baby. Since the summer and the delivery Ada's fixed it up, she's softened things. The baby hasn't hurt himself, and the place doesn't look decrepit anymore, though Harlan still hates it.

Tonight, as the baby sleeps on the floor and the season's first Christmas special ends—Andy Williams, always—Ada tells Harlan that she squared it today, and she can go full time with the new semester.

Harlan has *The Professor of Desire*, a thin one. The thick ones are mostly for show; the thin ones he reads, and likes reading.

"So if we want to change our minds we better do it now," Ada says. "Tomorrow they have to know for sure."

"It's fine with me."

"I suppose even if you get something right away, what can it hurt for one term? Yolanda says she doesn't mind having him, he's no trouble. If you get something soon she says she'll watch him days. I can be back by three or three-thirty if I have to, probably. Most days anyway. And you might wind up with something nights, who knows?"

There are beautiful markings in this book. No underlines: instead braces, the flowing symmetrical braces Harlan could never make. Until now he's seen only sloppy ink in these books, the recumbent reader's rude uneven ballpoints—and the silliest things noted, even he can tell that, and almost exclusively in the front forty pages, before the defacing bores the defacer. But these modest brackets preserve the right lines, Harlan thinks, important as far as he can tell. And the marks stay respectfully clear of the text, done off to the side in light pencil lead, number three, as if she normally didn't mark but couldn't help herself, she was moved. The braces are gently balanced like birds airborne, like soft sea gulls, and the ends fade out, not an arbitrary marking but a kind of gradual taking notice, which is how these things really happen. Harlan would like to meet her, mature past her years. It has to be a girl.

He rises from the good chair and drives the book back to the University Library. Then over to the mall, where he barely beats closing. His pocket money is just enough for a paperback copy and a yellow marker. At home he flips through the tight clean copy and highlights her early passages from memory.

The next day is bitter cold and it takes time to turn the engine over. He drops Ada at her engineering department, then he drives across campus and parks in the library's closest handicapped space. In front there's a newer, darker cement, and the curbs have been redone with ramps. It's a cheap school in what counts, he tells the baby in the back seat, but for the Feds they step lively. Harlan retrieves the spare blanket they keep in the trunk and he spreads it over the baby. He considers stashing the bundle like valuables, out of sight behind the driver's seat, but he'll be gone just a minute.

In the PS section the book hasn't been reshelved yet. He rides the elevator back to the ground floor, where a short foreigner is waiting with his cart. Harlan rides back up with him, sees the book, and slips off with it at the next floor. This tight school has only one copy machine, outside the second floor reading room. A paper sign hangs limply from the front of it, the paper fallen over itself, the Scotch tape failed. He tries it anyway, and it eats his dime. Ten cents they want here for a single copy.

"That's out, sir." A short, fat librarian, a young woman, has come out of the reading room.

"I guess it is."

"Is it an emergency?"

"Well, you wouldn't really . . ."

"Okay," she says. "I'll give you a note. You go downstairs, one flight, turn left, all the way around the big desk, that's circulation. Show the note and use theirs. You don't have much?"

"One copy. My dime's gone."

"Okay."

The fat girl almost sings this, and everything. She goes back into the reading room. Harlan figures that to avoid questions downstairs he needs a sheet of paper, so he grabs the out-of-order sign. For all he knows it's against some school code to copy these little jacket cards.

She returns with his note and on the stairs he promises himself to forget it if they insist on doing it for him. But nobody even asks to see his note, they just wave him to the back. He removes the small card from its pocket in the back of *The Professor of Desire* and makes a copy. When you copy empty space, the air, you get this ugly grainy gray. These dirty motes cover most of Harlan's page, and they bother him. He leaves the out-of-order sign on this machine.

With Paul Favolaro's card he borrows the book again, with the same due date, since all books must be back by semester's end. He signs the card he's just copied, and they take it away. One more thing while he's out. From the library he trots past his car and down the hill to the bank.

Miss Winfield is on the drive-up now. A quick promotion. Just as well, she'd lost that fresh-from-University-High look that hooked Harlan when she'd trained in the summer. She'd probably turned eighteen recently, or nineteen even. Lately she takes her break inside the bank, banters with the others, and doesn't look so serious and pure.

Harlan jumps lines as discreetly as possible, but it still takes time. They don't use the velvet herding ropes as most banks do, which used to be an advantage, since he could always line up for Miss Winfield. Today Harlan again withdraws twenty-five dollars. He hasn't seen the inside of the passbook since he lost his job. He doesn't want to know. He slips it across and looks straight at them until they slip it back, leaving it open as they always do, so like a blind man he fumbles it back into its plastic. It's been long enough since he's looked so that now he honestly has no idea how much is left—any day soon he expects a teller to tilt her head at him and say, "You want what?" He never uses the drive-up, by the way, Miss Winfield or no; he'd sooner hunt parking for half an hour and walk inside. "Emasculating" is too strong, but something about the drive-up seems unnatural.

Up the hill he hears no noise from the car, so he allows for one final thing. As soon as he marked his paperback last night he regretted it. He wants a fresh copy. It's a good bookstore, he'll say that much for the school. He buys a trade size, and immediately he likes the heft of it, and the firmer, whiter pages. It'll sit untouched for a long time, and whenever he opens it he'll wash his hands first. He spends $6.95 on it. No tax because he says it's for coursework. He likes the way the "yes" flies right out of him when they ask; the spontaneous lie invigorates him.

In the car the baby has worked its big head most of the way down and under the driver's seat. By now his crying is exhausted, raw. A vein in the purplish forehead throbs. Harlan wraps him in the blanket again and drives home with the bundle in his lap, the baby's astounding weight slowing his braking and footwork. At home he reads to him, reads from the copied library list over and over, and swings him in the baby swing until he falls asleep.

The dorm directory, Harlan figures, is the place to begin. The next day he goes back to the library, finds theirs, and carries it out under his newspaper. After Ada goes to bed he looks. Of the eight borrowers—not counting his two Paul

Favolaro signatures—not one is in the directory. This is good. He wants her to live off campus, do her own food shopping, maybe work a job.

Next step is the phone book. But theirs is a 1979, one of Paul's old ones. They don't get phone books because legally they don't have a phone. Their line is actually someone else's. Paul Favolaro knows as much about wiring as anyone—he worked the electrical end for the cable company while Harlan drove the van and showed the customers their new channel box. Paul rewired Harlan's bedroom jack to its old number, someone else's now, someone never home weekdays. Harlan bought an old princess phone at a yard sale. Ada won't have any part of it. Their phone can't ring (Harlan doesn't know the number to give out, anyway), so it's outgoing calls only, which is fine considering it's free. Harlan looks up all the last names on the card and makes a list of possible numbers. Monday he'll be all over that phone, he tells himself.

All Friday night the baby has a rough time. Ada wheels the crib up close to her side of the bed because the baby likes to hold her hair, which is getting long. The baby doesn't look like either of them yet—and so heavy, it's hard to toss him or even bounce him for too long. Even Ada admits he's still homely, and when he cries he looks uglier still. Tonight he can't seem to stop, and at two-forty Ada announces that all hope for eight hours sleep before tomorrow's departmental ice skate has officially expired. Harlan carries the baby out to watch HBO, which they're still getting free with their basic cable even though Harlan's been terminated, because the day after the scramblers went in Paul Favolaro came back, off the clock, and pulled them again. Paul got them all thirty-six channels. This is *Last Tango in Paris* again. Harlan gets the baby to push some of the buttons but can't make him notice the corresponding channel change. For Harlan, *Last Tango* is old and dull; the fourth time it doesn't do a thing for him. The baby's heavy breath makes Harlan think he's asleep, but he keeps looking down to find the eyes open. The baby's probably coming down with something. With the TV volume as low cover, he rocks him in the swing and reads again from his card-sized Xerox sheet—since yesterday the grainy paper's all been clipped away.

"Mary Henning, due March 15th of '79; John Young, due April 21st of '79; Terry Krausse, due October 24th of '79; Sandy Geer, due December 1st of '79; Laura Frallic, due July 8th of '80; Lewis P. Lockhart, due November 11th of '80; Alice Dempsey, due September 16th of '81; Angela King, due November 4th of '81; Paul Favolaro, due December 23rd of '81."

Ada's needed a haircut for a while, and she knows a place that does a good job for eleven-fifty, but since Harlan lost his job she won't go. She can keep it from flying away, her hair, but there's still too much of it. It seems to grow out; it's as wide as it is long now. Ada used to smoke Old Golds and she quit, as promised, the day she found out she was pregnant. She used to buy them by the wholesale carton from her mother, who half owns a restaurant three states south of them and who's doing very well. After the baby, Ada went looking for them again but Old Golds were gone, off the market. Ada's on sugarless gum now, and the baby loves the bubbles.

On Sunday Paul Favolaro comes over for the last week of

the NFL regular season. A quiet weekend for Paul, who, when he worked with Harlan, would often demand a stop at the Surgical Supply on Friday lunch hour for some props for weekend bar hopping. Today he borrows a bathing suit of Harlan's because they keep it so warm inside for the baby, who is coming down with something. Paul eats sandwiches with them and goes home after "60 Minutes." Ada has the Sunday paper all around her on the couch.

"Did you see anything in here?" she asks.

"No, nothing yet."

"Have you even looked?"

"Some." Harlan leans from the good chair to hoist the baby off the floor. "Silly to, before the holidays, really. If we're at your mom's for more than a couple days then I'd have to blow off my second week on a new job."

"I suppose," Ada says.

"Nobody fires right before Christmas. It's after the holidays they let them all go."

"Wait it out through the holidays."

"Right." Harlan fingers the fleshy rolls on the back of the baby's neck.

"So not till after the holidays." Ada spreads her hands over the couch. "So this is really seventy-five cents wasted, then."

"It's all right."

She's looking at him.

"Hey," Harlan says. "You can't start on that piddly stuff. That's a good way to go crazy."

"It's not all piddly," she says. "We can talk about thirteen ninety-five a month just to watch TV."

"But we're only paying for *basic* cable," he says. "By rights we should pay thirty-four ninety-five. We're all right, Ada. It's not that bad."

"Not, you say."

Harlan shrugs at her. He bounces his son, and the baby rasps through its nose, where the snot's hardened all around. To wipe it off would make the kid scream. Harlan remembers that he forgot to ask to borrow Paul's phone book.

Monday Ada drives herself to work and Harlan sleeps until one o'clock, which is when the baby screams with the discovery that Ada's missing. From the start most of Harlan's visions involve Angela King or Alice Dempsey. He hopes like hell that Angela King is whiter than her name sounds. John Young and Lewis P. Lockhart are out, obviously. Terry Krausse and Sandy Geer are probably girls but might be men; their signatures don't give it away. Of all, only Terry Krausse's is in pencil. If Mary Henning's still enrolled here, then it means she marked the book as a freshman, which he can't believe. No Hennings in the '79 directory anyway—she's probably dorm then, and graduated now. Laura Frallic read it in the summer, and that's not what he had in mind; this girl's away all summer, traveling, or house-sitting in the country. Plus he likes those two names best, Alice and Angela, and the names are important.

All goes well until he looks at the princess and panics. He's never used the phone much—never went through a have-you-got-Prince-Albert-in-a-can stage—and though he thought it would be easy, when it comes time pretenses fail him, and in panic he can't conjure a single good lie. He spends an hour of the afternoon rummaging closets and kitchen drawers for things pencil-written months and years back. Research. To see if pencil marks age at all. Even alone, he feels foolish doing this. But he doesn't want to discover too quickly, he doesn't want to exhaust the chase before the holidays.

When Ada comes home he's long since quit for the day, not touching the phone, taking it a piece at a time.

Tuesday morning he does a little shopping and then drives idly around the campus, but the cold today stings and most people use the underground. When he comes back Ada's awake and dressing for her afternoon of work. She just looks at him.

"You're kidding."

"What?"

"What, right," Ada says. "On your head."

Harlan flips the sunglasses back down over his eyes.

"There's a glare out there, honey," he says. "In wintertime there's a glare."

Ada pushes the shaggy bangs from her eyes, where there's the sparkle of temper. "They look real sharp."

"It's winter. You want me to go blind?"

"No, fine. They're fine. No problem."

He walks to the baby and wipes its face. The kid has a nose bridge like a moron—it's as thick up there as down by the nostrils. Harlan can't stand the mess the baby makes of himself.

"I stopped at Rite-Aid," he says.

"Terrific," she says. "Nice mark-up over there."

"Hey, they're good durable ones. They'll last. Shades for the eighties, all of them."

"I say they're lost by March."

"I'll take good care," Harlan says. "And they weren't all that bad, either. Nine and a quarter."

"Fine, Harlan. But let's take them off in the house."

"Hey. Just go easy. You don't have to drive at three and four o'clock in December."

"And you do."

"Ada," and he does take them off. "We use a tank every three weeks. It keeps me out of the bin. It's cheaper than a shrink."

"Shrink?" Ada's mouth opens wide and she chokes out a laugh. "Just read your books, Harlan. The library was a great idea. For while you wait out your holidays. But you stopped with the books, in case you hadn't noticed."

That night Paul Favolaro comes over and they head for the mall. Yolanda is out, so Ada takes the baby, cold and all. She ducks into the fabric store, where she's done most of their Christmas shopping. She gets in some knitting every day before work. She just needs touches now, nearly everything's finished. While they wait for Ada and the baby, Paul and Harlan sit on a fake brick wall and watch the gaggles of teenagers pass.

Paul is tired and he doesn't come back to the apartment. Harlan has the cable on late. Before she undresses, Ada says she's sorry if she snapped, and she kisses him. Once she's in bed he looks, without any luck, through some computerized grading sheets she's brought home. He didn't expect this girl to turn up in Engineering anyway. What he does find in Ada's satchel is a blank civil service application. Harlan puts everything back exactly as it was.

After he drops Ada off on Wednesday afternoon he comes straight back to the house, puts the baby down, and goes for the phone. It's the only way he'll ever get it done. But he still can't think what to say.

"I'm looking for Sandy Geer. Is Sandy there?"

"No. Sorry."

"Will Sandy be back soon?"

"Sandy went home for Christmas," the voice says. "Who's this?"

The baby cries in the living room. Harlan doesn't know what he's doing, or why he's doing it. He reaches behind him on the bed for a pillow to cradle. Paul Favolaro has a theory about pillows, that they're in strict inverse proportion to economic status. Rich people content themselves with one, while the poor lay them in like sandbags at the head of the bed. Harlan thinks how Paul Favolaro would be a hundred times the detective he is.

"Who is this?" says the voice.

"This is Mr. Winfield at the bank. Sandy has a free gift coming from us. And . . . We need to know whether to send the . . . necktie . . . or the kerchief."

"You're from the bank?"

"Just . . . Are we talking about a man or a woman, can you tell me?"

"What bank?" the voice says.

A guess. "Marine Midland. Sandy pulled off the drive-up before we could give it to her, to Sandy. Sandy's one of our newer . . ."

"Hey now, asshole."

As he hangs up Harlan feels better. Readier, like after a first roller-coaster ride. He wants to line up and go again. It wasn't bad—it was fun, even.

First he paces a little, then watches the baby—asleep now with clenched fists. He checks all thirty-six channels for helpful dialogue. Then he goes back to the bedroom.

"Hello, Paul Favolaro from University Library calling, is Alice Dempsey there?"

"No, isn't she there?"

"Hnn?"

"Who's this again?"

"Paul Favolaro, University Library. It's about a book."

"The school library?"

"Right. Paul Favolaro calling."

"Well she should be there studying. She's got the world's latest possible time for a final. In the reading room maybe?"

"Oh, very good. What's she wearing?"

"Why?" returns the voice, louder. "Maybe she just stepped out for a minute. Does she owe a fine?"

"Oh no," Harlan blurts. "A rebate. Really. She overpaid, for the copy machine. You see the student one's broken and she left a dollar with us down here in circulation."

"Alice? Left a buck?"

"Yes, but there's no charge. I have the dollar right here. What does she have on?"

"Now before you said it was about a book, not copying."

"About a book? No I didn't."

"Oh."

"What's she wearing?"

Harlan sees the baby waking, so he lowers him into the swing and gives one big push. Some physics law is bound to help him here; the baby's bulk will keep him rocking for a long time. Harlan speeds the half-mile to school and leaves the motor running in the handicapped space. He looks for the dark hair/yellow sweater, and finds it. It's not her. Maybe it's Alice Dempsey, but it's not her, not who he's looking for. But that's all right, since it means the holidays aren't over.

Harlan's looking at the penciled brackets in the book when Ada comes home, a few minutes early. This is the twenty-third, her last day until January. She owns two sensational work outfits, and this is one of them. Nice skirt, snug wool sweater, terrific colors.

"I cleaned up a little," Harlan says.

"Great."

She goes to the bedroom and comes back in Harlan's baggy swimming trunks and an old shirt.

"Hey."

"I'd melt in the other," she says. "It's just too warm for that in here." She lifts the baby, and he claws at her hair.

"He got all fours moving together today," Harlan says. "A little bit."

Ada puts him down again. The baby rolls around on its face.

"I think he's holding his head up better," Ada says as she sits him upright.

"I don't see it," Harlan says. "But the cold's not as bad."

"He's had it since day one." Ada blows a sugarless bubble for him.

"Much worse last week, though," Harlan says. "You can't argue that."

Ada gets down on the floor with the baby. "Any mail?" she asks.

"My check from the cable."

"There it is," Ada says. "Last one."

"I know, last one, but it's money. 'Good' might be the thing to say, not 'last one.'"

"You know that money's spent twice already. It's not exactly relief."

"Ada. C'mon. It's two days before Christmas."

She gets up and retrieves her satchel from the bedroom. "Can you sign this please? It's for after the holidays, all right? I filled it out for you, since there's a deadline."

"What is it?" Harlan asks, and the stall, the lie, reminds him of being on the phone.

"At the post office annex, eight-fifteen in the morning, Tuesday, January five. It's for the civil service exam. An application. I filled out the whole thing already. No muss no fuss just sign it."

"What'll this do?"

"Make you a mailman maybe, I don't know. There's a booklet with jobs and pay scales. Wait a minute."

Harlan signs his full name and puts the form on top of the refrigerator.

Ada says, "Under 'Reason left' for the cable TV thing I put down working conditions."

"I saw," he says.

"What's Andy got?" Ada points at the floor. It's a dust bunny, plum-sized, going into this mouth.

"You said you vacuumed?"

Harlan shrugs.

"Well honey you've really got to *do* it, if you're going to do it." In another minute the machine is out of the closet. "This thing's practically worthless. When you do it you have to bear down. And go slow. You can't just scan it."

The vacuum starts up. It makes the baby laugh. After a minute Ada turns it off, and touches Harlan.

"I mean I appreciate it, and everything. But once you've gone over it you have to unhook it and clean the brush with the middle pipe—or else this stuff just goes right back on the rug."

After supper Harlan says, "It looks much better. I just quit after a while."

She kisses him. "It's this old thing. It's half dead."

"We could really use a new one."

"It's way down the list," Ada says.

As she does the dishes Harlan lifts her hair and kisses her neck. "You're terrific. I wish your mom could see how well you can manage on practically nothing. What you can do with a dollar."

"Harlan."

"She'll see soon enough with the presents, though, everything made from scratch." He laughs. "But she'll send you straight to the hairdresser, you know."

Ada moves away from him a little.

"You're really quite . . ."

"We're not asking my mother," she says.

"I didn't say."

"I won't borrow from her."

"Did I say? I didn't say."

Before they leave for Christmas there's laundry to do. Ada won't allow more than a single washload done at her mother's house; the rest must be clean when they pack it. That night Ada climbs into her other nice outfit and leaves for a department Christmas dinner. Harlan's invited but he can't think of any reason to go. He can't relax with those people. No leads lurk there, and if they did, if his bracketer, his bracketress, had friends at the Engineering party or was there herself, he wouldn't want to know.

When the laundry's organized Harlan takes the baby upstairs to Yolanda, who's in a green leotard as she answers the door. Harlan steps carefully on the exercise mats that cover the floor. She's watching "Aerobicise," on Showtime. It's something Harlan and Paul try not to miss, though they both think the exercise girls are a little too painted; the pure white studio is nice but the dancers don't look quite fresh enough, and their mouths are always, always open.

"Ada says you guys are leaving tomorrow." The baby is reaching for her, and she takes him. "I hope it's a good Christmas for you, I really do. Sometimes these are the ones that are."

"What these ones?"

In conversation Yolanda stands about six inches closer than most people would. To Harlan it's very noticeable. The baby could reach back from her shoulder and touch him now, Yolanda's that close.

"Faux pas, faux pas," she says. "Never mind. Forget I said it. Hoof-in-mouth disease." She closes her mouth gently around the baby's pudgy foot. Harlan makes a polite snort.

"You mean the cable job, I'm guessing."

"Wait till it hits you," she says. "I mean it's good that it hasn't—the holiday season and all. But wait till it does."

Harlan always does the laundry. Ada can't stand the place, she gets hot and uncomfortable there. Every ten or eleven days Harlan lugs everything up the hill in an old mailbag and crams the big front-loader ("Pack It Full!" it says) and feeds five quarters. No one else is out doing laundry on the twenty-third of December.

When he pulls his jeans from the dryer he finds his note from the reading room librarian, the one for the downstairs copy machine. He never really looked. All this time sitting in his pocket. It's legible, none the worse for the washing. On the bottom next to SIGNED it says "Krausse." Terry Krausse, due October 24th of '79, is the chubby reading room steward. He's not sure whether to be cheered at the progress or discouraged at another possibility vanished.

To Harlan clean clothes seem heavier than dirty ones—senseless, since you leave behind the dirt and sweat you came with. As he struggles in the dark with their wardrobe's full weight across his shoulders, it helps that he can see their building from the moment he starts out. Their first floor is dark, but above that Yolanda flutters like a green bird he's spotted, arms spread in exercise, bobbing and flapping in the second-story window.

He walks with the sound of his heavy boots—Ada's mother's gift last Christmas—on the new powder snow, a continuous grating without ever a gap, one leaden foot always grinding the ground, the effect unsettling, like a soundtrack crescendo stuck before the critical release, or like a creaky revolving door, or like the labor of jet engines at takeoff, grinding hard against a runway headwind, but never the release, never the break that comes with winning safe altitude.

And then Harlan thinks of *The Professor of Desire* on the back of the couch, and remembers that tomorrow it begins to be overdue.

It's still dark as they rise on the twenty-fourth and pack for their seven-hour drive. By about ten they're on the road. Ada declined her mother's offer to fly them down and back; if he thought it would have made a difference Harlan would have argued for accepting. Instead they drive south, through enough traffic to demand full concentration. Harlan's boarded a plane only once and, besides actual flight, what struck him was how weightless it all was, how light they made things. They gave him the wrong meal and he tensed his arm to hand the tray back—it's the shock of nothing being there that he remembers. He thinks about this now for several miles at least. In his arm he can still feel what it was like. For some reason he and Ada don't talk much when they're in a moving car. Later he wants to say something about not flying, and about her refusing her mother's Holiday Inn offer, but he doesn't. Her mother thought that since Ada's bedroom bed was a single they might consider it, all of it her treat. Ada's mother has some money: Harlan's always been nice to her, though she pays him back hardly at all, in his opinion, tolerating him like teachers do C-minus students, the ones too smart to be projects, and too dumb to win favor.

Night driving makes Harlan quiet and irritable, and before they've arrived it's turned dark again—the sun gone so early at Christmas. To calm himself he thinks about the best part of all hotels, their padded runways, the long carpeted corridors down which, preferably barefoot, you couldn't help but run.

But on Christmas Eve they find twin beds in Ada's room, pulled together. For the baby the small anteroom shows bright new paint. Ada's room on the top floor is dusty and warm. It's as she left it a year and a half ago. The fuzzy throw rugs are everywhere, her high school cosmetics ferment in the drawers. The posters haven't fallen—she says they should film a Scotch tape testimonial there. After dinner Ada gets a gold necklace from her mother, thin and light and very expensive, and Ada wears it all night. After the guests leave Ada's mother takes charge of the baby, and they drink a little and listen to records. Christmas Eve high up in that room brings a marathon of silent sex that ends with Ada stretched face down over her old homework desk.

They return on the twenty-eighth, and in the dark at five-fifteen Paul Favolaro is at the door. His new partner, Ray

Ziegler, is drinking coffee in the passenger seat of the Cableview van.

"Want to go see *Ragtime* tonight?" Paul says.

"I heard it was all right," Harlan says. "Not great."

Ada says either come in or stay out, but close the door.

Outside Harlan asks him, "Is it down at the Walnut?"

"No. Out at Cinema One-Two-Twelve."

"I don't know," Harlan says. "Eight bucks is a bite right now."

"I'll pay for both of you," Paul says. "I'll spring for a sitter."

"Sitter's free," Harlan says, jerking his head toward above. "Whatever."

"It'll be on HBO if you can wait a year."

"I can't," Paul says. He hops to keep warm. "Let's go."

Paul has a thing for Elizabeth McGovern. When *Ordinary People* played on the cable this fall, three times a day for six weeks, Paul had it timed: he'd try to test people's pictures when she walked home from high school down that leafy street, in that plaid skirt. Or the other scene when she comes out of her house in the morning. He'd stall the customer, create some technical problems, run up the pole outside again, and fiddle until the divine moment. It's still at the point where people will accept any lie you want to tell them about how cable works, especially when they're minutes away from getting it themselves. With three channels running the movie, Paul could get her a couple of times every shift. After a while Harlan saw what Paul did, and so he feels the same way. They both know she does a nude in this one.

They leave the baby with Yolanda. Ada sits between them in the car, in the movie, and in Rockett's afterward for a drink and a sandwich. Paul pays here too. He calls it a Christmas present. Ada shows him what her mother gave her, the necklace.

"I got a watch," Harlan says, and shows it. "She got us both something light because she figured we'd be flying."

They come to the apartment. After Ada retrieves the baby she goes to bed. She has a doctor's appointment first thing tomorrow. Paul asks Harlan what he thought.

"I don't know," Harlan says. "It's like I didn't get the whole picture, you know? I forgot to look at her face. I didn't put it all together. It could have been anyone. I'll have to see it again."

Paul grabs his arm. "Yes," he says. "That's just what I said. You like it better the second time, you see more. This was my second. I went with Ziggy after work last week."

They watch a movie on Cinemax and talk for a while. The baby wakes up and Harlan holds him. Paul falls asleep on the couch for an hour, then goes home. Harlan comes close to telling him about the library book, about the penciled lines, but he doesn't. He still hasn't told anyone. Except the baby, he talks straight to the baby. The baby has heard every dull detail of the detective work.

Here's how Harlan lost his cable TV job, all truth now. They worked the day after Thanksgiving. Only a skeleton crew, only those who hadn't arranged weeks ago for the time off—but Cableview was open. The manager had made several dozen promises for service by that week, and he wanted it done. Harlan and Paul Favolaro had their busiest day. Harlan found some surprising and unprecedented frustration in work, in the hardest work of the year, on the Friday after Thanksgiving, the one bonus day left to a Monday-holiday world, a free weekday without design, the perfect pagan meal-less holiday of a dozen foil-wrapped snacks, and full refrigerators, and leaves left as they are in the dinner table because nobody does anything this day. Purposeless and utterly free, it was Harlan's kind of holiday.

But, home from work, these people called about their promised cable, and they kept calling, and at the shorthanded Cableview office the manager himself answered the phones, then radioed Harlan and Paul Favolaro. At five-forty they were still out there working, in the dark. It made Harlan remember that he'd risen for this long day in darkness, too. The hell with it, he said. He drove them to their fifth-to-last installation by way of Rockett's. Out front he turned the motor off, but Paul talked him out of it before he left the van. They were near the office, so Harlan drove back there for a soda while Paul waited outside. The Coke machine sat against a back wall, at the end of the only long corridor in the place, and as Harlan marched down the runway to it, the manager—this being one of those occasional days when he chips in, when he's always at large, when you can expect at any time the surprise of a meaty hand clapped on your shoulder, when he rolls up his sleeves for the effect, when he parks his jacket over a chair but lets the vest hang unbuttoned, when he comes out of his office to fray nerves for two hours at a time before he grows tired of helping and retires again to phone cronies, this day being the first legitimate occasion for his pitching in, there being only two other workers in the office, the manager answering phones all day and giving information, promising, answering phones standing up, on the fly by a desk where one's ringing, this day also being the occasion of a visit from the district manager, visits that invariably move the manager to grand displays of skipperish, foremanish, reinsmanish administrative zeal—the manager, with the district manager behind him speaking calmly and dully in his district-manager-for-life drone, not at all caught up in any of it, the heat in the kitchen, the manager stepped from his office not ten feet away from the Coke machine, stepped with a peculiar ebullience, a hyperactive bounce, as Harlan accelerated toward the red Coke light, takeoff always the most dangerous part anyway, even the million-mile pilots still sighing a little when it's over and cleanly done, and the manager threw out his meaty arm straight as a toll gate and said "Hey there, buddy" and Harlan, almost there, charged through, broke through, surprised in that fatal liberating instant, in that moment of turbulent release, surprised that the obstruction was as light as it was (it was no prohibitive barrier, it turned out, it was an affable where's-the-fire gesture, a helmsmanish we're-all-pals move after all), and after crashing the arm he plowed ahead through the surprise, through the shock that was the main obstacle now, to obtain at last what Paul Favolaro seems forever pledged to call, with half-mock reverence, "the twelve-thousand-dollar Sprite." The manager claimed a split knuckle against his office doorframe (his back-thrown fist like a circus tomahawk just grazing the district man's ear), and people say the wrappings are still on it. Harlan drank his Sprite as he walked home for the weekend, and on Monday the five unlucky customers finally got their cable from Paul Favolaro and the new man, Ray Ziegler.

"Miss," Harlan calls softly to the reading room librarian.

It's January now, 1982, and the library is open again. Harlan stands near the desk. She's behind it, crouched and back turned, sorting magazines that arrived over the holidays.

"Terry," Harlan says softly. He still has no idea what he's doing.

It's Ada's first full-time day at Engineering. The baby is with Yolanda. Paul took them to *Reds* and *Pennies from Heaven* last week, and on New Year's Eve they showed briefly at a party for Cableview people. Harlan hasn't looked for work. His New Year's resolution was to sleep regular hours, and that's shot already. His bedtime's been pushed ahead and ahead and around the clock, he's on twenty-seven-hour days seemingly, and like the baby he sleeps in spurts. Last week he was napping at midnight. When he stands in the reading room at nine-twenty on this Monday morning it's actually just before his bedtime. He knows he looks like death so he wears his Rite-Aid sunglasses.

"Miss Krausse," he says, much louder.

"I'm Mrs. Krausse," says the squat little librarian as she turns around.

"I'm sorry, Terry."

She looks at him. "Oh, you don't want me . . ."

"I'm sorry," Harlan blurts. "You look like a young girl I know. I thought you were her from behind."

She gives him a strange look. To see his face, she can't watch what she's doing. Her eyes stay on him as she blindly straightens magazines on the desk. It's not so much her height and weight that are unappealing, Harlan thinks, as it is her oldishness. Another twenty-three-year-old doing her best to look thirty-three.

"Can I help you at all?" she says.

"I'm sorry about that." Harlan offers his hand. "I'm Paul Favolaro."

"Dorothy Krausse." She's still looking at him. He's glad he bought the sunglasses.

"Could I have the last two *Newsweek*s and the last *Sports Illustrated*?"

The librarian isn't Terry Krausse, but she's married to Terry Krausse. There's no evidence, but evidence has been getting him nowhere. She might have been about to untangle some of it if he'd just kept his mouth shut another minute. Harlan thumbs through his magazines. There's only one Krausse in the '79 book, Dr. Arthur. Harlan still doesn't know what he's doing, but he doesn't feel bad about it. In ten minutes he's back at her desk.

This early the reading room is empty. There's no need to whisper.

"Then you're Dorothy Krausse. Dotty Krausse. Your husband never told me you worked here."

"You know my husband?"

In his head Harlan sees the phone book clearly. "Been to see the doctor."

"His dad? Professionally?"

"Right."

"Oh. You mean when you were in high school."

"Right," Harlan says.

"Then you're from the area?"

"Yes."

There's a pause while Dorothy Krausse seems to wonder to herself why, exactly, she's standing here talking to this guy.

"Your name was?" she says.

"Paul Favolaro."

"From whereabouts?"

Harlan names a nearby town he's never seen.

"Who do you see now, Paul?"

"Who?"

"I hope you don't mind my asking. Since he retired most people have been driving over to Gray."

"Gray, right," Harlan says. "Well, I tried Gray and I didn't much like him."

"Really? Why not?"

"Personality clash I guess."

"Really. Who do you see now?"

"Well," Harlan says. "Well, nobody really. I really don't have the problem much now. I'm kind of glad you can't tell. That's good."

"Yes."

A weightless peace comes over Harlan. He's happy here, he realizes.

"You really can't tell," he says again. "Good. Says a lot for the doc."

"What was it?"

"Guess," he says.

"I don't know. I don't see. What?"

"Go ahead and guess."

"I don't know," she says. "Eczema?"

"Nope," Harlan says before he thinks.

"Psoriasis? I don't know, what?"

For a moment Harlan can't remember the third one. "It speaks very well of Dr. Krausse, doesn't it? Not a trace. Speaks very well of him."

"I guess it does. Gil really didn't call me Dotty to you, did he?"

"Gil?"

"Do you know him by something else?" she says, excited. "Does he have a nickname I don't know about? Oh good, I can get him back."

"No," Harlan says, undisturbed that Terry Krausse could still be anybody. Right now nothing drags him down. "Gil was all I heard anyone ever call him."

"Well he didn't really call me Dotty, did he? He knows I hate it. It has certain childhood connotations—rhymes and the like, you know?" Harlan's new ease must be contagious. "Only his mother still calls me that. Constantly. At least once a week since the wedding. I ask her nice but she forgets. Forgets and forgets. Woman's written three books and she can't even remember her own phone number. Have you met Gil's mom?"

"No," Harlan says, but feels the answer a waste. "Almost once, though. Actually, I just missed her a couple of times."

"You know Gil well, though."

"Years back," Harlan says. "I had the thing in high school. This is old times, 'seventy-five or so. Prehistoric. I met Gil at Dr. Krausse's office. Seborrhea is what it was, it was seborrhea. My own damn condition, and the name got away from me for a minute, I went to the other guy one time, Gray, but your dad, or rather your father-in-law, over on Frontier Ave., he did the trick."

This is as good as Harlan's ever felt. He's been awake all day and night but he's newly alive, he's released, he's airborne. There's a liberation in winging it. Lying is flying, it's weightlessness, it's leaving the earth. Terry Krausse could be man or girl, could be unlisted or graduated or dead, and it's the new year and Harlan's made little progress—but it's all thrilling today. He's never had so much fun.

He zips home and reclaims the baby from Yolanda. He talks to her, first in the doorway and then from a chair. Her cable is on: she stands on her head, she does sit-ups, she does shoulder lifts and side pulls. "You get so heavy over the holidays," Yolanda says. She tells Harlan the baby's a dream, it's practically maintenance free. Anytime, no trouble. Harlan watches her exercise and tells more lies—not all flattering, but all about himself.

He stays awake all afternoon and is watching New Mexico calf roping on the cable when Ada gets back from her first day full time.

"You're here," she says.

"You're surprised."

"I don't know what I am. Ill mostly. I had a dream, I think. I don't know."

She gets her coat off, then falls into the good chair. Right away the warm house melts the snow on her boots. What she's wearing is not one of her best outfits.

"You OK?"

"Wiped," she says. "I feel sick."

"Want a back rub?"

"No, that's OK."

"C'mon. You'll feel better. You don't have to move or do anything." Harlan begins to lift her by the arms. "You can sleep through it, even."

"If you want."

He lets her go. "It's for you. Do *you* want?"

"It's all right," she says.

"C'mon. No effort required. Just some daylight between you and that chair."

She looks at him.

"Did you type?" Harlan says. "All day, I'll bet."

She slides to her knees and crawls slowly to dry carpet.

"Would you rather the bed?" he asks.

"This is fine."

"Shirt on or off?"

"On," she says.

"You'll be changing anyway, right?"

"Just go ahead."

To rub her neck and shoulders he must move her hair, but it's hard to gather in one hand. He holds what he can. The other hand kneads. He straddles her, his knees framing her waist. He's careful not to catch the new necklace, thin enough to be nearly invisible in a room lighted only by the brown of the TV rodeo. After a minute Ada tries rolling onto her back and is trapped.

"Thanks," she says.

"Enough?"

"I think."

He lifts a knee so she can roll over, then he clamps again.

"Feel better?" he says.

"The truth?"

"What, worse?"

Her hair fans under her. It spreads to all sides. Ada sighs. She rolls her eyes back until she can see the baby asleep in the swing behind her.

"You've got to use the whole hand. You pinch, with the fingers, and you twist. Use the palms. And lighter."

She tries to lift herself to kiss him, but she has no leverage. Harlan waits a moment, then he moves, gives her a hand up, and she hugs him.

"You look dead yourself," she says. "Paul wants to drink

tonight. He stopped by school at lunchtime. He won't quit spending his bonus money on us."

"What bonus?"

"Christmas."

"Christmas bonus." Harlan lets her go. "He tells you and not me?"

Ada just looks at him.

"When do we go?" Harlan says.

"Seven o'clock at Rockett's. I told him we both get up early tomorrow."

"We both?"

Ada's gone to the baby. Now she turns back. "You have not forgotten the civil service thing. I know you haven't. You'll just piss me off if you pretend you have."

They go to Rockett's for drinks, and an hour after they return Ada is in bed. Paul and Harlan and the baby stretch out in the living room.

"I've been awake thirty-one hours," Harlan says. He's pretending he's as drunk as he wants to be. He always enjoyed it, that feeling. In high school he made every party, friends or acquaintances or half-hostile strangers, just to sit in a corner and float.

Harlan points a foot toward the screen. "This girl reminds me of the old receptionist. Alva."

"Nobody on TV reminds me of anybody," Paul says. "When I watch I don't think of anything, my life vanishes. It's a trance. I think more in my sleep than when I watch TV."

"But doesn't she though?" Harlan says.

"Which now?"

"In the pool," Harlan says.

"Where in the pool?"

"Wait a sec, they'll get her again." Half a miute goes by. "Come on, show her. There."

"Her?"

"Yeah."

"You're crazy," Paul says. "Not even close. Alva was older, more like Ada's age. You know, much more mid-twenties. More just-past-the-peak-looking."

"Ada's twenty," Harlan says.

"No."

"Yes she is."

"Get out," Paul says. "You say it again tomorrow and I'll believe it."

"Be twenty-one the first of April," Harlan says. "I married a nineteen."

"You're shitting."

"Swear to God," Harlan says. "Four, one, sixty-one. If I could move I'd prove it."

"I can't believe it," Paul says. "I mean not that . . ."

"I know," Harlan says. "Even the long hair doesn't help. She went to a junior high PTA, even, they wouldn't blink."

"I wouldn't go that far," Paul says.

Paul is on the couch. Harlan stretches across the floor on the cushions from the good chair, at an angle to both the couch and the television. The baby, who can sleep anywhere, is at the foot end of the couch, half off Paul and half on him. The baby rattles away; he still has his cold.

On the cable are eighty-seven low-rent minutes stretched across five wet T-shirt scenes. They've all seen this movie at least twice before. The fourth wet T-shirt interlude, a team contest between the sorority debs and the mothers of the townie girls, is just ending.

"This is sick," Paul says.

"With the moms, I know. What else is on?"

Paul reaches over his head for the January Cableview guide. "Seen two seen 'em all," he says. He reads aloud all thirty-six channels, none of them fresh, everything old.

They talk about music. They trade cold-weather stories. Paul talks about his new partner, Ray Ziegler, and Harlan wonders how much of it he's making up. The baby rolls over, and as he begins to fall from the couch Harlan winces at the noise it's going to make. But Paul Favolaro catches the baby between his calves and slowly lowers it, groaning from the effort.

"Nice stop," Harlan says.

The baby sits up for a moment. The weight of its huge head seems too much. Without a sound it overturns and goes back to sleep.

"He's a load," Paul Favolaro says.

"My son," Harlan says in a mock old-world accent.

Paul watches him sleep. "It's unbelievable," he says. "How long do they stay this calm?"

"Till the teeth," Harlan says. "Not much longer. Once the teeth start they raise holy hell. But for now he's got a terrific service record, that's what Yolanda upstairs says."

"Who?"

"Upstairs, Yo. She says he's maintenance free, practically. You know her?"

"What's her name?"

"Yo. Yolanda. I've introduced you at least once. Yo with the leotards. With the legwarmers. She takes the baby. Says he handles nice and easy, Yo-Yo does."

Paul starts laughing.

"It's what the Yo-Yo bird says," and now Harlan's coughing and laughing. "Yo-Yo knows." He always coughs more when he's tired, but he still might be catching the baby's cold.

Paul leans off the couch to touch the sleeping baby. To pet it, really.

"Not the world's best-looking baby," Harlan says. "Son of mine."

Paul laughs. "But probably not the ugliest," he says, drawing out "probably."

"He could be close, though," Harlan says, starting them off.

"Within range."

"In the neighborhood."

"On the block."

"My son," Harlan says again.

"Kind of the Casey Stengel of babies," Paul says.

"The Karl Malden of babies."

"The Elmer Fudd of babies. The Leo Durocher of babies."

The baby wakes up.

"The Walter Brennan of babies," Harlan says.

"Lyndon Baines Baby."

"You guys are real funny," Ada calls from the bedroom. It's a very small apartment.

Brought down from sleep by the baby's crying, Harlan staggers from bed at ten the next morning. He can't keep his eyes open, quite literally cannot, and he does as much of the baby's maintenance work as he can with his eyes closed. He brings the baby upstairs but Yolanda is out. Ada arranged a ride to work today; their car sits ready across the street, in a dusting of new snow. Today is Tuesday the fifth—civil service day. Very late last night he found Angela King's address in the current phone book Paul finally left him. He bundles the baby and takes him for a ride.

The cold air doesn't clear Harlan's head. To himself he still seems all up inside it, drifting and hovering. After an hour's watch, they see someone scarfed up to the eyes enter the house. Harlan writes Angela King's name on a blank envelope and seals it. The baby cries when Harlan opens the door to leave. The girl at the door takes the envelope and writes a downstate address on it. Angela got a local lit professor into a bit of a jam and she's starting at a SUNY downstate this semester, by her own choice. Angela never liked it here; she found the work pointless and she'd avoid the whole campus for three weeks at a time, in the heart of the semester. The girl who tells all this to Harlan is black.

Driving home he's stopped floating, he's finally awake. Yolanda's just going up the stairs. For the first time she sulks a little taking the baby. Harlan says he's been awake for two, for three straight days and he has to sleep, he's desperate for it. And in another hour he's back in bed, the old floorboards creaking in endless jumping-jack rhythm above, Harlan half-dreaming that the baby's weight warps the floor and then breaks it, and that the baby sleeps soundly as he falls through onto Harlan's bed.

That night he resents it when Ada comes in. A light goes on and then off. There are noises. A draft shoots under the covers when she settles next to him. Harlan's territory is halved. He must endure small movement out of his control, jerkiness, turbulence. With her face turned away, Ada's hair covers all of her pillows and some of his. Harlan's been robbed of his warm levitation. Ada settles in, sighing, bracing herself. He won't get back. He knows she'll keep him grounded.

"You're not sick, are you?" she says.

"No." He's surprised by the question.

Another minute passes, then Ada says, "Do you remember me waking you this morning?"

"I can honestly say I don't." Just a moment ago, dozing, a lie would have seemed impossible.

"You slept through a fight, Harlan. That's a pretty neat trick."

"I suppose a replay's coming," he says in groggy singsong.

"Ada says honey get up. She says honey please get up. She says you'll miss this civil service thing, and Bob Marks is coming out of his way to pick me up. She says you'll really hurt me if you don't go for this exam."

"I'm sorry, I was exhausted," Harlan says, and thinks then that being awake in bed is the worst. If sleep is flight, then waking life is at least mobility, a chance at land-roving. But to be here is to be mired, a sitting duck.

Ada doesn't say anything. She seems intent on it. Harlan won't break the quiet either. It stays just that way for a long time, until finally there's more turbulence, Ada's light involuntary convulsions, the sign that she's gotten there first.

On his lunch break the next day Paul Favolaro knocks on Harlan's door and hands him a letter. "What the hell are you doing?" Paul says to Harlan. Paul comes in for some food and they watch "Aerobicise" on the cable. The letter Paul brought is the overdue warning from University Library.

While they're eating Harlan's own mail comes. It's just the fuel bill for December. No other pieces, no buffers. The fuel bill like special delivery. Harlan expects something high, but he's staggered anyway.

Paul takes the book with the light penciled lines, saying he'll pay this afternoon. Harlan only half-protests. With options dwindling, Harlan feels freer to imagine her. Almost without his knowing, the picture's been building through the holidays.

She's a sophomore. She turned nineteen in November. She's in an unused pocket of the library, a remote study area, tilting her chair back some, her long legs set one over the other along the desk's front edge, book snug—no hands—in that triangle of thighs and calves. The number three pencil rests lightly in her fingers. She never twirls it, or presses her teeth with it, or rests it near her face. In full concentration she has no tics, and now she's absorbed in a book, not merely doing her time. She wears jeans and a blue workshirt, sleeves folded neatly past the elbow. She's here on student loans; her family lives far away, in a neighborhood with one-car garages. Her blond hair curls in long spirals, like a straight-haired's ten minutes out of the pool. The ends play in and out of her workshirt collar. And above the slight breasts, that marginal do-or-don't button is closed; she's not dressing for anyone. Around her neck are pearls small as seeds, each an inch apart on a tiny gold chain, a chain with no slack. She doesn't wear makeup. Winter's taken her tan, but she's not pale. If she stood she'd be five-nine. Her blue eyes aren't spectacularly so, you need to look hard to see what color they are. And somehow—here, the miracle—she either doesn't know or doesn't care that she's pretty, she's shunned beauty's old concomitance. Why not bequeath her everything, all he could want? What makes her fully ideal is some imperfection Harlan can't see. Somehow she's not longed for, some convenient and irrelevant mystery lessens her appeal, excludes her from the campus elite. He goes no further. He doesn't think, doesn't need to think, how this unlikely last might be possible.

Harlan is out all the next afternoon. When he comes back lights are burning. Ada's home. Before he opens the front door he pockets the sunglasses, doing as he's done since the day she first saw them.

He finds her in the bedroom. Their dresser has been pulled from the wall.

"Bugs again?"

She's on her knees. The flashlight blinks off and he sees that she's been crying, still is. When she speaks it's softly, from the front of her mouth, without vocal cords.

"Please tell me you've seen the necklace."

"You lost it? It's really missing?" He walks to the kitchen. He lacks the mettle for this, doesn't enjoy it. His heart sinks with responsibility.

As the kitchen light makes its first fluorescent stammer Harlan thinks he sees bugs from the corner of his eye, prowling the refrigerator door. But they don't move. They're only thin black magnets: fixed to the door like a summons, finally, is a note from the savings bank, a warning, a financial pink slip. It happened by mail, in the end, and not in person.

Harlan sits at the small kitchen table, facing away from the refrigerator. He picks at the label on the gallon of cheap cola, the flat syrupy bargain Ada's been buying since Thanksgiving, to save money.

He hears Ada rummage in the living room. Under the sofa, down the sides of the good chair. At intervals he hears rasped curses, obscene oaths leaned on, invested in, as if, made hoarse and sibilant and strong enough, they might acquire the power to retrieve.

"Just wait awhile, honey," he says without turning. "Things turn up if you forget them a couple days."

He hears her in the bedroom again, then in the bathroom, on her knees to shine light at the porcelain paws. From the bedroom the baby cries. Ada's steps suggest she's relieved by the diversion.

"I think he's ready to cut one," she says, back in the kitchen.

"Uh-oh," Harlan says. "Nice while it lasted."

"Go see if you can see, up top and on the right."

"Here we go," Harlan says. "The party's over."

He visits the baby and comes back, sits just where he was. Ada's running water for the three days of dishes that cover the counter. Though the steam makes her sniffle more, she's calmer now. But Harlan knows it's not real calm, it's only another bracing.

"Did Yolanda see?" he asks.

"This afternoon."

"What'd she say?"

"About which?" Ada says.

"About which? About the baby."

"She said he's probably ready to cut. And she said we might want to spring for a stomach X-ray if the necklace doesn't turn up soon."

"But that was a joke."

"Yes, that's right," Ada says to him.

"Ada," he says, "please try not to worry."

Water darkens quickly in the single-basin sink. Suds die young, and dishwashing is difficult. Glass mixing bowls clang dangerously against the porcelain sides. It's the sound of heads bumping, of skull on skull, and it makes Harlan's front teeth hurt.

Ada lifts their ancient heavy skillet. She runs the water too hot and curses again. Hands wet, she shoulders her wild hair back from her face.

There are jokes: heavy skillet, housewife, bank notice, and the henpecked, shitlisted husband—but Harlan can't frame one immediately, and he knows it's wiser not to try. When Ada drops her steel wool it bleeds a filthy wet rust.

"She also said," and her voice startles him now, jerks him down, its power restored, the vocal cords back. "She also said, when she was down here and she saw our mail today, she said she'd be willing to loan . . ."

The baby starts again. Harlan goes in there. He thinks he'd like to come back to the kitchen with the necklace, he'd like to make her happy. But he comes back empty-handed.

Ada does silverware by the handful, a dozen at a time. The plastic rack on the counter beside her is overflowing; half her piping-hot handful falls back to the sink.

She takes a breath. "You're waiting on Punxsutawney Phil, Harlan, is that it? Is Groundhog's the last, or is Valentine's included? Don't try St. Patrick's, because that's after the eviction, that's Maytag-box time. We're in corrugated cardboard by then."

He tries to laugh at this but she won't let him. Just the way she holds her frame prohibits it.

"Tell me which," she turns toward him. "Which goddamn holidays are we talking about?"

She keeps her gaze straight, thwarts tears. She stares him down from wherever he's been.

"Soon," is all he can say. And later, when she thinks to search the floorboard crevices, "Try and don't worry."

It's a rough night for Harlan. He had his heart set on a final day tomorrow. He comes close to providing the necklace, but doesn't; the night goes on, ten minutes at a time, and Harlan finds himself failing to deliver. After nine he keeps clear of Ada. Cruelty's less trying at a distance. He carries out the trash, walks down for a magazine, sits awhile in the car.

Even the baby seems to know it's the last holiday. Pitching through half-sleep the next morning, Harlan hears Ada do the changing and the feeding, and rummage the same territory she's searched the night before, and close the door sharply as she leaves, then he's uninterrupted until near noon, when the baby can't sleep any longer and begins to cry.

After Harlan feeds him and holds him he showers and dresses himself deliberately, he grooms himself well. He takes the necklace from hiding, and replaces it with his wedding ring. He finds the campus notebook he bought yesterday. He finds his trimmed Xerox page. On the notebook's inside cover he apes Terry Krausse's sweeping signature, and then lays the necklace inside. If this still won't lead him to

Terry Krausse, he'll indulge himself and find the cleanest, freshest young girls to ask if they've dropped it. Whatever, he needs an ending today. They're out of money, simple as that. It can't go further, today's the last holiday.

At her door Yolanda stands back further than usual.

"How're you today?" Harlan begins, flipping his sunglasses up.

"Oh, all right."

"Hope you don't mind."

"No, I don't think so," she says. "Not today."

Harlan's stuck for how to get started. There's a pause while he searches for something to say. The baby leans from his arms, looking to fly this extended distance into hers. Finally, Harlan says, "Are you going out?"

"No."

He takes a breath and leans against the door. "I can't leave him for just this one last time?"

"No thanks."

"You're serious."

"You'll need the practice, Harlan."

"An hour," he says. "Tops."

"Take him with, wherever it is. Maybe they won't mind, your companion, or companions. He won't be any trouble, he's very quiet. I don't imagine you're decked out like that for an interview."

Harlan is two beats late. "You got it."

"The hell. That's no hiring outfit, unless Rockett's needs more bouncers."

He sighs. "Last time, promise."

"No."

"Why?" he says.

"Because. Just because. I don't want your kid weighing me down today."

"Company coming?"

"You take him."

"Please," he says.

"Just do it," Yolanda says. "It's not that bad."

"Are these Ada's instructions?"

"Listen," she says. "I say so, that's why. You go play house for a while. I'm tired."

"Tomorrow I'm looking for jobs. The truth. But today, just forty-five minutes."

She says, "I can't think of new ways to say it."

There's quiet. The baby's stopped reaching. Harlan thinks she'd like to close the door on him but wouldn't dare, never would.

"Do you at least believe I'm looking in the paper Sunday?"

"Maybe *I'll* get a job," she says. "So I'll have a good excuse. And when the other comes I'll pay to have you keep them both downstairs."

Harlan looks at her.

"You did get that news," she says. "Didn't you?"

Though stunned, he nods.

"I'm kind of surprised she told. She asked me first. She was easing you into it before the trimester, trying to keep her options open. She wasn't going to drop another ten-pounder all by herself. I said go ahead and tell. Another wouldn't drive you off, not to worry. But I was just saying that. Wouldn't surprise me if it did."

He sits in his living room for a while. He leaves the cable off, his coat on. Just sits: two hours, maybe longer. The baby cries and sleeps on and off. In time Harlan again feels ready to go, and he decides to take the baby with him, why not, the single-dad look, he saw *Kramer vs. Kramer* on the Movie Channel this summer, maybe it'll score him some points.

He wraps the baby against the cold and settles it into the stroller. But the sidewalk snow's too dense for the wheels, and Harlan must carry it all on his shoulder. And though the baby makes laughing noises now he'll have no memory of this, of the wheels that lifted off and flew him a half-mile over snow once. It's wasted on babies, Harlan thinks; after a time they suddenly come to, without any recollection, as after a colossal bender, a four-year roaring drunk. What adults, what the world, could make of the favor extended only babies and lunatics, that luxurious amnesia.

For the baby, the flight ends for all time as they touch down in Student Records and Financial Aid, which teems with victims of the new semester's paperwork. Rather than wait here Harlan tries the library. Dorothy's round face shines at the sight of the stroller. She abandons involuntarily her reading room pitch.

"Is that your baby?" she nearly squeals.

"No, just watching him," Harlan hears himself say, for no reason, he supposes, except that he's still on holiday.

Dorothy makes gentle faces into the blankets. It's another minute before she looks up.

"It was Carl, wasn't it?"

"Paul Favolaro."

"Paul, yes, I'm sorry." She wiggles three fingers in front of her. "Whose is he?"

"Oh, a neighbor of mine. Single woman up above."

"And how old?"

"Five months." Here the improbable truth is enough.

"Five months. You're not serious."

"It's for real. He's a load. He's been big enough to ride this since about five weeks."

Still squatting, she asks, "The mother's divorced?"

Harlan shakes his head sadly. "No, just single. And another on the way, though that's just rumor. She's . . . you know . . . talking to men she stands very close, for instance, for whatever that's worth."

Dorothy reaches behind her for the Kleenex box.

"But listen," Harlan says. "This necklace here. A friend of mine found it with the notebook. I told him I knew you and Gil, because, I don't know, I thought maybe you knew a Terry Krausse, a female one."

Dorothy stops dabbing at the baby. She stares at Harlan. "Sure I know one," she says. "So do you."

"Ah, no, I . . ."

"That's right, you never met." She looks at the gold in Harlan's hand. "Oh, that's nice."

"The real stuff," Harlan says. "At least it looks like."

"I've never seen it on her."

"No?"

She takes it from him and looks closer. "Must be from Christmas."

"Must be."

"They just came back north on Monday."

"I see."

Dorothy finally stands up. "Where'd you find this?"

"Upstairs here. In the fiction section. Like I say, my friend found it, actually."

"That's weird," Dotty says. "Thanks much for returning it, though. She'll be thrilled. She loses stuff all the time."

"You'll see her?" he asks.

"I hope so. She lives the same place I do."

"She does?"

Dorothy looks at the baby, then back at Harlan. "How well do you know Gil?"

"Oh, not very," he says. "Not for years. Bet he didn't even remember when you mentioned me. Or have you?"

"No, sorry, I haven't," she says.

"That's all right."

"I'll see this gets returned, though. Tonight at the latest."

"Well, I really should do it," Harlan says, gently taking it back. "There could be a mistake. Is this her notebook?"

"No idea."

"Well, if you could just tell me where to find her. There's no need for you to get mixed up in it. In fact the kid who gave me this is far from the most reliable. An airhead, more or less. Flighty. Far from the most responsible. So anything's possible, a joke, even. Some kind of joke on me is highly possible."

"What kind of joke would this be?"

"You never can tell, not with him. Far from the most dependable."

"Nice guy," Dorothy says. "This friend's not the father, is he?"

"The father?" Harlan says.

She nods her head toward the stroller. "He sounds like a perfect match for your lady upstairs."

"I never thought of that."

"Just an idea," she says.

"Hey, you know," Harlan says, and possibility rises sudden and delicious—more abides in his world of lies than he alone could ever think of. "They do know each other. I've been up there with him. She wears high-cut leotards all the time. High-cut here, low-cut there."

Dorothy squats and looks into the stroller. "Is this guy heavyset? More than you, say?"

"A little maybe," Harlan says. "I know he's stopped by her office at lunchtime. He's seen the baby, too. Won't have anything to do with it, hardly. Once he called it Lyndon Baines Baby."

"It's awful," she says. "But it's all circumstantial."

"So far," Harlan says.

"Well, whatever." Dorothy stands again. "It's none of my business, really. It's just too bad. Take good care of him when you can, Paul. It's worth the trouble, to keep an eye."

"I'll be doing more," he says.

"I hope it turns out hers," Dorothy says. "It's gorgeous. She should be in her office still."

"In her office."

"Uh-huh. History, third floor."

Excited by all this, invigorated, Harlan still hasn't figured, he's overlooked the obvious, he's still thinking Gil's sister, a grad student probably, here for the peanuts Ada says they pay teaching assistants, her "office" a seedy storage room shared five ways. Early to mid-twenties, well past his ideal, but enough to finish on—it's been a good last day. Maybe a last, he thinks now, wavering for the first time; with his fabricated kingdom expanding like this he half wants to keep going, no matter that it's impossible, no matter that they're out of money, and that things lie nearly ruined. Across the parking lot to History he's flushed with lively new fictions, all more outlandish than the simple truth he hasn't figured yet. He wheels into the foyer where, in this stingy school, there's not even the letter board you'd find in any run-down medical building, only a copy sheet taped to the wall. Still, it's enough, her name in type, an inked confirmation outside his house and his head, and this sight propels him to the elevator and up to three, three-thirty-six the first door so her three-oh-three's a full long corridor away. He misses all the signs, young sullen types loitering in the three-thirties, this end clearly lower echelon, and he wheels the stroller briskly along, down the long corridor with purpose, speed enough to flutter the flyers and sublet sheets tacked to the walls, to waver their fringed ends, as the offices of the associate and then the assistant profs flash by now in the three-teens. Harlan still not putting anything together, having trouble with fact, and then the baby roused again near three-eleven by the literal wind in its face, Harlan going that fast, the load in the stroller making stirring sounds, and Harlan behind it in the commuter's half-trot now, still not knowing what he's doing, none of it seeming foolish, to the end ignoring the obvious, a joke on him indeed, as the numbers at last descend to the given one and on the odd side he finds her finally, in the office as promised, the published scholar, Gil's mother, the dermatologist's wife, Dotty's forgetful mother-in-law, whom he'd have found on day one if he'd supplanted the dorm directory with the card catalog, a history professor in an evergreen dress that sets off nicely her short silver hair, Professor Krausse standing relaxed and smiling behind her tenured desk, in the first week of the new semester, with a line of five or six freshmen in front of her, all tall teenagers, freshboys (her martial survey with its 1066s and 1789s a real male draw anyway, Harlan in his own way having found the callow pledge's most popular campus female), a reverse here in the last day, ending with a woman and boys, boys patient in passing the two or three insignificant minutes it requires to get her soft penciled lines next to their computerized names.

By now it must be close to five o'clock. The big parking lot has been kept clear, and Harlan can wheel the stroller. The sky's a rich blue still—the days stretching longer, January's subtle steady improvement—and now at five or later there's enough light to see. Engineering sits at the other end of this lot. The car shows itself immediately. Harlan eases the baby to the back seat and lowers himself down into the driver's, but he doesn't turn the key. Ada should be only a few more minutes. When he sees her emerge he puts the notebook in his pocket and looks to hide the necklace. Anywhere lacks plausibility, though the glove compartment might be best, or under the seat, or better in the cleft between seat and back rest, where it might have unclasped and fallen. But it is time to start something new. As the handle clicks under her hand he holds the necklace in his, trusting himself now to trade his truth for hers, and do it before they pull away, to sit rooted here until it's out and over with, maybe even done while there's still some light left.

PARTNER

Okay, I dropped my wife off at work and I was driving back out through the east side of town. This was about two weeks ago. It was early in the day for me to be doing anything—usually either my wife takes the car to work or after I drive her I go right back to bed. I wasn't sure where I was going, to the mall to play video games maybe, who knows? Maybe change my oil, maybe get a paper.

Up ahead on one of the main streets out of town there were these two guys, one older than the other. They were on the opposite side of the street. They could have been two brothers, or maybe father and son. Two girls were walking down the street, going the same way I was. They were headed right into this family thing. The language being used, the filthy words. These two guys were cursing so hard it was making them cry. Each had hold of a parking meter for support. Even over the whine of my Datsun I could hear it. For me, I don't know, that kind of heavy-duty swearing is soothing, the dirty words in there on a regular beat; it sounds like junior high used to. I could listen to that stuff all day. This was serious though, it was a family matter, and that's where you get injuries, you get maiming. The street was quiet—it's early, remember—and there was only one other witness; he'd passed through already but he was still watching, walking swiftly and skillfully backward, like news photographers do.

I came up on the two girls before they reached this family thing. I rolled down my window and said, "Would you like a ride out of this?"

I don't do that sort of thing often and I got the feeling that they didn't either.

They were clearly a pair, partners. I sensed that one was visiting the other—there's a college here and one of them had probably bussed up from the old hometown. That's what they looked like. When I gave them my line they faced each other and you could see the wheels spinning. This would be an adventure, a safe one; they could laugh about it over the phone next month and it'd be something to say when people asked about the visit.

Now I'm trustworthy but my face won't tell you that—you have to know me. I don't have a friendly face. There's a spotty beard to cover where I got burned in college. I know my face won't win anybody's heart, and it doesn't produce instant trust. But they were a team. They felt safe together. What bad happens in a Datsun, anyway? Plus it was so early. How evil could things get at nine in the morning?

They were older than I thought, maybe even a little past college—from a distance they'd looked younger, and taller, too. Between them they had one hairstyle. One wore a pink sweater and the nice simple blue jeans you don't see anymore. The other dressed the same but looked altogether different—she had the build of a buoy, kind of, not obese but bottom-heavy. A long face and a wide round ass and short strong-looking legs. Her contents had definitely settled; you got the feeling there was something in her tugging down, drawing her substance out the bottom of her shoes. It's been my experience that when two opposites like this are together they're usually partners for life.

"I figure they'll be picking up big rocks any minute," said the squat one, who was in the back and kicking my seat while she hunted for leg room.

"They do like their cussing down here," the other said.

So I was right about one of them visiting. I've got that knack.

"Is it all right if I put my shoes on the seat?"

As we were driving, I was wishing that this was over. I could have used a fade-out right after I rolled down the window and gave my line. Just the idea of picking them up and delivering them from danger, that was enough.

"You're going where?" I said.

They were quiet for a while. The pink girl, the one who was rummaging through my glove compartment with her eyes (there's no panel on it—it's just a hole), finally answered. "Out to the Green and Talbot's."

"We need to pick up some stuff."

"She doesn't have any food in her house."

"Yeah. We're having a party tonight." This was the round one talking. "It's a going-away party for one of the guys where I work."

"Alphonse Gluck, from Hamburg," her partner said.

"Right," said the one in the back seat. "Where are you going?"

"Out that way. I'll drop you off."

When you sit in your car in the parking lot at the mall or the supermarket you may think you're alone but you're not. There are always a shocking number of other people sitting out in their cars, waiting.

The two girls didn't get out right away. This was the same supermarket my wife boycotts because of the stupid, low-budget TV ads, the talking shopping carts. I thought about offering them a ride back, too, but I didn't.

"Thanks for the ride," the pink one said.

I realized that in back the other was writing. What she gave me said: Ann and Vicki, 148C Chestnut, 10pm, BYOA (for anything).

"Which is whom?" is what I said, but they didn't hear me. They were away already, toward the store, and even though they were just walking I knew they were talking about me without speaking, the way lifelong friends can.

The sound of all this probably makes you think I'm dumber than I am, except for this last remark, which probably makes you think I think I'm smarter than I am. What I am is from a good home and college-educated, a near-graduate. I went to Michigan for three years. My wife Denise went there for four years. I spent finals week my junior year in the hospital and I never made up the work, but by then I was barely hanging on anyway.

A national chain of newspapers hired my wife after she graduated; she works in their traveling fix-it department. Actually I'm not sure if she works for the newspaper chain or the consulting firm, but so far we've been to three small cities while my wife's group brings the local paper into the twentieth century. If you've ever been outside the big city you know the kind of rags I mean. My wife works with six other people—they come in and re-do the graphics, get a style section going, beef up the sports, cut down on the international wire stuff. It's a good company, whoever they are; in Youngstown I was stunned when she brought home the fat shiny benefits package. A half-dozen glossy booklets about dental plans, stock options, everything. No place I've ever worked had that.

Youngstown was our first stop, then Wheeling, then here. Frankfort's next and then Brockton, Massachusetts. Beyond that the future hasn't been scheduled. We usually stay five or six months; we came here in May so we should be leaving by the end of next month, November.

I don't have any kind of job right now. I try not to hang around the house all day—you tend to wind up in the bathroom; with nothing better to do you secrete a great deal and whip through rolls and rolls of toilet paper. I'm not trying to be funny. The bathroom gets depressing when you're in there all the time. In the past couple of weeks I've been getting out for a drive every day. I've learned lately that it's important to get out in the morning. It makes you feel like something. Things are so much easier when you do them early. Ever call a utility company at eight forty-five? Walk into a post office at nine? Go to the market at nine-fifteen? You'll sail right through. I've been doing it for the past couple of weeks; I try to get going while the cars are still wet. It feels good to get out early. If I don't have anyplace to go I'll just drive for a while. I'm always back by noon, so it's never a long grinding day. In the afternoon the streets get mobbed and the people get less interesting. I don't go far; mostly I drive around town. Every Saturday morning I fill the gas tank. That's another good feeling—doing things on Saturday mornings: getting gas, driving to the dump, washing the car, airing out the house, shopping with the wife, browsing the hardware store, fixing a door or a window.

From my parents' roof you can see part of Denise's house, the windows of her brother's bedroom. It's on the next block, about halfway up the street. I met my wife on the first day of fourth grade when Mrs. Van Durant rapped on the desk and introduced her as the new girl from Flint. Denise was always the tallest in class. We're both twenty-four years old and we've been married six years. My wife, incidentally, still holds a share of the school mile-relay record.

Outside of our wedding the big event in my life came in May of our junior year at Ann Arbor. It was a house party, mostly wrestlers; through special coursework and the like their school year was already over and they were celebrating, even though it was finals week for the rest of us. It was an especially long party, standard stuff, I won't burden you with much of it. But the hard-guy fad among the wrestlers that year was silverware fights. It started in mid-semester with the white plastic Sweetheart stuff and just kind of escalated. Near dawn I needed some aspirin and I walked into the kitchen just as somebody was one-upping with a Pyrex coffee pot. Of course the pot had boiling water and I caught it flush in the face. I've made myself forget exactly what it felt like. I went into the hospital and I never caught up in school. I painted houses and waited for Denise to graduate. Her degree is in mass communication, by the way.

In these places there isn't much work for five or six months that I honestly would not mind doing. Cabdriving, you probably say, would be good. Well, forgetting that there are maybe ten cabs in this town total, I don't think it would much suit me anyway. Just driving is what I like. It's good. It involves you but doesn't wear on you, it's like light exercise, but still exercise, like isometrics. It's like doing the *TV Guide* crossword puzzle.

I feel safe when I drive, I know I'm good at it. And I'm good without being cautious, particularly. I'm not a slowpoke. When I drive around it's not as a samaritan. I don't have cables and flares in my trunk, and I'm not a vigilante, I don't scan the police bands or hunt for the citizen's arrest. And I don't cruise the streets looking for action. I picked up those girls on about five seconds forethought. I never pick up hitchhikers, it isn't the same.

My wife's group hangs around together, understandably. Their chief is a tall guy named Don. Don is about fifty and he always dresses in brown, at least when I've seen him, and when he laughs he doesn't move his body. You sort of have to see him to believe it; when he laughs he sits dead-still except for jerking his head around a little.

We have the biggest apartment and my wife invites them over. I usually stay out of the kitchen—and so does Denise, we eat out often—but last week I broiled up some steaks for them all except Don the vegetarian. It was World Series week so we had the TV going during dinner; Denise thought it was rude but she was overruled since they were all heavily into the office pool.

"Who's going to Frankfort?" one of them was asking. They tend to talk about their next city a lot.

"Everybody, I think."

"We'll have to get started before Christmas."

"No we don't. I heard we don't. Don and Denise have to go there early. But for us I heard no. We're free until after New Year's."

Don sat still and laughed. "Christmas in Frankfort."

My wife took her car keys out of her pocket and began to jingle them, for holiday music. There was much laughter; Don was rigid with it.

"What a team these two are," said one of the others. "Don and Denise. It sounds like an act, even. Somewhere in this tank town there's a perfect spot for the act, Don and Denise. You should have heard this one today," pointing at my wife. "For five solid minutes she had us crying."

"These things happen," my wife said, deadpan. She really can be very funny sometimes.

All these people were laughing so hard it was making them cry. When at last they got their food they all sat around the TV.

I always root for the American League since I'm from an American League area, a Tiger fan. It was a good game but my wife's group kept talking shop. Except for Don they all disdained chairs and spread themselves out on the floor and leaned their backs against the walls. They were in a long, free-form gossip about people at the paper.

I said: "What I don't get here's the wives. They keep showing the wives. What's the point? The little woman who sits at home. So what?"

They got quiet and watched the TV. Don began moving in his chair, sitting up, crossing and re-crossing his legs. A few of them sat on their hands. One tugged carpet threads like they were blades of grass. There wasn't a smoker in the bunch.

I got up and went into the bathroom. I smoked a cigarette and washed my hands. Some water splashed on the big poetry book that sits on the back of the toilet. I forgot to mention that my wife reads poetry in the morning. Her father did it, too. She says it gets her going in the morning, bad poetry or good, just reading the lines gives her a running head start.

I took a run down Chestnut Street the night I was invited. It didn't look much like student housing, the address they gave me. There wasn't any party—I had no trouble parking on the street, and there was only one light burning in the house. It had the look of a very nice place. I didn't go in; I sat out in my Datsun awhile and smoked and listened to the radio. The street was on a hill and I could get almost half the country from there. I couldn't see anything happening inside.

My wife and I had one of those weekends last weekend. All sorts of small things adding up, you know what I mean? We weren't mad with each other, it was just a calamity weekend. We left the house hardly at all. Denise didn't have the energy. We forgot to go to the bank so we didn't have much money. Whether we watched it or not the TV burned for the whole day and night. My glasses slipped right off my nose once, when I was leaning out the front door looking for mail.

The side piece, or whatever you call it, was bent and all weekend it dug into the skin behind my ear. We stayed up for a Marx Brothers movie and it was dull and not nearly as funny as I remembered.

I poked Denise in the eye once, accidentally, when we were on the couch. Saturday I didn't get into the shower until about four-thirty—I didn't do any of the usual Saturday morning things. The water in the bathroom sink comes on very hot and twice Denise burned her hand a little. Ever had a weekend like this? On Saturday night she just sat there, planted on the couch, complaining about the garbage they put on television. She was really worked up, berating every little thing that came on. My pulse raced just listening to her; I agreed but I wanted to tell her to shut up. After a while I reached up and turned it off but she said it made no difference, she knew it was still there.

All weekend my clothes felt uncomfortable on me—the laundry needed doing and I was wearing old shrunken T-shirts that rode up on my back. She asked me, several times, how many more weeks until Monday. I put about a pound of Bisquick and a dozen eggs and milk in a bowl and we ate pancakes all weekend. The dishes stayed where we ate, as if to mark the spot, and soon there were sticky plates and milky glasses in the kitchen, in the spare bedroom, on the living room floor, on the coffee table, and on top of the TV. Each time we'd hunt a clean space to eat.

The one time I left the house was for the Sunday paper. I took the wrong coat. October can be like that; as soon as I closed the door behind me I knew it, but I didn't go back in. Not wanting to look foolish carrying a down coat around I kept it on me, and I worked up a full sweat walking to the corner store. The Sunday paper got Denise going. She read it sitting on the floor; her hair kept falling in her face and she threatened to cut it all off. They'd blown everything in the new Lifestyles section, nothing had been done according to plan. Barefoot, my wife kicked and kicked at the Sunday paper until it floated down over every part of our living room, but that didn't seem to make her feel any better.

This week I've been taking the same road farther and farther out of town every day. You can go for a long way on these roads before you cross anything else that's paved and lined. Each day I cover maybe fifteen minutes of new ground before I turn around and come back. It looks a little bit like Michigan out there—the wait for new scenery gets longer every day, of course, but more interesting. I had to gas up the Datsun in the middle of the week. Friday I got back just barely in time to pick up my wife.

She didn't show right away. I waited in the parking lot a while longer, then I saw her sticking her head out the side door.

"Don's really cracking the whip," she said. "It's square-onesville." It's one of those thick steel doors, the kind you'd never open because of the buzzers and bells that would probably go off.

"I didn't know you'd be staying." I was careful not to say "Well! You could have called!" like some cranky housewife.

"I tried to call," she said. "What was for dinner?"

"I was going to pick up a pizza."

"Go ahead then. You can eat most of a whole one."

"I don't have any money," I said.

"You want the checkbook?"

"Cash would be better."

"I need all I've got."

She went back inside and I sat on the steel railing, trying I guess to look happy-go-lucky. You'd probably like to know more about my wife besides that she's funny and she ran track in high school. I don't know, I think I'm too close to say. When she brought out the checkbook she gave me a kiss that smelled like coffee. "Sorry," she said. "I'll get a ride home."

So now I had to go to the bank, too. I was driving through town in the traffic. I was stopped at a red light. There were people all over the place. I was wondering what time it was, whether the bank was open. In the mornings things are truly so much better. I was really working up my hate for this hour of the day, whichever it turned out to be. When I pulled out on the green light I hit somebody on foot. Never saw him, this pedestrian. All I saw was the green and I went.

On the ground was exactly the kind of guy I'd hit, exactly, if I ever hit somebody. We were fated to meet at the front end of my Datsun. I would never nick a pretty woman or an eccentric old man or even a pathetic foreigner; I'd hit this—I don't know, trainee-plumber maybe—this chubby guy in the army jacket.

It was not that bad. All I really did was knock him over. He must have gone two-thirty and my car, with me in it, was no more than a few hundred pounds going at ten miles an hour. After I backed the car out of the intersection I went over to him.

A few people had gathered but not many were staying, that was how harmless it looked. He was about my age and he had long, rod-straight hair that fanned out under him on the street. He had been carrying a pocketful of sunflower seeds, more than a single bag's worth, and when he went down the seeds scattered all over the street.

This tall bony woman was right up in front. Even though it was only October she was all bundled up. "You do not move him," she was saying. "Don't ever try to move a victim at the scene of the accident." She had no color in her face that you could tell. I guess this was her natural condition. It occurred to me that she was one of the bank tellers, meaning they were closed and I was out of luck. She had just stepped out of McDonald's with what looked like dinner for six, all wrapped up in the biggest white bag they had. She sat the bag down next to him like it was a doctor's kit.

To me he looked stunned but not in pain. But he didn't move. We listened to this woman. It was our accident, but we did what this woman told us to do. "I feel a little pain in my back," he said. It looked like his watch was broken. Birds were bouncing around nearby, wanting at those seeds. My car was as far off to the side as I could put it, but it still blocked traffic. The guy had shells in his teeth; with his tongue he was trying to fish them out, with dignity, on his back in the big intersection downtown at Friday rush hour. I tell you this is just the kind of guy I'd hit.

The woman jogged across the street to the pay phone. She removed her sunglasses and let them dangle from her hand while she did this.

"Load of seeds you got there," I said to him.

"I gave up cigarettes. These relax me. Something to do. Otherwise I'd be picking my lip all day." LeBlanc was the name on the army jacket, but you knew it wasn't his name.

"Look, partner," I said to him, stroking my bumpy face.

"My car is tying everybody up. There's got to be a hundred people looking at us right now."

So he finally picked himself up and I gave him a ride home. I told him I'd pay for the watch but he said it was broken already, he wore it just for jewelry. He lives in one of the older neighborhoods. I counted at least four cats and a dozen flower pots on the porch when I pulled up. I offered to pay any medical he might need but he said his mother's insurance covered that. His mother has the voice you'd expect; she answered the next morning when I called to see how he felt. I don't think he'll sue me. We both just want to forget it. Maybe he will, but I just get the feeling he won't. You know what I mean?

SLEEPING TOGETHER

Dwight and Laura get into bed at seven-thirty and they don't get out until ten past one the next afternoon. That's eighteen hours, just about.

Laura's family is gone for a week and a half—one of those fall vacations her father prefers, jerking all the kids from school and hiring three cabins at some mountain ski resort long before the rush. Only Laura and her big brother Kenny are permitted to decline; Kenny is away at college and Laura is a high school senior. Once Mom and Dad and the six youngest kids have gone, Laura and Dwight take great care to arrange the downstairs playroom, where two of her younger brothers normally sleep. They move the twin beds, which lie corner to corner, out into the center of the room. Laura spends most of an hour binding them together with kite string. They take clean king-size linen from an upstairs closet:

sheets, contour sheets, and pillowcases ready for her parents' bed. They carry the newer of the color portables down from the living room. They bring the two soft, rust-colored chairs from the den. They find the only large cooler the family has left behind, fill it with ice and with stock from the main refrigerator, and put it right by the bed, or beds. Laura's mother has told her to please eat what's in the refrigerator before it spoils, to keep the doors locked, to forward anything that looks urgent in her father's mail. Laura has told her mother not to worry.

Dwight has told his mother the truth. He'll be at Laura's house for the week. It was accidentally perfect timing; he caught her with the dishwashing, somehow less likely to react with both hands lost in a half-foot of gray water. There is little for her to say anyway. She's been divorced a few years and working full time and dating, and has never kept her only child bound to the house. What Dwight's mother did say, head inclined over the running water, was that she hoped he wouldn't miss too much school because of it.

They're seniors at the same high school, Dwight and Laura. She is one year older—all her family had missed a season of school when their father took them along to England a while back. Dwight has worn a beard for six months, but for the most part he and Laura look like everyone looks, they dress in modest variations of the uniform. Still, among the crowd they are rarely seen: when Laura does come to school she is most often late, and armed with a dismissal note that claims a medical appointment shortly after lunch. Dwight enjoys school and tries to go every day, but as the crowd empties to the parking lots in the afternoon or trudges in groups of three or five down the hill (the building sits on a large hill—"the school on the hill," the fight song calls it in three different places), Dwight often leaves himself behind. Nothing extracurricular keeps him, he simply dawdles, relishing the empty-stage quality of the school at ten past three. A dozen scattered students remain, and the routinely harried custodial staff, and the younger teachers—all of them aware of this shift to a more behind-the-scenes sort of scene. Dwight can't ever quite get over the sudden and flagrant lack of a crowd, this notion—as best he can put it—that he stands in a place that's the same, but not at all the same, as it just was.

New light into this peculiar new bedroom may do it. Or the sounds of first neighborhood traffic. Whatever, they are both awake. The television burns from last night.

"Hello," Laura says.

"What time is it, you guess? Six-thirty?"

Even before meager lines like these there is pause. Through no special effort the words carry weight.

"The dream I just had," Laura says. "We were talking to an actor. To the actor who plays you. Nancy Gillerman and me, we were talking to the actor who plays you. Don't ask me why Nancy Gillerman. Your mother, the actress who plays her, she wasn't around. It was weird. They were moving cardboard walls and doors around and more people were coming over to hear what he had to say."

"What did I say?" Dwight says.

"That was all. You woke up and asked me what time it was."

"That's a great picture you get down here. Sharp."

They stay in bed, neither moves to silence the TV. One of

those ultra-competitive morning shows comes on. It makes them both jumpy and a little dizzy to watch it, all the quick cutting: the forty-five-second features, the ten-second previews of forty-five-second features upcoming, and the thirty-second commercials in between. Dwight falls back to sleep first. Laura has to get up and use the bathroom before she can sleep again.

It's not the sex that's new—it is the retiring for the evening, the turning-in, the actual physical resting, side by side, overnight. They have found the time and space for sex mostly in Laura's car, a few times in spare rooms at parties, two or three matinees at Dwight's empty house, and once on the dewy eighth green of the municipal golf course. Last winter, after a party celebrating someone's early acceptance, they sprang for a motel. The year's coldest night, they rode around in it, Laura driving, for two hours or more before they agreed on a spot and pulled in. The motel was about twenty miles from their town; it was inexpensive but looked clean and well kept, managed by a forthright Nielsen family that lived behind the office. The oldest son—about their age, it looked—worked the desk. The lobby was nice; it had a side area with inviting chairs and matching sofa, and a massive TV that played a repeat of the late local news. Dwight approached the desk and paid cash, signing his own true name and address on the register. Laura plucked one of each of the travel brochures from the small rack, and she read aloud from them as they walked down the orange and brown hall. Then, deftly, she plucked the key away from Dwight.

But there was someone behind their door. They could tell, they could hear noises. Laura—and she surprised Dwight here—put one hand over the other and turned the key anyway. Most of the bed was hidden from view by an orange and brown partition: all that showed was a horizontal pair of feet. The same rerun played on this TV, it was the only light in the room. They were bare, rigid men's feet, parallel and pointed as if on skis. Laura laughed, but the feet never moved. "There must be a tag on one of those toes," she said. They returned the key to the desk and the boy-clerk gave them another. As if either to atone or to punish them further, he had assigned them a room as far away as possible, easiest reached across the icy parking lot. Dwight, at the top of his lungs, complained about the cold all the way over. On the bed they thawed out and made love and both went right to sleep. In the morning Laura took for her own room the fine-printed placard of motel policy and state law, and Dwight left a dollar for the unseen chambermaid, suspecting that years ago his father had shown him it was the thing to do.

When Laura sleeps she tucks her head down. She keeps her chin on her chest and seems to study her body, protect it through the night, keep watch.

Dwight is fitful. Even at five in the morning, in his deepest sleep, he tosses and turns. These are grand and sweeping moves, full of energy. Most of his body leaves the support of the bed; he gives a near leap, then spins in the air and settles on his other side.

Occasionally Laura says something: it's in a voice mumbled but still strong, a loud, belligerent, near-male tone. The words are indecipherable, but it sounds like she's explaining to someone, answering interrogation, pleading her case.

It is late September, and for the first time the weather settles near fifty.

All the blankets and spreads for the king-size bed are locked in Laura's parents' room, so they have spread a single comforter across their legs and taken separate, twin-size blankets for their top halves. Underneath, the king-size contour sheet is too big—it bunches in places and comes loose in one corner, exposing bare mattress. The kite string still holds, but without its original strength—their lovemaking and Dwight's sleepy, leaping twists have not helped—and the crack between the beds has widened some.

Laura sleeps with her hands kept close. Pretty hands, feminine, they seem always poised and closed—rarely has Dwight seen in them the strain of muscles and tendons working. When on her back her hands meet with what seems like mock gentility across her lower belly; when on her stomach she buries them beneath her, or else makes of one a light half-fist between her face and the pillow, as if she were taking a call, like they were patching her through to heaven. Sometimes they rest at her sides but always near. Her hands never hang over the floor, or over him.

Dwight sleeps best on his stomach, his right arm bent under the pillow, his head facing left. From this position he seems least inclined to move. In the early morning Laura—sleeping better once accustomed to Dwight's sporadic rocking—shifts to her side, and for warmth puts her hands between her knees, which are bony, and which now bend and come clear across the bed's median. For the actual sleeping it is much better, clearly, to be alone.

It disturbs Dwight that Laura has no dead-set sleeping position. He watches her for a while, after midnight, with the television going in the playroom dark, some ninety-minute movie about a bounty hunter. For now she sleeps crookedly, as if she imagines the head of the bed to be about two feet over and one down from where it really is. After nearly a year, Dwight has yet to find in Laura reliable traits, out of bed or in. He would not be pleased to learn that Laura has no particular seat at the dinner table, that on the nights she finds herself home she slides into any opening. Though Dwight would consider that unthinkable in a large family—or any family—he would admit it as typical of Laura, as unmethodical as could be. It is a tough, brawny name, Laura, a girl's name to be sure, but not without some muscle and gristle to it. A chewy, hard-to-cut quality. And she looks muscular to him this week, for the first time ever, when his head is between her legs and she is on her back; he sees her legs tightened and her breasts flattened by gravity and she looks solid and powerful, the TV glowing on her, tree-trunk thighs and a well-developed muscular chest. Laura is a tough name to write, too. Dwight always prints, and to print her name becomes trouble when you come down from the "u" and have to lift the pen from the page and go to the top for the "r." It rarely comes out right, and never at all if hurried—the "r" inevitably loses itself in the "u." Dwight scribbles the whole name, or avoids writing it.

"Hey," Dwight says. "You can't do that."

Laura is leaning like a figure skater or a ridiculous piece of art. Her head and chest dangle from the bed, she is supported by one knee; her other leg waves in the air over Dwight, for balance.

"Hey. You don't know what's floating in there."

With a plastic cup she dips into the big cooler like it's a river. It is early afternoon, the ice has been there all night and now the surviving cubes are floating, along with a dozen or so apples, cellophane rolls of cookies, and soda bottles. Dark specks abound in the chunky water, too.

"Hey, Laura Murray," Dwight says. Her full name has lately become a kind of endearment, her only nickname.

"I'm not getting any," Laura says, and it's true. She has trouble supporting her weight. The cup is shaking. She keeps coming up empty. "Maybe I should just stick my head in."

Dwight rolls onto his feet and jogs up the stairs. "I'll get ice water," he calls back. Naked, he notices himself as he moves. He has never gone freely without clothes for any real stretch of time; but like most other liberties, it seems, more than anything else, merely new.

The Murray house is split-level, and large. The upper level seems to stretch forever, corridors big as the school's. In the kitchen Dwight looks for the cabinet with drinking glasses. The family bulletin board is surprisingly bare. Only a recent phone bill and the schedule at the local rec center. The Murrays' refrigerator has a door that gives ice water. Dwight fills two glasses.

He walks to the living room window and raises a drawn shade clumsily, with his two free fingers. It's a small disappointment to him that he hasn't set down the drinks and full-fisted the thing. He's always found that satisfying, raising the shades, letting them fly. After every filmstrip several gradeschoolers will vie for the privilege. Outside it is not a sunny day. Dwight moves down the hall. He finds the door to the master bedroom locked, as Laura claimed. He can't quite say why he hadn't fully believed Laura when she said her mother stockpiles things in there, hoards away from the kids the items that go too quickly, like ballpoint pens and cases of Diet Pepsi.

Holding the ice water out from his body, Dwight walks farther down the main hall. In Laura's sister's room his bare flanks are warmed some, just by the air. It seems thicker in there. The bedspread is thick, too, sky blue and impossibly fluffy. There are four different rugs on the floor and action posters of hockey and football players on the walls. On the dresser is a Plen-T-Pak of Wrigley's Doublemint gum. Dwight doesn't take any.

He walks back to the living room. The dog has gone on vacation with them, but from habit Dwight keeps his eyes low, ready for it. There are Hummels everywhere. The glasses begin to drip. He puts them down in the corner, on top of the electric organ. He doesn't know how to play the thing, which has to cost five thousand dollars, easily. The organ's got everything. He flips the power switch and touches a button that says "WOOD BLOCK." It's a catchy, clip-clop sound. He turns it up a little and taps out a few notes, keeping in time. The glasses make rings so Dwight shuts the organ down and lifts them. Dwight is naked; he has nothing for wiping the rings, so he leaves them there. But he is careful not to spill water on the stairs.

Laura sits on the bed, drinking cooler water from the plastic cup. "It took you so *long*," she says.

Laura was born in 1962 and named for the perky young wife on *The Dick Van Dyke Show*. Dwight was born in 1963 and named, naturally, for the former President, his mother's favorite. She had been saving the name for three years, since the Democratic takeover, waiting to get married and have her first son.

Strangely, the Murrays have met Dwight's father—who lives on the other side of the country—but they have never met his mother. When the Murrays were in San Francisco for an FAA conference Dwight's father looked them up. He is a former liquor salesman who has remarried into some modest vineyard money, and his days are mostly free and clear. He and the Murrays shared most of an entire day, including lunch and dinner. Stranger still, it was at this FAA conference in San Francisco that Laura got her job at the fancy downtown liquor store back home. Names came up, as they might, throughout lunch and dinner; it turned out that Dwight's father knew the owner, who was looking for a young, attractive, dependable girl with some personality, so Laura got the job. What Dwight got out of this FAA conference was a modest-looking silver watch, a gift from his father that the Murrays brought back. Strangest of all, Dwight already owned a watch and his father knew it, or should have, since he was the one to buy it the Christmas before he moved away.

The wet roll of cookies is under Laura's leg. Naked in midafternoon, she sits cross-legged at the head of the bed.

"What about next year?" she says. "Maybe we can go to Houston?"

"Who still wants to go to Houston?" Dwight says.

"Everybody says there's jobs again there. Let's face it, things are brutal where we are. We could work in a tool factory, or we could be exterminators. We could rob banks. You pick it. We could manage a motel. Motels are about the greatest thing." On her back now, Laura sometimes kicks up her legs and cycles them in a small tight motion.

"We can't go," Dwight says. He sits, also without clothes, in one of the rust-colored chairs hauled down from the den. His new soda bottle sweats a burning drop or two into his leg. Laura lays Fudge Stripe cookies like rings on each fingertip; she eats them like that, rotating her wrist and nibbling around. Dwight peers into his bottleneck and the gathering fog.

Laura says, "We'd eat these constantly, just like this, with a gallon of milk, all the kids down here watching TV. All the kids and my grandmother, on this hideous couch we had. She wore these puffy-sleeve dresses and she laughed herself sick at the dumbest shows. That couch would cut right through our bed here. One end stopped at about where my knee is. Nanna always sat right in the middle of it. Laughed until her face was wet. We had this real big black-and-white, thirty-four inches or something, so when we were real small we could walk up to it and sort of fit, you know. Hunch right up *in* the picture."

"A thirty-four-inch television?" Dwight says. "Nothing personal, understand, but you're a fucking liar."

Laura laughs. She takes a bite of cookie and then talks before she starts to chew. "We could go to Houston, you know. We could go to school there. Everybody always wants people from far away. TCU, SMU, anywhere, all those places, they'd be honored, I bet they don't get many from New England. Harvard wants them from all over so now everybody else does. I mean it. And they give full scholarships, if you're an out-of-towner with fourteen hundred on the SAT you're in. That amazes me. For a fourteen hundred people far away will pay *you*. What's that for us, another thirty right answers? We're five-fifties, right, eleven hundred overall? Just another thirty-forty lucky guesses and we write our own ticket. We should take it again, nothing's impossible."

This is largely performance. She doesn't talk this way in life, it's a mechanism of hers, heard only by Dwight and by her family. She uses it in the house exclusively, always has: the leapfrogging ideas, the word-blitz that precludes conversation, the calling attention to herself, it's useful in a large family.

"Maybe we'll find true love down there," she says, brushing crumbs from her chest. "I'll get my derrick man and his season tickets on the forty-five. You'll get a coed, a nice blushy one."

"Wait," Dwight says. "I want a rich girl."

"What rich girl. You want a rich girl?"

Dwight raises his bottle. "Just like the second girl that married dear old Dad."

Laura laughs. "I'm a rich girl."

"You're not a rich girl."

"I'm a rich girl."

"Your folks have a little money. But you and me, we're on the poor side. We'll be thrashing around. Don't get it confused."

"We're comfortable," Laura says. "That's my Dad's word. Ask him if we're rich and he'll say we're comfortable." She is riding her inverted bicycle again, defying gravity, and laughing. "You want a rich girl, you want me."

■

Shortly past sundown they are wrestling on the bed when the front door opens.

"Shit," Dwight says. He is frozen.

They hear ponderous feet on the stairs, then the opening of the refrigerator.

"Kenny's home," Laura says.

They appear before him shortly, Laura in a tattered tan bathrobe and Dwight, shoeless and sockless, in his jeans and a sweatshirt. They look as just-dressed as can be.

"What are you doing home?" Laura asks him.

"It's Friday," Kenny says.

"It's Friday." Laura sounds a little surprised.

"I'm getting some things." Kenny sits at the kitchen table with a sandwich. He appears effortful, hunched over his food like a man intent on good penmanship. "I'm going to Hyannis tonight—in a few minutes, actually."

Kenny doesn't look directly at Dwight, but he sends out a half-smile, a signal-flare of friendship. "Heard from Mom?" he says.

"No, actually," Laura says. "You?"

"No."

"She'll call soon, I bet," Laura says. "How's school?"

"Weird," Kenny says. He has a mouthful. "Things change. It's weird. There's this girl following me, I think. I see her all over the place, usually when I'm with Alice. She might be after Alice, I don't know. She looks kind of dyked-out."

"Really," Laura says.

"We see her everywhere. Life in the big city, I guess. Things change fast." Kenny keeps eating as he says this; he seems to make the effort not to sound too worldly-wise, too big-brotherly."You told anybody about this?" Dwight asks.

Kenny keeps his eyes on his plate. "I'd feel kind of stupid if I did. It's just some wacky girl, you know?" On this last he looks into Dwight's area.

"Life in the big city," Dwight says without malice.

"There's some real changes," Kenny says. In no time he has finished his meal. He rinses his glass and his plate and within minutes he is gone.

"He's a riot," Laura says, and in the center of the kitchen she reaches for Dwight's belt.

Dwight and Laura didn't quite tumble into their school's operative categories. They did not rove with the academic, athletic, or pharmaceutical subsets, nor with any of the small, odd-numbered squadrons that hung together for less simple reasons. They didn't see many other students outside of school. But they weren't the tidiest match—indeed they sometimes did and said things so bewildering to each other that a cessation followed, a period of pause while their awesome, utter opposition was observed. These were rarely critical. A few weeks ago, in the July heat, they stood at an ice-cream take-out, at the screen window outdoors, waiting for service from a single employee who had customers inside the store as well. Dwight felt a real pang for him—the minimum he must have been making, the unending file of customers and that endless, happy chatter you get in ice-cream lines, the genuine labor of digging the stuff from its carton and balancing it on a cone, the horrible sticky hair on his forearms. "He's just a soda jerk," Laura replied, "that's his job." She said it with a firmness that staggered him, as much as his limp comments had surprised her. After that came one of the silences, their long effort at comprehension.

They are side by side in the dark.

"Should we make an appearance at the football game tomorrow?" Laura says.

"An appearance is it? What time?"

"One-thirty."

"I don't think I'll be awake by then."

"You don't like to go anyway," Laura says. "You don't like sports. Or the band, or sitting out anywhere where it's not seventy-two degrees."

"You'll see plenty of football in Texas."

"You object to even a brisk fall day, a beautiful day for football." Laura's hands are on him, but not tenderly. "We *should* take off. You'd dig the Astrodome. That's your kind of room."

"I don't like the crowd at school games," Dwight says. "That's what I don't like. That stupid mob scene."

"Same as my father with the crowd, beating the crowds."

"I don't like your father much either," Dwight says.

"You don't like anything."

"I like steak," Dwight says. "I like you in overalls."

A pause.

"Well now," she says. "That didn't sound too silly. It should have, my favorite things. But it didn't, it sounded all right. It must be the dark."

"I know what you mean."

"Even this. Right now. Like that commercial where she calls the guy in the morning and says, 'You snore.' That's what this should be sounding like, cute enough to gag on. But it's

OK. That's news about the overalls, incidentally."

"Well I mean it."

"I'll have to pick up some more."

"Clothes cost," Dwight says.

"Don't worry about money. We have money."

"You're not being realistic."

"I've got five thousand saved up," Laura says. "I take home about three hundred a week."

"From work?"

"Yes."

"Three hundred dollars?"

"Yes."

Dwight tries to see her through the dark. "You steal. Is that it?"

"Right," Laura says. "I am afraid you are right."

"You steal money. You tap the till."

"There it is."

"Wow," Dwight says.

"Uh-huh."

"Wow," Dwight says. "Feel better now?"

"Who says I felt bad?"

Dwight pulls a sheet over his legs.

"We can go anywhere," Laura says.

"Do you take from your parents, too? Somebody I know confessed that the other day. They stopped recently. I take it you haven't stopped."

"Not really, no."

"Somebody told me they took thirty dollars at a time. The folks never missed it."

"Who's this?" Laura asks him.

"Somebody told me."

"You won't tell me who. Dwight? It's pitch dark in here. The confidences are flying, my God. I've confided. Yo tengo confido. I thought I'd take that secret to the grave. I really did. It was the only possible way. I kept it all to myself. But there you have it. It's dark in here and who knows what time of night and bang, it's out and I can never have it back. Dwight? I'll confide another thing—it sounds pretty weird to say your name. We don't say names much, you know. It's like we shouldn't even bother having them. You there?"

"Right here."

"It's an art, kind of. I think I do it well. I knew if I never talked, or never even thought about it much then there'd be no suspicion. We have those old, old cash registers—part of the atmosphere. Everybody thinks they're great. But sure as shit they're not theft-proof. The NO SALE button makes no record. The machine doesn't keep track. I can hit NO SALE when people pay any kind of round total, and I keep a running count in my head. See how all of this comes pouring out. I'm surprised."

"For how long?"

"Since I was there about a month. I never think about it, that's the key. I forget it. I do it automatically. I think I could pass a lie detector, really. I'm not sure, of course. I've never taken one. But I like my chances. It's amazing that I'm saying all this."

"Yes it is."

Laura rolls over onto her stomach. "You couldn't do it everywhere. It's the right place and the right kind of trade. They're elite, they're fancy, but not so much they send the help over to buy for them. Then you'd be sunk. It's young city types, go-getters, who drop dead before they flinch at the prices. They don't know from receipts—at least that's what they make out like. Not everybody, though. You have to sense who the right ones are. I don't like them much anyway. It's the kind that walks away from one cent, two cents change. With a $4.99 wine you hold out their penny and they say keep it and walk off. I think they're despicable. And they always wait until you hold it out, too. Keep it, you bet. I keep the whole fucking thing. That's how I built my empire, brick by brick, $4.99 at a time. It's funny—there's something athletic about it. You do it an hour a day at the most. It's draining. You have to be up for it, have energy. Big old Ms. Katz would be proud."

"Girls gym," he says. "This year she's Ms. Eckmann or Beckmann."

"My goodness. Somebody actually married her."

"Somebody divorced her," Dwight says, swinging his feet to the floor. He's trying to remember a time when Laura sounded at all like she does now.

"Look for openings," Laura says. "Keep your poise, work on misdirection, sense the rhythm of people's attention. It takes some talent. With the misdirection, it's like magic. It'd look so obvious if they knew what was coming. But you make sure they're diverted, and usually they divert themselves. And you don't flinch. It can be terribly easy if you do it right. And if you believe in it, you know?"

"You sleep like a criminal."

"Come on. Hey. Don't call me a criminal. It's our money. It's earning interest. I didn't piss it away on a new pool table or something."

"I said you slept like one. It was sort of bugging me. I just figured it out."

"How do criminals sleep?"

"You worry about your hands, you protect them. Like they're holding something. You watch over yourself, and you don't make sudden moves. And you explain things. You just sleep like a criminal would. It was bugging me."

"So now you've got me down," Laura says. "Just like that."

Later Dwight gets out of bed and goes upstairs. He spends a moment in Kenny's room, naked, reclined on the bed. The window shows the backyard; Dwight imagines its appearance in each season, and a few years before, when the young maples were even scrawnier, braced by wood and wire. Before he goes to the living room he takes Kenny's tennis racket and pauses in the hall. He tries hard to get closer to the threshold, to the point just before he'll flail at the flimsy lock, beat his way into the master bedroom.

His bare skin on the polished organ bench is among the strangest things he's ever felt. He begins with the series of green buttons in the "Swinging Fingers" section. Eighty-eight keys and nearly twice that in switches and buttons, dials and levers. Some of them are labeled unintelligibly, in Latin, like obscure body parts, and there are mysterious inch measurements painted on some of the switches. A five-thousand-dollar organ. He hits one of the purple RUMBA buttons, starting it out low and a little faster than a heartbeat. It's no tape—it will go forever if he wants, a dependable, rich, vital sound. The main keyboard is in the traditional black and white of old pianos, but there are colors, every color, everywhere else. The long rows of plastic levers stretch across the top; pools of buttons and switches lie on either side. What do combinations sound like? It would take all night. There's a military feel to it—more here than could ever be used. He switches to RUMBA II. People think the organ is funny; it always gets a laugh; it ranks only behind the kazoo and the accordian, for some reason. Dwight gets off the bench just once, to turn the thermostat a little higher.

FOREIGN OBJECTS

First there were the spare pillowcases—old and scratchy, weeks in storage, brought out for an overnight guest. When my mother left, and my father sold that house and all it contained, I lost their smell completely until years later and my first handful of money fresh from the automatic teller. Something of the cedar dresser in them, I suppose, and the sort of thin linen that feels dirty even when it's clean. It was a smell I hated—I stood in the guest bedroom and stuffed pillows at arm's length.

In 1967 we had the most visitors, and did the most housecleaning. My aunt Kate came, and so did my mother's younger friend Harry from Minnesota, and an overfriendly froggish woman I was required to call Dr. Maple. My granduncle Terrence, the machinist on my mother's side, came to call before his lungs gave out. We got quite a few who knew my father when he worked in California; trim, middle-aged people who claimed to remember me well. They were all cheerful, the ones who stayed the night and the dozens of others who didn't sleep over but still came, in ones and twos, to visit and sit up later than usual with my mother or my father, or with both of them. In the morning I'd find ashtrays and adult dishes, coffee spoons stained in the hollows, cups and small plates, and a stuck wet sugarlump on the tablecloth or the edge of the sink.

"Go help, Roger," my father would say in his driest voice on the morning before guests arrived, or the morning after they left. I did the work I could stand (hauling plastic bags, dusting and some vacuuming, clean-hands jobs) and did it whenever I remembered—but our house always looked lived in. My father had stopped lecturing about it, and he had stopped helping to keep it under control. He did enough of that for a lifetime, as he liked to say, when I was a mewling, dribbling little baby. He gave this an extra flourish that made it sound warmer, a little, than it normally would. "Just how this place has grown even worse since then," my father said, "I cannot imagine."

A cleaning lady came Tuesdays, but by the weekend her work had disappeared. That my mother kept house badly was in our family established fact. "Your mother insists on believing that soap gets things clean," my father said when the big washer choked with Cheer and flooded the room next to mine. "Soap doesn't get things clean. Water gets things clean." I'd seen worse, at my friends' houses, but my parents didn't know these people, they had their own friends, and there seemed nothing other than truth and reason on my father's side when he toured the rooms in the hours before our hosting, examined things with one hand—his left, and barely moved from its place by his thigh—and winced. It was all he did, but he did it often.

I had guests as well. There was no objection from my mother, and if there had been I knew that I could plead that it wasn't fair, it was a double standard, and if I kept it up long enough I could drive her, submitting, from any room in the house. Harold McGuire's parents were tougher, but on a Friday night early that winter he had permission. Harold was a year older, my one friend outside fifth grade. We'd been at the same school all along, but had really only met that year. All I recalled about him was how as a first-grader he couldn't get his jacket on; he got the sleeves bunched around his head and shoulders and needed help from Mrs. Swerm. Though he had improved, and no longer suffered open taunting, I found that I spent time with the group of my other friends, or I spent it with Harold McGuire.

The date was Friday, December 1st, 1967. The details, the facts of that day, have always been at my command. Harold came over at five-thirty. He brought a large bag, one they'd make you check at an airport. We wrestled that down to my room, in the basement, and Harold roamed around. "I love this house," he said. He wore a sweater that zippered in the front. He had a homemade haircut. My mother held dinner until seven, but when my father hadn't come by then, she and I and Harold McGuire ate center-cut pork chops, corn on the cob, and a big store-bought salad. It was terrific food, and my mother let us eat until there was nothing left. She sat at the dinner table afterward, but we were excused.

"I'm going to win the Selectmen's Prize," I told her when Harold was in the bathroom.

"That's wonderful," my mother said. "Congratulations." I wasn't boasting. My fifth grade lacked any real competition. It was going to be a formality.

"Is there a presentation?" my mother said after a while. "Is there a certificate that goes along?" I shrugged but she wasn't seeing me. She seemed to hunt around the kitchen for something else to say. Then she stood up and cleared plates. "You should be extremely proud," she said as Harold McGuire returned.

Harold was flatfooted and had a funny walk, as if he were cycling uphill. He hadn't ever lived in another town. You'd see his father steering an orange public works truck, rumbling off to somewhere, one of Harold's two much-older brothers often in the cab working with him. Both brothers had married and moved out. This left Harold alone in the upstairs and made it easier for him to do his fake radio show, a daily affair, three to five on weekdays and twelve to six on Saturdays. Harold went straight home from school and did the show every day. He played records and conducted celebrity interviews, he told jokes, or he scanned the newspaper and commented at length. Most segments of the show ran long. Harold felt no pressure for variety. If he liked a song he'd play it for a while, a dozen times in a row or more. Today, he said, he'd done the second hour on marriage and the worth of it, working from the newspaper and the ugly front-page image of Eisenhower's grandson and Nixon's daughter.

I had never witnessed this. I had to rely on what he told me. His parents were not in the habit of entertaining, or asking Harold's friends in from the yard. The one time I entered the house—it was a Sunday, no radio show, his parents at church, Harold skipping—I spent the whole hour snooping with him in closets and drawers, and then panicking to find, under the double bed, scattered alien scrawl, pages of bedlam: the first I'd ever seen of shorthand. Harold took the sheets from me casually. He told me his mother had this on records, too, and sometimes he put them on his playlist.

On December 1st, Harold McGuire and I watched "The Wild Wild West" and played Chinese Checkers, and then we took the marbles and made up a new game. We spread flat across the floor and tried to roll them closest to the other's face without touching. During "Tarzan" with Ron Ely, I asked my mother if I could make popcorn. I found her sorting clothes at the laundry hamper. When the popcorn was done I dumped parmesan cheese over it and ate more than my share, since Harold didn't care for it, though he took some anyway. After "Gomer Pyle" he went to inspect the refrigerator.

"This is such a great house," Harold said when he came back. He'd found the cookie cupboard, and in returning had paused outside the den to study the bright concentric circles on the walls.

"My mom painted those this summer," I said.

Harold wound his Timex. There passed a half-hour or so when we couldn't find anything to watch. We left it on "Judd for the Defense" and Harold talked about how Jimmy Ellis would bloody Oscar Bonavena the next day. I was just a modest fight fan, though I'd grown more interested recently. The only thing Harold didn't like about boxing was that it wasn't as good as professional wrestling. I heard my mother over in the laundry room, loading the machine. I didn't know why she'd be doing this at night, except maybe somehow to impress Harold, or my father later. When she finally stopped for a minute, came in to sit with us, it was after ten o'clock. We'd turned to an NBC special, "Same Mud, Same Blood": Frank McGee was reporting on his four weeks with white and Negro troops together in combat conditions. She watched a few minutes—Harold was quiet, so was I—then she left the room. There seemed no reason to stop eating. I went up for cereal and milk and found my mother in the kitchen.

She stood at the dishwasher. "When are you going to bed?" she said.

"We want to watch some of Johnny Carson," I said. "We're almost there. We want to see the monologue."

Harold and I had Sugar Pops for a long time, pouring from the box or the milk carton as we needed. We talked about people at school, mostly about the girls. Harold seemed to doze for seconds at a time. News stories were about Vietnam and the early snowfall.

Then the vacuum started upstairs. I knew it was silly, but the sound made me lose my breath—it shocked me that the machine could even function, was at all capable, that late at night. We laughed hard when Johnny Carson came on. There were some minutes when I thought I might throw up, but they passed. I was sipping cold milk from the bowl. The guests were Bosley Crowther, Gig Young, Peggy Cass, and Sarah Vaughan. Laughing inspired Harold: he picked up what he'd been pursuing the day before—he was intent on making me see that the Globetrotters would romp over the Knicks. "Of course they would," he said. "Who's going to cover Curly Neal? Jackie Jackson? *Meadowlark*? Just imagine the two teams on the court. Just picture them. How could it be any other way?"

We were still in our clothes and there were marbles all

over the den. Harold then told all about the vacation his family took last year, on the Cabot Trail in Nova Scotia—he remembered it day by day, especially his brothers scuffling with the customs police. My father's car still wasn't outside. Then, as sometimes happened, I pictured his sudden death. More notion than image, it was much like what surfaced at the airport, in the back seat of our double-parked car, my mother sliding over to drive, the trunk slamming and my father leaning at the window to shake my hand and hang a quick arm around me. It would be nothing gory, in fact quite dry and routine, and with a small announcement on the news, and with obituaries beside a handsome and casual picture—bigger and more near the front of the suburban paper. My father worked in magazines, and had some local notoriety. I saw myself failing to get an accurate count of the dozens of perfumed, cologned people in the house, saw them eating imported food and talking and joking a little and flipping through the slick paper in his magazine, unable not to grease up the margins, but mostly empty-handed and stumped in the extreme for what to say, like after my granduncle's funeral, resorting every so often to hopeful call-and-response conversation with my mother's hired people, who worked at a clean house both before and after the event, and more discreetly while it went on.

Around midnight we left the den. In my room Harold unpacked; he had record albums in his bag, a big clock radio, many changes of clothes, and a floppy pile of magazines—one about wrestling, one with women in bathtubs with other women, one with the words to all the hit songs. We put a mattress on my floor for him. I said my prayers in the bathroom, with the sink running. My mother was washing more clothes and this had a small effect on the water pressure. Harold McGuire had a funny body—he had calves like drumsticks, a collapsed right nipple. His pajamas were paisley and he gargled. He did a few minutes of arm and leg exercises. He wore his watch for this, and everything. He had a blister like a balanced ball at the end of one middle toe. I sat under the covers and watched him, amazed.

Harold said, "My dad does these with me, every night." Ten minutes later in the dark, he said, "Thanks for the dinner and all the rest. I forgot to tell your mom it was good. Remind me."

I lay listening to the noises of housework above, frightened only a little, and for the first time. It was lost in the sound of Harold sitting up. "I just counted to three hundred," he said. "I like the color your walls are. They even look great in the dark. Mine are just white, except where I write on 'em." The night went on, and we were awake in it. Harold said: "Let me ask you something. Why do you flush before and after you go?"

"I was taught," I said.

"I like this room," Harold said. "I'd like having a roof that doesn't slant. Imagine a giant hotel, with all the rooms like this."

"But your room has three beds," I said. "Doesn't it? It must, it's got to be bigger."

"But yours is a perfect square," he said. "It seems a *lot* bigger. It's just a great room. I love it." On his back, Harold crossed his legs beneath the blanket figure-four style, ankle on knee, and then jiggled his foot so he appeared to share the bed with robots, or tame animals. He kept talking. "I think my father's mad at my mom, for letting me come over."

"Your dad must have thought it was OK," I said.

"I don't know. He didn't really want me over here." Harold sat up a little. "But here I am."

"My mom never wins an argument," I said. "Not that I can remember. My dad's undefeated."

"Do they hit?" Harold said.

"No."

"Do they hit you?"

"No," I said, then told him about the one time, which didn't make much of a story, really, the high point being the reach of my father's hand, blinding—he'd boxed—over the quick distance from his place to mine at the table, but still less a jab than a move you'd make to stop a box falling from a shelf; and the tape recorder I'd got on my birthday, a miniature that I enjoyed leaving to work in grown-up rooms, wedged in magazines or behind the breadbox; and the overnight guest across from me when I revealed it during dessert, played it back for all of them, barely discernible over the kitchen's hum and knocking, nothing embarrassing in their words that I could tell, everybody's voice on tape but my own, which I never recorded because it sounded like someone I didn't know; and the serene precision in this adult guest—it was Harry Bragg from St. Paul, come to see my mother—when he reached and took the machine from me and cracked circuits and gears, worked his fork in it like it was shellfish, then handed it back; and that first, smallest squeak of my objection that brought my father's hard open hand and a look that said You'll never understand, I don't imagine.

"My kids," Harold McGuire said. "I don't care, I ain't hitting 'em. It just won't do any good. There's nothing gained from it. They step out of line, I'll just look at 'em. I'll go: Cut it right now. They step out of line again, I'll go: Come over this way. I'll go: Learn. Then I'll put holds on 'em."

This made me laugh. "Holds," I said.

"Beat kids up, it won't solve things. No, sir. They step out of line, they go right into the sleeper."

"Submission holds," I said. I was laughing. "Use the Piledriver. Use the Boston Crab."

"Depends on the situation," Harold said. "Probably, my main one would be the Iron Claw. Right in the solar plexus."

Harold's older brothers went to the matches at the Garden. Next time, they said, they were bringing Harold, and Harold's father.

"What if they don't submit?" I said.

"They have to. A fifty-pound kid won't take it for long. Even Bruno can't always fight out of a sleeper."

"It's fake, Harold."

"Not the championship matches!" Harold said. I thought he might have been loud enough for my mother to hear. "The ones on TV might be a little fake, okay. But in the Garden. When they step inside that squared circle, for the title. Swear to God."

Now he was wide awake again, telling the stories his brothers told, dwelling in particular on the manager's antics outside the ropes, and on the blood. George The Animal Steele was biting all through the title match. Bruno Sammartino retained the undisputed heavyweight crown on a draw, which was called at the twenty-minute time limit, both wrestlers unconscious outside the ring.

"That was the real stuff," he said. "It was all over the place. Bruno needed thirty stitches." During the night Harold went into the closet to kill the light I always left burning. The chimes on the clock in the hall woke him several times, and his stirring woke me.

In the early morning I had one dream about school. It ended with a crack; Harold's arm hit my dresser as he tossed on his mattress. Once we were both awake, we began to wrestle. Harold did the announcing in a rapid, croaking voice I could barely follow. I was in his grip, but not for long, before I became aware of how hungry I was. My room got the sun before noon, especially in winter. I broke sweat right away; Harold was dry as a tire, though something in the touch of his skin told me he'd been clammy during the night. He marched me around in a headlock; the face of his watch, which he wore backward on his wrist, fit neatly between my lip and chin. I imagined I could feel the small gouges in it.

Harold held the upper hand for a time, then suddenly he let go. "New match starts," he said. He left the room and came back with stiff posture—smiling, waving. He removed his pajama top and struck bodybuilding poses; he kissed his imagined muscles. Then with a flourish he got down to his underpants. He folded his tops and bottoms perfectly, and bent to set them down in a corner.

"What'd you say?" I said.

"Ref's not looking," he said, still turned. "Ambush me." So I did. He covered up, rolled on the ground. It was older, large underwear; over one hip the cloth flapped free of the elastic band. "Choke me with my jacket," he said when I fell on top of him. He gave all his directions in a stage whisper, then resumed the garbled announcing.

Our expanded, empty stomachs made what we did feel more reckless. I twisted Harold's arm, and he slapped at his shoulder like it was coming apart. On the rug he let me come close to a pin, then made desperate escapes at the two-count. I faked some hairpulling when I dragged him to the windows. "Now I get the momentum," he rasped from under my arm. "Let's run the ropes."

I flung him against my wall of shelves, and he bounced. He couldn't run a perfect line, but he dodged furniture and his bulky luggage and made it look, in his gyroscopic trot, as straight as he could. I couldn't understand a word he said. I began running between the other two walls. The second time we crossed he caught me with a knee, gently, and I went down hard. Harold looked woozy, but fired up. He winced and staggered gamely. He held his neck and rolled his eyes, he struggled to get his bearings. He shook the cobwebs. He was *in* the ring. I was trying, too. I lay on the rug, rolling weakly and clutching my windpipe; it was harder for me, in my own room. Harold held his foot above my neck and looked around, asked with his eyes if the crowd wanted mercy.

More than smell it, I could feel his breath when he kneeled over me, pretended to bite my forehead. He snapped his head away expertly. He looked displeased with my rendition of searing pain.

He came even closer to whisper: "Let's get blood."

There were supplies of all kinds in the closet just outside my room, a pantry loaded, reserves for a month. I came back with a thirty-two-ounce bottle of Heinz Ketchup. I thought the excitement was about to choke me and bring tears.

"New match," Harold said. "I'm the bad guy." He stayed from the room for an extra moment. When he lurched through my door, a bit disoriented, he was a medley of evil: fascist from the Eastern bloc, lunatic gaucho, forest savage, shifty oriental. He crossed my room in a backstep full of swivel and glare at the ringsiders, or more ethereal hecklers. We stood still while the referee checked us for foreign objects. At the handshake he Pearl Harbored me.

We had the bottle uncapped right away. The stuff was warmer than I expected. We poured ourselves handfuls. We smeared it, at first anyway, only after a devastating blow.

Harold liked to swat at his own forehead after I hit him, hoping to start a genuine trickle down his face. We rolled all over my bedroom.

It wasn't during the lulls, but at the height of the action, the leaping and swinging and staggering, that I imagined being heard, imagined getting caught at this. I couldn't let myself go; still, I didn't stop. I let Harold smear more blood. We kept going at it. It wasn't not caring, it was just not stopping.

I was trying a full nelson on Harold, locking our arms, burying my cheek in a wet clot between his shoulders. He made a heroic show of struggling to his knees and finding a neutral corner. He groped there, and palmed the white bottlecap.

"Foreign objects," he said in a rasp. He broke my hold with real force. Then he closed the cap in his fist and brought the knuckles across my eyes, rapidly but lightly. Then he hid the cap in his shorts and strutted around while I lay on the mat in a daze, the feeling in my stomach nearly a vibration. The ketchup had gone cold on me. Harold licked a little of his. Then he proffered his empty hands to the crowd and the referee. Harold was good; he could have fought the match by himself. He swung around, fished the cap out, and charged me. He ground it harder this time against one eyeball. While Harold stood erect again, while he made a handle of my hair and asked the crowd what to do with me, I reached an arm back and looped it through his big empty bag, and then I swung it. Harold went down in a package. The zipper caught him under the nose. No real blood, but a white welt.

I stood up, leaned over him, watched the welt get bigger. Harold looked under his wrist, blinking to focus. "It's eleven-thirty already," he said. He whined a little, but with his other hand over his tender nose it came out like transmission, like air-traffic control. The ketchup on him was completely inauthentic. It collected in places where nobody bleeds, away from surface vessels. There was a lot of it in toe gaps and behind the knees. The rest was on the walls, the carpet, and the furniture. One clump in the shape of a damaged parachute held to the spines of thirty records. For some reason little stuck to the sheets. I couldn't see all of myself, but I knew I had more of it than Harold. It was most neatly coated on the inside of one thigh. On my arms it was drying; hair reappeared through it. I used my pajama bottoms to wipe my face and ankles. I wore my bathrobe over the rest of it. Harold had rolled away as if he meant to go back to sleep, though he hadn't taken his hand from his nose. I looked around my room, then I went upstairs.

My father sat at the polished dining room table with the unopened newspaper in front of him. My mother would be back in eleven days. The next time, in 1971, would be for good. My father had folded the note twice and put it into his breast pocket. He was in rumpled clothes, yesterday's, and drinking coffee.

He saw me coming and reached out at me, a move quick

but still close to awkward. He wound up touching me on the forehead, handling me really, then again on the tight skin below the temple and just in front of the ear, a gesture to reassure me and to make me go away. His eyes looked large and dry behind his glasses, but his knuckles and his fingertips shone with his own spit, and the dumb, sticky smell—the smell of droolers and nailchewers, of kids who'd stayed back twice already—was distinct through the stench of ketchup and everything else. My father went out to stand in the backyard. I went to the bathroom to stand at the mirror for a time, and then to wash and wash. In my bedroom Harold still lay on his stomach, his talk easy and steady into his red fist. He was on the air.